THE BASKERVILLE DUSTJACKET

BY

RICH/

THE BASKERVILLES DUSTJACKET

THE CHANCE DISCOVERY OF A VERY RARE COPY OF AN ADVENTURE INVOLVING A FAMOUS HOUND SEEMS TO SET OFF A CHAIN OF SINISTER EVENTS WHICH ENDS DRAMATICALLY ON THE SHORES OF LAKE GARDA

BY

RICHARD HAMILTON

Copyright: © Richard Mannering Hamilton
1 January 2020
Published by the Author 2020
The author retains all rights to the contents of *'The Baskervilles Dustjacket'*, and no extracts may be copied and printed or used elsewhere without his permission

PREFACE

It must be stressed that all the characters in this novel are fictional and any similarities with known individuals are quite coincidental. A few of the incidents which happen to the narrator, Monty Warnock, are based on true events. Any organisations which can be identified will be pleased to read that everything said of them is entirely complimentary and that includes a certain lakeside hotel along the shore of Lake Garda. Gardone is a lovely village and I am sure that the authorities there would ensure that nothing dangerous or sinister could ever occur to spoil the peaceful beauty of this magical place. I do hope that all Arthur Conan-Doyle enthusiasts will pardon my use of a very famous creation of his, and the quite regrettable production of a dust jacket, which never existed outside my imagination.

To my daughter, Rachel, who read much of the text and asked many relevant and clarifingly helpful questions,

Many thanks, Dad

CHARACTERS IN ORDER OF APPEARANCE

Monty Warnock	Secondhand Book Dealer, Narrator
Daniel Harrison	Peterborough Police, and Fellow Book Enthusiast
Cynthia Brownley	Elderly Friend, Husband to Ernie
Mavis Morrisy	Friend of Monty Fellow Church Goer
Fr Blakeston	Priest at St Petrie's Chapel
Joseph Mallings	Trumpingtons Auction House
Charles Sedgfield	Trumpingtons Auction House
Wendy Goodison	Friend and Neighbour of Cynthia
Fr John Evans	Retired Clergyman
Fr Andrew Hutchinson	Retired Clergyman
David Jenkins	Organist
The Dean	Peterborough Cathedral
Lucinda Ellerton	The Dean' Wife
Junaid Anwar	Police Officer
Henry Tay	Book Restorer, Trumpingtons
Jon Mostang M.P.	Member of Parliament
Nat Lawton M.P.	Member of Parliament
Muriel Missily	Sister to Mavis works for Kenneth Peterson
Kenneth Peterson	Resident Leopold Mansions, Philanthropist
Tony	Chauffeur to Ken, Artist
Anthony Breakspeare	Friend of Monty, Travel Agent
Mathias Poynton	Neighbour Ken Peterson, Neurologist
Two London Police Officers	
John Prendle	Solicitor to Jon Mostang
Joanne Prendle	Wife to John
Rosemary Lawton	Wife (separated) of Nat Lawton
Angela Lawton	Daughter who lives in Spain
Benjamin Lawton	Son, European Travel Courier
Genevievre Renoir	French Opera Singer
Pierre Renoir	Brother, International Lawyer
Jean Renoir	Brother, Student -Pianist
Anik Anwar	Brother of Junaid, Private Security

Sanjay Bhatt	Reformed shop lifter, friend to Junaid
Kieran Overton	Reformed shop lifter, friend to Junaid
Ch. Sup. Matthew Tomlinson	Peterborough Police
Husani El Masry	Brother to Late Noura, first wife to Daniel Harrison
Mrs Bhatt	Sanjay's mother
Kabir Anwar	Youngest brother to Junaid and Anik
Andreas	Agent bidding for The Hound of the Baskervilles
Eileen	Mother of Andreas
Stephen	University friend of Kabir's
Sergeant Armstrong	Peterborough Police
Angelini	Receptionist, The King's Tower, Gardone
Giovani Baptista	Manager, The King's Tower, Gardone
Frederico	Book Dealer, Salo, near Gardone
Fabrizio	Owner of Restaurant in Salo
Alberto	Taxi Driver

1. CROSSING THE FENS

If there is an urge to combine a feeling of nostalgia with a drive across peaceful and seemingly never changing countryside, then the journey from Hunstanton to Peterborough can often provide all that's necessary. There is enough of the Edwardian seaside town left to make one feel that time has stood still, especially if one's memory doesn't reach back to before the railway, pier and station disappeared. To stroll through the gardens, past the bowling green and along towards the old lighthouse until that view of the pink striped cliff-face comes into view, provides scenery that is perhaps little changed in a hundred years. On a clear day one can look out to sea and just spot the coastline close to Skegness. Looking in the opposite direction, across the gardens and coast road is an attractive row of Edwardian Villas. My own feelings of nostalgia stem from memories of annual Sunday School trips from Kings Lynn, by steam train to the seaside, organised by The Reverend A W Allworthy, and how appropriate was his surname, Vicar of St John's Church. Races on the green followed by sandwiches and buns in a nearby hall doesn't seem very exciting by today's standards, but to a small boy in the very early 1950s it was heaven. To come back to Hunstanton from time to time has a quality almost of a pilgrimage in which I can drift back in time and just wallow in nostalgic pleasure.

On my way back I have perhaps detoured through Kings Lynn, Gaywood and past Highgate Infant School which I attended, along Loke Road where I lived, to the town centre and the Tuesday market square. My father worked on Saturday mornings and on occasions I was allowed to walk into town to meet him.

As a special treat he would buy tickets and we would cross the River Great Ouse and as I remember this, I recall the time when the motor ferry's engine conked out and we drifted down river towards The Wash. To me it seemed a great adventure but to adults perhaps there was some sense of apprehension about what might have happened had the ferryman been unable to restart the engine. On some Saturdays our neighbour's lad, older than me by a few years, was given extra pocket money to look after me and on one of these child-minding afternoons we took a train to the village of Middleton. Unfortunately, I ran up a grassy bank straight into a barbed-wire fence and ripped open my upper lip; I still have the scar to this day. More fun than reminding myself of a scar was to remember that a lady, who found me pouring with blood and with John, the lad from next door, who didn't know what to do and probably frightened about the consequences, took us to her house and called an ambulance. With bell ringing, probably to cheer me up, we were driven to the hospital in Kings Lynn where my lip was stitched. I don't think much can have happened to John, because he looked after me on plenty more occasions, and there were other mishaps too. That's the best kind of nostalgia, to relive past excitements, not to lament past times and try and put the clock back, because that's the route to discontentment.

And what of the drive back to Peterborough? Far stretching vistas of farm-land countryside, fields showing acres of autumn-tide ploughing, long, long furrows of black soil and of course, endless skies reaching to remote horizons. Along the road, signposts draw one's attention to out-of-view villages – Tilney High End, St John's Fen End, Gedney Hill (a hill, in the Fens!), and the now, by-passed Thorney. Along the road itself – wayside stalls selling seasonal produce, tumble down barns, disused and rusting farm equipment, isolated cottages, and the occasional cyclist. Not often but on some days, there might be little traffic and very few people about. The view either side is always good because for much of the journey the road is on a high embankment and the fields and buildings to both sides are a couple of meters lower. Let one's imagination run and there is an amazing sense of timelessness about it all

But as the traffic begins to increase on the outskirts of Peterborough, the nostalgia fades and the carrier bags on the front seat remind me of my little two-day trip to North Norfolk: bed and breakfast near Kings Lynn, visits to Wells-Next-The-Sea, Fakenham, Holt, to hunt out secondhand books and pamphlets from dealers and numerous charity shops. After much loving care and restoration, together with a dose of good luck, I might just make enough profit from their sale to cover the cost of this trip down memory lane.

Monty Warnock dropped off his hire car, called a taxi and returned to his terrace cottage in Crawthorn Avenue. This was where most of his older childhood and teenage memories lay as his parents and he moved to Peterborough when he was a small boy. Unlocking the front door of the house he had known ever since, he put down his various bags, walked straight through and out into his small walled garden. Long before 'experts' started talking about the 'outside room' as they put it, he had laid it out with a variety of narrow block paved paths which followed an intricate route around this tiny area, curving past small bushes, stone urns, specimen roses and three different seats in small arbours. Everything had a pleasantly aged and decayed appearance. The smoky red brick walls which surrounded the garden were covered with masses of flowering roses, ivies and fruiting espaliers, these last bearing witness to his patience over ten years or so. In fact, some items dotted about he had 'dipped' from skips; only a little imagination required, and they gained a new life. Nearly all his own work, he frequently strolled out into this small garden whenever he returned home. In the far corner was the smallest of sheds totally covered in a flowering creeper and containing the minimum of essential tools with just enough room to hang his old but essential bicycle from the top of one side; he had abandoned ownership of a car soon after his mother had died. His occasional need to drive was satisfied by a hire company and this as an annual cost was a fraction of that caused by actual car ownership.

He returned through the French doors to the one large downstairs room which he had created once he was living there by himself. Monty's father had died when he was at College so when he qualified and started teaching, he had returned to Peterborough. He hadn't planned to be with his mother for the rest of her life, but circumstances just seemed to bring that about.

His father had worked for the Civil Service so had a pension and some of this passed to her. With early-onset dementia, companionship had gradually become care, and this had coincided with the need at his school for some staff to be made redundant. Being of the right age Monty had been able to opt for early retirement; he wasn't the best of teachers and he had been of a nervous disposition so perhaps these factors were taken into account and certainly his pension expectation was greatly enhanced. Once he had got used to his single life he had set about modernising where he lived and laying out the garden to his own designs dictated by minimum maintenance. He was reasonably handy with tools and had enjoyed undertaking much of the work himself, buying in help when the need arose.

When he had waited for his taxi, he had been able to by some food supplies and he put these away in the kitchen corner and switched on his computer in his book corner. He thought of his room in corners, there being a further one for television, and from the last, rose the staircase, constructed from old reclaimed oak and delightfully noisy it was when he clattered up and down. The carefully placed desk, pine kitchen table, and the two settees, divided the whole area into three rectangles and left a straight walk from the front door through to the back. Any spare wall space was given over to book shelving and everywhere you looked there were books – all overflowing from the book corner. The upstairs was more traditional and retained the original layout, two bedrooms though one was given over to more books. There was an old and very heavy cast iron book press, kept now as a large display item, as well-sprung hand clamps were easier to use. There was an ancient desk rather littered with tools associated with minor book repairing. An old 'put-you-up' made possible the occasional guest. The remaining room upstairs, an original looking bathroom which seemed to have brass pipes and taps curling over and around the ancient ceramic and cast-iron fittings, completed the floor. Combined with a toilet the whole was decorated in old period tiles. The attic above was totally empty; one day it might have to accommodate yet more books. The roof space was quite high so a good size room could be created, evidenced by some of the nearby houses, with access through the study/bedroom.

It being late afternoon now he knew Daniel would be arriving soon, so malt, water and ice were taken to the furthest seat in the garden where the sun would still be shining and despite it being autumn the brick walls ensured the warmth remained. Monty had met Daniel some ten years previous, having found themselves standing shoulder to shoulder at a local auction. They were bidding for the same box of books and quickly agreed for one of them to win and share the books amicably; totally against all the rules, but fortunately no one noticed, and later when they divided the spoils they didn't so much as dispute one volume. Although fifteen years apart and both single, one, a retired teacher and the other, a widower and still serving police officer, they shared a great interest in old books. With this in common, the acquaintanceship grew, and the Friday afternoon malt quickly ceased being occasional and now regularly signalled a delightful moment at the end of the week for Monty and definitely the beginning of the weekend (if he were lucky) for Daniel. Chief Inspector Daniel Harrison, formerly of Scotland Yard, still worked and if work were to interrupt this pattern, a phone call would advise Monty to put out only one glass; an absent friend would receive a toast.

"Lovely weekend coming up I think," said a hand whose fingers were just reaching over to the gate latch. At seventeen stone and at a height to suit, Daniel strode in, glanced approvingly at the preparations, and collapsed onto his end of the bench. "It better not rain, as I'm off duty for two days." He celebrated this thought with his first malt; the next was sipped most gently, lasting their entire conversation. A less aggressive drinker, Monty just sipped the one.

One of that morning's finds from somewhere in Norfolk was a first edition paperback of an early Marjorie Allingham and this was passed to Daniel, he being an avid collector of classic crime novels of the middle twentieth century. For himself, Monty bought anything quirky and off-beat and as most of his buying was for selling on, he and his auction-going friend rarely fell out when bidding. Titles which had come Monty's way in recent months served to prove the notion that he went for the 'quirky' – Nineteenth Century Funeral Customs, Aboriginal Art, Round World Motorcycle Journey, Bed Bugs, Small Arms Ammunition, Centurion Tanks, among many, many others. Careful to avoid prying into police affairs, Monty enquired after his week only to find out, as usual, that it had been humdrum and with too many meetings to suit Daniel's more active temperament.

"What, nothing in the local crime scene to match your reading interests?"

"Yes, well, when the 'local crime scene' as you describe it, begins to match an Allingham plot, I'll write it up and retire. Actually, we're in the middle of a mini wave of petty shop lifting. The same youngsters, or at least that's what we think."

"I thought all that sort of thing was caught on camera these days," said Monty, perhaps somewhat naively.

"Well that's what television would have you think. But so often the equipment isn't working, or it's not been switched on, or the camera happened to be pointing in the wrong direction or, whatever excuse you like to think of. It ought to solve more minor crime than it does, but it doesn't. Rather frustrating from our point of view."

"Well, as I think I told you some months back, it was the camera opposite the door of Oxfam that identified the pickpocket who was helping himself to my wallet, so that was at least one camera's success."

Monty picked up another book. "Remember this?" he asked

"No, you have got several thousand books in there you know."

"You gave it me the other week in exchange for another Allingham, but then the dust jacket was rather screwed up."

"Ah yes, the tatty old Observer."

"Not so tatty now, the dust jacket has ironed out and is complete, the odd nibble, but really quite good considering how it looked. The first page which was torn and loose is now back in place and the rip closed very neatly, I've got rid of the old biro inscription very successfully and all the pencilled notes have erased cleanly. It is a copy of The Observer's Book of Automobiles from the first year they published it, 1955, and it might bring me enough for another bottle of malt, so I've done best out of this swap I think!"

Daniel smiled his approval knowing full well that his salary far exceeded Monty's pension and book sales, probably four or five times over. "Well, I must be off, badminton later. No doubt you'll be tapping at the computer all evening while I try to sweat away a few pounds and failing at the bar afterwards. See you next week if not before. Did I tell you I'm away for a couple of days next week? Being sent to a two-day conference in Birmingham – 'Defence Against Cyber Attacks on National Systems', hope it is more interesting than it sounds. Don't forget to send me an email and let me know the date of the next auction."

"It's a week tomorrow!"

The gate closed and a hand acknowledged the shout as Monty gathered up the glasses, bottle and book, and smiling to himself, made off along the path all organised for his ready-meal or, if he really stretched his imagination, he could call it an individual homemade Beef Wellington. Sometimes he regretted not being able to cook beyond the essential basics. Reflecting a little more about Daniel, he thought the conference could be very interesting.

2. AMBLING THROUGH PETERBOROUGH

Monty Warnock was strolling through the centre of Peterborough a week or so later, generally a daily activity of his, though more a slow meander than anything approaching a walk. He never saw it as part of a fitness regime, perish the thought would be his attitude to such a notion; he just enjoyed his own company as he wandered, gazing into shop windows, or staring above where the period architecture would cause him to regret the ubiquitous nature of the lower shop fronts and standard logos. He liked being with people but was not in desperate need of their company. He took interest in, or not as the case maybe, any temporary displays erected by the City Council drawing attention to the next event of the annual round and he would consider for a while whether to book a ticket or try and remember the free exhibition. Always meeting with his approval however, would be the planters and flower beds which regardless of season generally had something colourful about them and much as he enjoyed their bursts of nature they never failed to cause him to feel badly about the smallness of his own rear garden despite the very best of his creative efforts. He was fond of Peterborough although he recognised how it had changed over his lifetime, changes than some regretted, but he didn't. He enjoyed its more cosmopolitan flavour and was always fascinated by the range of foreign languages to be heard. It caused him to regret his total lack of language skill – just some schoolboy French was all he could lay claim to. One road he always enjoyed walking along was Park Road, from The Baptist Chapel to Westgate, only a short stretch but you might not hear a word of English and on the side to the east were small shops, hair salons, food stores, mobile phone outlets and most seemed to be catering for a different cultural group. He might have misunderstood all the distinctions, but he found it fascinating; Peterborough was a City of great variety.

 Standing now on the steps to the Town Hall and staring at the 1930s foundation stone which commemorated the visit to the City of HRH Prince George. How many residents would know who he was especially as there was a new Prince George for everyone to hear about. He debated stopping for a coffee at the bar he had just passed or on to the Bishop's Road Gardens where he could sit and do absolutely nothing; he did both, and also fitted in a five minute detour to inspect Oxfam's latest books, acquire a modest find (a small consolation for having bought nothing at the last Saturday's auction, an auction, which fortunately Daniel had had to miss.) About to move on to the gardens his thoughts were totally interrupted by a couple of lads charging across the road in front of him only to disappear around the corner in the direction of the Key Theatre. It was only when he saw a couple of staff emerge from W H Smiths opposite, did he think of the shoplifting which Daniel had mentioned. Like most eyewitnesses, he realised immediately that he could recall hardly anything about the two tear-aways, other than that they were probably young teenagers.

Thinking that he must remember to tell Daniel what he saw, he ambled on his way to the gardens and thirty minutes later found him sharing a park bench with Cynthia, an acquaintance of some years. She was fondling the ears of her elderly black Scottie, Barkie, so named for obvious reasons. Even though Monty was now retired, Cynthia, in her mid-eighties, made him feel quite young and in dog years Barkie probably matched his sixty. He made himself feel comfortable and ready to listen sympathetically to Cynthia's troubles, always, always now concerned solely with her elderly husband's dementia. She never used that word but everything that she mentioned and described gave a very clear diagnosis. Until a year or so ago Ernie would have accompanied Cynthia but even then, it was clear that his days of idle strolling were numbered. Monty had seen all the photographs – the handsome RAF Officer from National Service days of the early 1950s, the post-war engineer and proud owner of their first car, holiday snaps with their one daughter who now lived in Australia, later ones from retirement 'dos' and past-times, dancing, gardening, coach trips, 'evergreen' parties and then ones showing the gradual signs of that frozen look and then no more. These photographs, well-worn and studied, were as precious jewels tucked in the side pocket of her handbag, just ready for those happy nostalgic reminders. To be able to share them with someone, anyone, was just bliss. Listening 'between the lines' Monty knew that Ernie's days were spent sitting, and sitting, just sitting. He didn't like to ask but he suspected that Cynthia heard very infrequently from the daughter, perhaps not at all and she certainly never mentioned her. He also knew about Wendy from next door who came in almost every day for a 'cuppa' as Cynthia put it and how low she would be if there was no visit.

The garden visit for the day nearly over, Barkie was beginning to stretch, a sure sign that the mistress was about to return to her house in Bishop's Terrace leaving Monty to decide on a route back to his place on Crawthorn Avenue. Wandering back and thinking about Cynthia, Monty could understand the inevitability of her increasing loneliness, many of their friends finding it harder to get out, beginning to suffer those ailments that made them house-bound, moves to nursing homes led remorselessly to isolation and it caused Monty to realise what his mother's last years may have been like had he not remained in the area. He wondered about his own last years and still to come but put the thoughts away quickly; keep busy was his motto. He returned via the longest route (perhaps this was some unconscious exercise on his part), on the way collecting some quality 'ready meals' having long since decided that this was the best method of getting a good and varied dinner without too much effort, just some extra vegetables, and with the advent of 'meals for two', a bottle thrown in, he could save something for the next day and enjoy a tipple or two for the next couple of evenings. He deliberately kept himself a light drinker.

It being Wednesday he remembered that there would be Compline at St Petri's Chapel, a little-known jewel in the Cathedral grounds. This mid-week service was something he had been attending for many years and it never failed to give him a sense of calm and peace. For most of his life he had attended church together with his parents and then with his mother and now generally on his own. At college he had sung in the chapel choir. These days he didn't always attend the same church as he sometimes played the organ. Although he wasn't a particularly skilled musician, he could stand in when required. It was their friend Mavis Morrisy, who lived a few doors along the avenue who had introduced him to Compline. They had met at the Cathedral one Sunday morning and had walked back together for coffee at Mavis's house and there a friendship had started up, with both him and his mother who she used to visit some afternoons as she didn't work.

St Petri's Chapel was a most unusual 'Foundation' within the Church of England. It was built partly in the cellars of a small three storied detached house, 'The Chapel House', in the grounds of the Cathedral. The Cathedral being dedicated to St Peter there was obviously some connection. The 'Foundation' went back centuries but there was in effect a perpetual charity which funded one retired Priest provided he was over the age of seventy-five, unmarried and agreed to live in The Chapel House. It wasn't a stipulated rule, but most incumbents were appointed from within the Diocese. The appointment, which was in the gift of the Bishop of Peterborough, was for life and didn't expire until life had expired. Consequently, there were periods of time when St Petri's went unmanned owing to the ill health and advanced years of the incumbent. Although the Foundation predated the Reformation it had continued to exist because so much of the original documentation made it clear that the trust monies were in the name of the Bishop (Abbot originally and successors thereafter.) The only requirement in terms of work was that two services had to be conducted each week, one in an evening and the other during a morning. It was probably out of curiosity that he first went to the mid-week service of Compline but as time went on, he appreciated it more and from a personal religious point of view.

He needed to remember to ring Mavis later in the evening to see if their usual arrangement was on for the evening service. Another reason he went was the joy in hearing those lovely words from St Peter's Epistle and with which the service was commenced:

'Brethren, be sober, be vigilant; because your adversary the devil, as a roaring lion, walketh about seeking whom he may devour.'

How true he thought that to be for so many people, himself included. Any reading of the daily news will bring to the light of day how someone, perhaps the most unlikely of people, can fall to a temptation; this can be at its strongest when a reputation is at stake. Simple to say, easily forgotten, but we just must be on our guard if we don't want to be devoured.

At about 7.35pm he telephoned Mavis, which was very quickly answered with a 'see you in ten', answered by an 'on my way'. Whereupon he picked up his wallet and phone, locked the door and strolled along to be at Mavis's for her exit about 7.45pm and then they walked quietly on their way towards the Cathedral grounds and round to St Petri's Chapel. They said little, didn't need to really, having completed this little walk on a Wednesday evening for a few years now. The chapel was alight, and Fr Blakeston was already in place and as usual didn't look anything like a man now in his early nineties should look. There were a few familiar faces around, and he and Mavis were probably the last ones likely to arrive.

After a few moments of absolute quiet, Fr Blakeston looked up and began the service with quiet words of rest and hope:

"The Lord Almighty grant us a quiet night and a perfect end." It was spoken in a gentle but sonorous tone and he moved on to urge the Brethren, to be sober and vigilant. The service of Compline always includes the saying of one or two Psalms. Fr Blakeston's usual pattern was to say first one of those set for the service and then another of his choosing. Tonight, his choice was Psalm 51:

'Have mercy O God, according to Thy loving kindness.'

This was one of my favourite Psalms and known to many musically minded people, perhaps without their even realising. Gregorio Allegri composed a magnificent setting of Psalm 51, generally referred to as Allegri's Miserere. It is a piece of music which falls into the category of a 'once heard, never forgotten'. They always said the Psalms at compline in alternate verses, Fr Blakeston said the odd numbered verses and the congregation the even numbered ones. Monty always found the Psalms beautiful, especially when read aloud. They are sensitive poems or songs, sometimes in the form of prayers and they have a lovely structure. As pieces of writing they can be enjoyed by anyone, religious or not.

Compline continued and it ended as it began, with a sense of hope:

> As the watchmen look for the morning,
> So do we look for thee, O Christ.'

> 'The Almighty and merciful Lord,
> the Father, the Son and the Holy Ghost,
> bless us and preserve us. Amen.'

Only a short time was spent after the service in quiet greetings, handshakes and farewells before Mavis and I strolled back to the Avenue. I asked Mavis if she was familiar with the Allegri setting of Psalm 51. I was surprised that she didn't but kept that thought to myself, and I promised to lend her a copy of the CD of the King's College Chapel Choir's version. We bade goodnight to each other and I went along to my home. Before I went to bed, I checked my emails, found some enquiries about books which I was able to answer quite speedily. I poured a small nightcap, looked out the CD promised for Mavis, intending to pop through her letterbox first thing, and then settled down to watch some late night television, perhaps with only half an eye, was vaguely aware of some political discussion about security threats, troubles in the Middle East, MPs giving vent to their own opinions and ignoring others, but soon it was better to be asleep in bed rather than on the settee.

3. DISCOVERY

There is always a thrill in poking amongst bits and pieces, boxes, suitcases, bags and anything else that auctioneers use to sort out the lots in a general sale, endless searching that just might, only just, lead to something exciting. It doesn't happen to me or if it does the find never amounts to anything special. I'm after books and perhaps I'll spot an unusual signature, an interesting letter as a folded-up bookmark. This morning's sale had more potential for me as there was an unusually large number of boxes of books. I had ear-marked a few to bid for – one containing various atlases, another had a large number of booklets about places visited on many holidays, several boxes of history and also a good number of boxes with the usual mix – a mix not easily catalogued. I often bought boxes like these just for the fun of what might be discovered. As Daniel had telephoned me earlier in the week to say he wouldn't be at the auction, I could see that today's 'winnings' would lead to a taxi being ordered to get me and my belongings home.

By the end of the morning I had only spent about £25 but seemed to have a dozen or so heavy boxes of goodies. Fortunately, I knew the taxi driver and he gave me a hand with the heavier ones, and by the time they were all unloaded and inside my house I felt my fare of £10 was money very well spent, especially as the threatening dark skies were now dropping heavy rain. Some lunch first and then I would spend the afternoon picking over my lots: those for repair, those for recycling, those which could be sold straight away and the final group – oddities for further research. The recycling group filled a couple of black bags and I lugged these away down the garden. Those needing repair I took upstairs and left on my desk. The 'sell straight aways' I placed by my computer and I would start on those later. With more coffee to hand I began to pick over the 'oddities'.

An elastic band was holding together a group of small diaries, several of which turned out to be for horse racing enthusiasts. Several books, all of the same size, had been given brown paper covers and these were all early copies of the red Ward Lock guide books, mostly for the well-known resorts, but a couple of London ones from the 1920s were interesting as they contained maps for the London Underground, some collector appeal there. There were some very scruffy old gardening books which could probably join the recycling bags. The atlases all predated the first world war, so I was surprised they sold so cheaply. Close to the bottom of one box of oddities were two regimental histories – I would have to look those up carefully as they could be quite significant. Last, but hopefully not least, was another brown paper wrapped affair with an elastic band which seemed to be doing no more than holding the old paper in place. I didn't have to remove much before my fingers started to tingle, because revealing itself was an old copy of 'The Hound of the Baskervilles'! As well as the brown paper and elastic band some of the pages were held together with paper clips with small pieces of paper inserted at the front of each clip. Fortunately, these had not rusted and when I slipped off the first and read the publication details, I discovered this copy wasn't just old but was the first edition published by George Newnes in 1902. The paper clip also revealed the first page of text and there was an absolute dream discovery of breathtaking enormity, because across the top in very small neat writing was:

'Dear Albert, your father, and my good friend George tells me you love reading mysteries. As I am at present collecting some copies of my new novel from the publishers, where your father is employed, I don't mind writing this and handing it back to George to give to you.

Yours sincerely, Arthur Conan Doyle'

I could only suppose the paper and clip was to keep this writing clean. I removed the next paper clip and displayed, was one of the illustrations with some more writing in the same hand but smaller:

'This is the best, my favourite of the illustrations.'

So, what would the last paperclip at the end of the book uncover?

'Now that you have reached the end of this adventure, I do hope that you have enjoyed reading it just as much as I did in writing it. Arthur'

It was a very good job that I was on my own because I was speechless and shaking with excitement. I didn't know what to think or do as the potential of the situation dawned upon me, that I was holding something of very considerable value. I quickly tidied away the other books that I had rejected, I wanted to put this magnificent find down in its own prestigious spot with nothing cluttering it up. Then I jumped up and paced about, couldn't keep still, couldn't think calmly, what should I do, nothing, it was late on a Saturday afternoon. My book friend, Daniel was away, how he would have loved to share this moment. I telephoned Mavis as I knew she would understand my thrill and come and share it – we would have a drink! I didn't tell her why I wanted her to come but I think she sensed that something momentous was amazing me because she was ringing the doorbell very quickly.

"Mavis, oh Mavis, I am glad you are here, look, look at this book, isn't it staggering." Of course, I didn't allow for the fact she wouldn't recognise the volume as quickly as I did, but as soon as I pointed to the first bit of handwriting, she began to appreciate the scale of the find. "A drink, we have to toast the moment. I'm having a malt, what about you, a sherry or what?"

"Not a sherry! Like you, I feel the need for something more powerful; I'll have whatever malt you care to pour!"

I leapt up to go for the drinks and as I turned, I kicked over one of the 'tidied' piles of books. These were the scruffy old gardening ones. Lazily I just shoved them out of the way with my foot. When I returned with malt and glasses, I found Mavis had picked the books up and was just placing them neatly when she unravelled a piece of paper.

"This is a large piece of paper to use as a bookmark. It has got print on it, what is it Monty?"

I only needed the quickest of glances and in my shock nearly poured malt whisky everywhere. "It's a dust jacket, the dust jacket! For the Conan Doyle. Look, it has been folded with the illustrated side inner most. Is there more of it because this is only half, at the most."

Immediately we were both on hands and knees looking at more of the gardening books and pulling out various bits of paper which had served as bookmarks.

"Here's a bit more," shouted Mavis.

"And this is the rest I think."

We unfolded the three pieces carefully and laying them flat we could see a complete dust jacket to 'The Hound of the Baskervilles'.

"Can it be repaired?" asked Mavis.

"Oh, I think so, look, the paper is feathered at the torn edges so it won't be a case of trying to butt two edges together, they will overlap ever so slightly which makes for a more effective and far less noticeable repair. I won't attempt it, too valuable, needs a real paper restorer. I'll place the three pieces in a protective sleeve which will keep them safe and allow us to place it round the book like a complete dust jacket. Just a minute though, this doesn't make sense, I don't think there was a dust jacket with the first edition. That arrived with the first American edition, I think that's right. Let me get my laptop, I can check in a couple of minutes. I'm right, the first UK edition was red boards on which was an ornate gilt design with a black silhouette of a hound to top centre but no dustjacket.

"Sit down Monty. You need to calm a little. Let's drink the malt."

"Yes, indeed. Well, here's to Sir Arthur Conan Doyle, his friend, George and George's son, Albert. Arthur, George and Albert."

We clinked our glasses and sipped in stunned contentment.

After a while Mavis went home, having thanked me for asking her to share this great find. I tidied up some more and locked the 'discovery' in my cabinet. I began to wonder about its value, tens of thousands of pounds I thought, especially given the unusual autographing and the fact that there was a complete dust jacket - but a dust jacket that shouldn't exist. I needed to check that. Then I thought about who had sold it and that they couldn't have known of its existence, and nor of course did the auctioneer. That could cause some embarrassment. Monday would see me making some tactful enquiries. I felt bad that someone might have been unwittingly done out of a considerable fortune. Strictly speaking, I believe the law was entirely on my side and that the book was mine to do with as I wished. Even so, I didn't think I could be that mean.

Sunday found me very fidgety, so it was fortunate that I was booked to play the organ twice and that forced me to focus my mind, be organised. Even so, I looked at the volume many times, just to savour the feel of it. I turned all the pages to check that it was complete and to make sure that there were no other fascinating pieces of writing from the author. I found nothing but was able to satisfy myself that this copy was in very good condition, binding was holding well, the pages were clean and that when the dust jacket had been professionally restored, it too, would look very pleasing. I kept forgetting about the dust jacket being incorrect, even though with restoration it could look quite beautiful. I rang Daniel but as I expected, he was still away. I thought about leaving him a message but decided the matter was too grand to reduce to a brief voice message; I wanted to share my excitement in person. I started to look at the pieces of the dust jacket a bit more closely and realised the design incorporated some of the book's illustrations – the title to the top, below that one of the illustration of the hound as on the front board in a circular frame and two similarly framed below that. Each was just a small part of a different illustration. These were in sepia shades and round each some of the gilt design from the board was used as a miniature frame. On the back was a copy of a full-size example of another illustration, the one of Holmes shooting the hound. This was also completed in sepia shades with a gilt frame. These copies of some of the original illustrations showed an impressive talent. The fold-ins were plain. Feeling the art surface, I could sense some unevenness and I wondered if I was looking at original paint work, very talented artist. I wondered if its date was contemporary with the book.

4. POST-AUCTION EXCITEMENTS

I had some boring jobs to do the following week and I would probably complete them, giving only half a mind to each. I started with the garden which for most of the year looked after itself but periodically I must attend to the state of all my pots, large, very large and a couple of old baths. I changed and renewed some of the soil, added fertilizer, plucked the odd weed which had had the temerity to appear, and pulled up a small beech tree just sprouting from where a squirrel had left the nut. It was also time to get some new bulbs on the go. Some of the plants growing against walls and trellis needed fresh supports. The success of this garden was in what I didn't have to do – cut any grass, weed flower beds; oh, what joy! When I was a child my dad used gain much pleasure from growing vegetables but sad to say I never inherited this pleasure and despite hints from my mother I made no attempt to rectify this very distinct lack of enthusiasm and for which, I'm sorry to say, I felt no guilt.

In the middle of Monday morning I rang the auctioneers, Jones and Hewitts. I had thought about this carefully and had decided to just ask if they could let me know who the seller was of the lots that I had purchased. They were hesitant at first, but I explained that I had found some items which were somewhat personal, and I had wondered if they might not have been intended for the sale. I would be happy to return them if necessary. The lady I was speaking to suddenly chuckled and I was a bit surprised. She apologised, explaining that while I had been talking, she had looked up the lot numbers. The owner was now deceased and there were no known relatives or beneficiaries. Sad really, but she only wanted to see the funny side of it. I could take whatever I had to the crematorium and have them burnt and added to his ashes or I could hand them over to officials at the Treasury as they would be the eventual recipients of the proceeds from sale.

I thanked her, said no more, and felt relieved that I needn't take any difficult or embarrassing action. I wasn't too worried about not contributing to the nation's coffers. The only real losers were the auctioneers as their commission would have been much improved had they examined what they were selling more carefully; I imagined it was not an uncommon oversight though. I decided to do no more about the book until after I had spoken to Daniel, but I could see a visit to a London Auction House looming in the not too distant future and that would be exciting. Perhaps Mavis would care to come with me.

Late Tuesday morning and to engage my whole mind, was a planned visit to the dentist. This had all the potential for being a painful trip as an old and large filling had fallen out a couple of weeks back. His temporary stop as he had called it, was coming to a permanent end and now I was to be found with a very well numbed mouth. Some thirty minutes later, expert craftsmanship completed, I emerged with one elderly tooth saved. I went home to take a couple of paracetamol and to await life to return to my gum, hopefully, not accompanied by pain.

I didn't totally forget the other books which I had bought at the now famous, in my mind at least, auction and I began to list some on my website and others on ebay. I completed several minor repairs, making a few books and pamphlets look quite respectable. At first glance they had looked scruffy, but some old-fashioned tender-loving-care brought about excellent transformations. On Friday I abandoned bookwork and replaced it with housework. It is an easy house to look after and a couple of hours will find a finished result suitable for any unexpected visitors. I was just beginning to think about Daniel's usual visit when he rang to say that he was finishing work early and would call middle of the afternoon if that was OK; that was a change of plan which pleased me immensely. Thinking Mavis might like to hear what Daniel had to say I telephoned but she was not in, so I left a message making it clear she was welcome to call. I also sent a text.

When Daniel called, I surprised him somewhat by telling him that we needed to be in doors, at least for a while. I placed a malt to one side of where he sat and on the other provided a further small table. It was here that I placed with some elaborate care 'The Book'. Daniel glanced down but said nothing, obviously struck by my somewhat mannered behaviour. "Oh, I didn't know that was available in facsimile ………. goodness, it isn't, is that an original Monty? May I pick it up?"

"Yes, do. It may be very valuable, but it still requires handling and study. Go ahead, pick it up, have a very good look, particularly at the first and last pages of the text."

He took another sip of his malt, set the glass down and proceeded to do as I had suggested. There followed a good five minutes of total silence. It was as if two small boys were holding their breath and daring each other to do something which they thought dangerous and brave.

"Monty, how on earth did you, no, you couldn't have, you surely didn't bid for it deliberately? Where was it, when did you discover what you had found?"

"You're right. I had no knowledge of it until Saturday afternoon when I started looking at various bits and pieces in one of the boxes of mixed items. It was wrapped up in this brown paper and elastic band." I had kept all the wrappings including the paper clips and I proceeded to give him some idea of how the item looked when I first picked it up.

"Not wanting to sound mercenary, but have you any idea of its value?"

"Well, I have tracked down an American dealer with a copy of an equivalent item but a first edition of the American issue, signed and with its dust jacket and he wants US$35000. His is a complete copy as sometimes a few illustrations have been removed or lost. So, what do you think, £40000? At present there isn't a copy with a dust jacket on the market because there shouldn't be a dust jacket. Suppose I'll have to get it seen by an expert. Like the American one, this copy has all the illustrations."

"What do you mean, 'shouldn't be a dust jacket'?

"Exactly that. This dust jacket was never issued by the publishers because the UK first edition didn't have a dust jacket. This is a previous owner's creation and very interesting it is."

Have you thought about sending some scans to one of the London auction-houses? I wonder if any research will reveal the identity of Conan Doyle's friend, George? Obviously, they'll want to see it and check it thoroughly and see your proof of ownership."

"Well that's a laugh, I have one piece of paper listing nine lot numbers all described as 'miscellaneous books. I don't want to get ahead of myself, but I suppose I'll be liable for capital gains tax, that'll be steep I bet."

"Monty," spoke Daniel, a little firmer than usual. "You need to get yourself some good sound advice before you do anything."

"Yes, I expect you're right. By the way, and pardon the change of subject, but did I tell you that I probably spotted your thieves the other morning. I was near the town hall when two lads shot across from W H Smiths, carried on down the road towards the traffic lights and then round to the left. All I can say is that they looked about 13 or 14 years old, scrawny in build and very fast when it came to running away. I only thought about the shoplifting which you mentioned because I looked back towards the shop doorways and two or three staff emerged, glancing about, and looking rather annoyed."

"Ah, there have been a few more incidents. But they'll slip up one day and we'll catch them. Now, going back to the book, don't forget, you need advice. Anyway, another malt to celebrate, and then I must be off."

Left to myself I thought about the selling side of my book and decided to make some scans and send them off to Trumpingtons & Co. Ltd. This old firm had been long established and one of their specialist areas was with books and ephemera. They had come to mind because I had read of some high prices recently achieved in one of their sales. Elizabethan papers and a complete library from one of the big 'county' families. It was the same old story, maintenance costs of a country estate outstripping the family income, but to me it seemed very sad to part with a complete library. I scanned some shots of the three parts of the dust jacket, the boards, the publication details page, the three pages showing the writing by Sir Arthur and I photographed the book in a standing and partly open view and scanned that in as well. Trumpingtons website listed a Joseph Mallings as being Head of C19th and C20th books so I sent him an email with attachments, gave him my contact details, added the scans, and sent it all off to him. It was already gone 5.30pm so I was much surprised to receive a phone call ten minutes later.

"Hello, Monty Warnock? As you have just sent me an email, I expected you to still be there. This is Joseph Mallings, I'm working a little later than usual and I have just been looking at your incredible scans, what an amazing find!"

"Well, yes, it has been exciting." Truth to tell, I was a bit taken aback by the speed of the response. "I need to plan a trip down to London so you can view…."

"No, no! You mustn't do that, far too risky. We would like to come to you and by 'we' I mean myself and another colleague, Charles Sedgefield – he has handled several Arthur Conan Doyle sales and is also familiar with his handwriting. We're in Cambridge Wednesday afternoon of next week for an evening preview of a forthcoming exhibition and we'll be stopping the night. So, is the Wednesday morning a possibility, failing that, the Thursday morning. Oh, and would we be able to take some photographs? Good as your scans were, we would like to take some more specialist close-up photographs, especially of the rather unexpected dust jacket, it's never been seen before as far as we know. We never drive anywhere without camera and lighting equipment resting across the back seat."

Well, that all sounds very good, I think Thursday morning would suit me best, 10.00 o'clock or so be all right? I can email some instructions if you're driving or it will have to be a taxi from the station. I don't have a car these days so I can't pick you up.

"That is not a worry, some directions would help. Although we do travel by train occasionally, we'll probably drive. We're looking forward greatly to seeing this find of yours."

"Goodbye." The phone clicked off.

I was just moving away from the phone when it rang again.

"Monty, it's Daniel, I thought you would like an update on the lads you saw the other day. You'll probably be able to read about it in a local newspaper next week or so. The boys got picked up a few days after you saw them, caught in the act of rescuing an elderly lady, Cynthia, I only have her first name at moment. It's rather sad, seems she was attempting to drown herself when the boys arrived. One of them jumped straight in but the woman started to push him and they both got into difficulties, so the second boy got in and between them they pulled her to the bank. Anyway, police and fire brigade arrived and all three of them were pulled to safety. Cynthia was obviously in a terrible state and as soon as an ambulance arrived, she was taken off to hospital. Of course, the police started to ask the boys the obvious questions and it quickly became very clear that they were keeping back on something. Needless-to-say, it all came out in the end – they were truanting and had been doing all the petty thieving."

"What will happen to them? Do you know how Cynthia is now?

"Sorry, but I haven't heard how she is. The boys will have to be charged but by the time the local press get on to the story, the Magistrate will probably let them off with a sharply worded caution and at the same time praise their courage. Not so their mothers, as colleagues say they are both forces to be reckoned with. One of them is from India, came here as a child, she married a local guy. She is very small but has a tongue that more than makes up for any lack of height. The other mum is huge, apparently could knock her boy over with her little finger. No doubt their school will have to take some action.

"It sounds very sad about Cynthia, I know her, did I say? I will have to try and visit her. Oh, I nearly forgot, I sent some scans of the book to Trumpingtons in London and they rang back within ten minutes and have arranged to come and see the book next Thursday morning.

"It's all happening at present. If you like I may be able to sit in with you Thursday morning, I'll check and let you know."

"I would certainly appreciate that Daniel, I'm excited about their visit but I can't deny being a little nervous about it.

5. THE TRUMPINGTON VISIT

Although I couldn't keep my mind off Thursday's meeting, I did manage to visit Cynthia. She was still in hospital but very calm, probably some drugs I thought. Reluctantly she told me about a terrible time she had had with Ernie one day, he had knocked his soup all over the lounge and then struck out at her, she had screamed, her neighbour had come in, took one look and called the doctor. He didn't come but sent a nurse around. (Later I was to discover that she was from a community mental health team.) Before Cynthia really understood what had happened, Ernie was admitted for assessment. It seemed gradually that everyone left, and Cynthia was then on her own and just didn't know what to do. Then followed a long sleepless night and it was the following morning when she had gone around to the gardens where I often met her. She couldn't remember the next details but found herself just stepping off the bank and into the river, but she must have wandered a couple of hundred yards to get to this particular point on the bank. Her next bit of memory was fighting with boys as she put it and then waking up in hospital. It was only after the police had visited, did she learn that far from having a fight with them, the boys had been her rescue team and without them she would probably have drowned. At this point in her story she suddenly shuddered and started to weep, and it was a good fifteen minutes or so before she could speak again and then she only mumbled about not knowing what was going to happen. She looked at me quite blankly, almost as if she didn't know me, quietly she whispered the name of 'Ernie', in the form of a question as if I were Ernie. I thought she was getting a bit muddled, excused myself and went to find one of the nurses. She either couldn't or wouldn't say much but was clear on one thing, Cynthia would stay in hospital for a few more days as Social Service staff were intending to visit. I didn't learn much more, but I did tell Cynthia that I would visit her again and soon.

One of my never-ending tasks – pleasant one, of course – is packing up and sending off books, most days, and to anywhere in the world. This often leads to what I have called 'short-term email friendships' in that a customer will tell me why they have bought a particular book, what they collect, ask me to look out for particular items and which occasionally I am able to find. I also like searching websites to research and find books, sometimes spotting a bargain from a dealer. I have got in a muddle with postings and sent books to wrong people, tricky when overseas addresses have been involved and expensive to put right. As the end of the year begins to loom, I know that I will increase sales; books still make excellent Christmas presents. Whatever else I may have to do I can never get behind with the selling side of my life with books!

Daniel telephoned on the Wednesday to confirm that he would be able to join me when the guys from Trumpingtons arrived and I went to bed that night full of excitement and expectation. True to plan, Joseph Mallings and Charles Sedgefield arrived within minutes of 10.00am. Daniel was already installed, and I made coffee for all while Daniel introduced himself.

"Well, let me not keep you guys in suspense; this is the book!" I passed it over wrapped just as I had found it but without the paperclips. Over the years paper can get very brittle, didn't want to cause any damage. As Charles was the acknowledged Conan Doyle expert, he took possession first. He was totally silent and looked at the volume with meticulous care, using a magnifying glass so he could look carefully at the stitching and down the spine. Similarly, he studied the illustrations, by Sydney Paget. After a little while he looked up and smiled. "Well. I don't think that there is any doubt about this volume, a totally genuine copy from 1902. Here, time for you to share the moment, Joseph," as he passed the copy to his colleague. "Now, I know this is your copy, recently acquired, but what is your proof of ownership?"

"Not much, just one piece of A5 size paper," I replied. "I bought several boxes of books at the local auction Saturday before last and this was at the bottom of one of them containing quite a mix of books. My total bid value was exactly £25, and the one receipt just says: Monty Warnock, Date, 9 lots, numbers 24 to 32 Total value £25 plus commission at 20% £5, plus VAT £1. Total paid, cash £31.00. The firm's clerk has signed it and the paper is headed Jones and Hewitts, Auctioneers, Peterborough. I have made a copy for you. As yet, I haven't told the auctioneers about this book. Don't quite know how, but I know I can't keep the matter secret."

"No, you certainly won't keep it secret and if you did people might wonder why." Charles smiled, "It is not an unheard-of situation but that doesn't make letting them know any easier. The commission that they have missed could easily be in the region of £8000. Who was the previous owner?"

"I think that matter is at least straight forward. This sale arose from a house clearance, the occupant having been found dead and there are no descendants. Jones and Hewitts have already told me that the proceeds from the sale will be going eventually to the Treasury but I don't know who is organising that, local solicitor perhaps."

"Assuming verification of all that from the people you have mentioned, I don't envisage any problems, but we would pass all the circumstances to our company's legal adviser. As I indicated earlier, it is not a unique situation and we have certainly encountered it before, but to its value, I don't know. Other than you, who else knows of this book's existence?"

"Daniel, of course, and another friend of mine, also a neighbour, a Miss Mavis Missily. I haven't mentioned it to anyone else."

"Did you say Mavis Missily?" Joseph's head shot up as he almost shouted his question. "What would she be now, middle years, quietish sort of individual, has a sister similar age, can't remember her name, something similar if my memory is correct?"

"Yes, that sounds like Mavis, I have only known her since she moved this way fifteen years or so back.

Her sister, Muriel, works and lives in London. How on earth do you know them?"

"Well, this is going back a long time now, twenty-five, thirty years maybe. We were holding an auction of modern fine art, at the time very recent stuff. Part of the auction covered fabric designs and similar. Mavis, as I recall, had a few pieces in the auction and this couldn't have been that long after her finishing art school, they were in wool, knitting, but not as you might think of knitting, these works were very three dimensional. They were most unusual, abstract designs, very subtle colours and incredibly textural. They didn't make a lot of money, but they were commented on, they impressed some of the viewers. I remember her because I met her at one of the viewing days, she was with her sister and they were looking at her work and reading the catalogue, perhaps surprised at the estimates. That is all I know, never met again and never encountered any of her art either."

"That is certainly news to me and may account for her not being here. When I first told her about your planned visit, I didn't mention the name of the firm. That wasn't until last night when I rang just to say that I wouldn't be going with her to Compline – we have been going together for years now. I think I said something like, 'don't forget about Trumpingtons in the morning, about 10.00am.'"

"No knowing what may have happened, some people's inspiration just dries up, may have lost confidence, needed to earn more money. Now our name has been mentioned she may say something."

I agreed, but I knew that I certainly couldn't just raise the matter.

"Back to Arthur Conan Doyle, then. What do you think of the book Joseph?"

"Amazing! The dust jacket will repair well, but we need to think about that carefully as it can be better to auction an item as it is, give the new owner the choice about any restoration. Certainly nothing else needs attention. But most significant are the unusual inscriptions. I don't think I have ever encountered an autographed book in this way. Not uncommon for a book to carry a lot of notes by an owner who subsequently becomes famous and that is the reason for the book's value. But these are three deliberately thought about inscriptions for young Albert. It would be wonderful if he and his father, George, could be tracked down. I have no idea what publisher records still exist, and he might have been a very minor employee and the reference to George being Conan Doyle's good friend may have been nothing more than politeness. Now, Charles, you're more expert than I am with the works of Sir Arthur Conan Doyle, where would you pitch the estimate for the pre-sale catalogue?"

"Very difficult. I don't see it selling for less than £35000. When the dust jacket has been repaired it will be an excellent copy. And remember, the dust jacket only needs repair, not restoration – there are no paper losses nor surface scuffs causing loss to colour and there has been no fading. I can see it making £50000 so an estimate of £40K to £50K perhaps Need to think more and perhaps consult. One absolute certainty - as soon as its existence is known the interest level will be both enormous and world-wide."

"But what about the dust jacket," was my small interruption. "It is not original to the book and it looks like actual artwork, I mean it hasn't been printed. This is as an artist finished it, using material from Sydney Paget's illustrations and the board designs themselves."

"What do you think about it, Charles?"

"Monty's right in so far as it is not a printed item, so presumably it is a one-off. If its date is contemporary with the book, then it takes on some significance and repaired it will be impressive to look at; it complements the book extremely well. We will have to seek additional opinions."

The meeting was gradually coming to an end. Charles set up the camera equipment and took several photographs, some very close up. Joseph mentioned that the next most suitable sale for an item such as this would probably be early May when they would be including several lots of early twentieth century works of fiction and related ephemera – authors' letters, drafts, notes etc. They wanted to know about current security and insurance for the book which made me realise I hadn't given it much thought. In the event of them being given the privilege of auctioning this item they would arrange for secure collection and storage and insurance set at a level equal to the upper estimate auction value. I assured them that I wasn't in contact with other auction houses, asked them to give me a day or so just to think about it and then I would contact them regarding collection. At this point Daniel did mention that he could arrange temporary secure storage. The only alternative would be a short-term safe deposit scheme. I suddenly thought that this could all become an enormous worry so I asked Joseph to accept the commission for sale then and there and arrange collection just as soon as he could. How terrible was the thought were theft or fire to befall such a rare treasure.

After Joseph and Charles had driven off with promises of being in touch within 48 hours Daniel and I sat down to consume a recuperative malt, sizable measure too.

"I think you did the right thing Monty, get them to take on all the immediate responsibility. After all, they are experts and the firm enjoys quite a reputation. So, I shouldn't be surprised if the book isn't on its journey before Friday's out.

"That will give me peace of mind. Exciting as the last couple of weeks have been, I now realise the responsibility of ownership is very considerable so I shall be pleased to pass it on. Minor by comparison, but I must call on Jones and Hewitts and tell them about the book. I'm going to be a little economical with the truth – something like 'Ah, hello, thought you might like to know that amongst all those books I bought the other week was an early Arthur Conan Doyle. It's a bit outside my usual range of activity because it is a signed copy so I'm sending it to London for some book specialists to auction it. Not done that before so see what happens.' Something like that, what do you think?

"Yes, that's all right, keep it fairly low key."

Joseph Mallings of Trumpingtons was speedier than I expected as he was on the phone late Thursday afternoon to let me know that a security firm would call on me by nine o'clock Friday morning to collect the book and also for me to sign over responsibility to them along the lines of the explanation they gave Wednesday. There will be a copy for me to keep and the driver would also be giving me a receipt. He promised to keep in touch with results of any research. He also said he would send me information about forthcoming auctions which might appeal, inviting to come down to London and soak up some of the sale room atmosphere. He mentioned that their firm had an arrangement with a local hotel, 'The Williams Hotel', about thirty yards from the back entrance to Trumpingtons, and that if I ever wanted to call at their Auction House on this matter or to visit another sale they would be happy to make a booking which would save me about 20%. I thanked him for that, said that I may well take up the offer.

Trumpingtons' security driver arrived as promised and exactly on time. He dealt with the paperwork very efficiently and was on his way within 20 minutes. In a way it was quite sad now, not to be able to have a look and perhaps gloat over my find, not perhaps the best of behaviour though.

6. THE PASSING OF A FRIEND

With the departure of my 'treasure' an excitement suddenly left my ordinary life, its ordinariness had been unexpectedly interrupted and now it had to be resumed. It was some days now since the meeting with Trumpingtons and I had taken up my book repairing and selling again, punctuated with everyday shopping, strolling about Peterborough and the many other day to day activities. I had also visited Cynthia a couple of times and was pleased to find her much better.

I was still thinking about all this when the phone rang. "Hello, is that Monty Warnock? This is Wendy Goodison, Cynthia's neighbour, I don't think we've met."

"Yes, this is Monty and you are right, we know of each other, but we haven't met. How can I help?"

"Sorry to tell you but I have some sad news. I believe you knew Cynthia's husband, Ernie. I'm afraid he passed away last night, heart attack I believe. Cynthia called to tell me this morning and asked me to let you know as you are one of the few people who kept in touch."

"That is sad news Wendy and I'll try and call on Cynthia's later today, she may well need some help with arrangements. If you can tell Cynthia that I'll call later, that would be kind of you Wendy.

I had a few bits of book business to complete before lunch and get a couple of items in the post in time for the last collection. It was about two o'clock when I called on Cynthia, needless-to-say I found her very upset, but she seemed relieved, perhaps comforted to see me. I sat with her for quite a while and we talked about Ernie. I looked at her photographs as she relived memories of happy times. As she mentioned her daughter, I asked if she had been able to let her know about her father. Cynthia explained that she was going to write, her way, I think, of letting me know that she didn't expect her daughter, Jean, to be coming home. I ask about plans for the funeral and clearly, she was at a lost to know what to do, looked rather bewildered. She explained that she was on her own, no close family folk to call on. It made me wonder if there might be a financial difficulty, so I offered to make some enquiries for her. Cynthia seemed very relieved by this suggestion and I promised to see her at some point over the weekend.

I don't know why I took it upon myself to help Cynthia, but I had a scheme which could easily be put into effect and nobody other than me need know the financial details. I knew who to see and found myself ringing the doorbell of Fr Blakeston's residence.

"Monty, this is an unexpected pleasure, come in, come in. I've just made a pot of tea so you can share that with me. How can I help?"

"I want to arrange a funeral and would like your help."

"That's an unexpected request, somebody close to you? I had formed the impression that you had no relatives, was I wrong?"

"You're quite right Father. This funeral is for the husband of a dear friend who I have known for many years, known but never known closely. Cynthia Brownley is in her eighties, and her husband, Ernie, who died last night, was of a similar age. Over the last two or three years he had been developing dementia and recently attacked Cynthia. He had to be taken into safe residential care. He had only been there a few weeks and last night he suffered a fatal heart attack. In their younger days they were an active couple and used to go to the Cathedral on Sunday mornings although I don't think they formed any close friendships. They have a grown-up daughter who lives in Australia and who doesn't keep in touch. I used to see them frequently about the town and often sat with them in Bishop's Road Gardens. He had been in the RAF as a young man, qualified as an engineer and worked in this City for most of his adult life. They lived in a small house in Bishop's Terrace where Cynthia still lives, with 'Barkie', a pet Scottie. One of her sole sources of comfort is a collection of old and rather dogeared photographs and she likes to look at them frequently, show them to whoever is willing. She has a very loyal neighbour, Wendy Goodison. She was involved when Ernie attacked Cynthia and she rang me this morning to tell me of his death. Immediately after Ernie went into care Cynthia was so upset that she attempted to drown herself but two teenage boys, acting very quickly, were able to save her. At the time they were truanting and shoplifting but that's another story. I suspect Cynthia has little money and I don't think they owned the house. When I asked about funeral arrangements, she seemed very overcome and worried, hence my request."

"Well, Monty, you do realise that you may be incurring considerable expenditure? But, certainly, I am willing to help all I can. I presume you would like the funeral to take place here, at St Petri's Chapel. I can ask the Dean and his staff if anyone remembers them from when they used to attend the Cathedral."

"That all sounds most helpful. I am not worried about the cost. My real concern is that there may only be half a dozen mourners as Cynthia has never talked about relatives and over the last few years, I think they have lost touch with local friends."

"Oh, don't worry about that, God will look kindly on whoever attends and it has always been my experience that more people attend these occasions than is expected. Will it be a cremation afterwards? You go and see the undertakers and then come back to me. I have no commitments in the next week or two, so any date will be fine as far as I am concerned.

"That's all truly kind of you Father. I'll call on the undertakers shortly and then let Cynthia know what can be arranged and if she wishes me to continue. Thank you again and thanks for the tea. I'll let myself out."

"Goodbye Monty, God bless."

"Bye Father, I'll be in touch."

My next stop was with the undertakers. I went to the Co-op as I remembered them being most helpful when my mother died. Explaining my circumstances, that I was unsure who was paying for the funeral, they were extremely understanding. One phone call to the crematorium, and quickly a date and time was arranged. They were intrigued by the funeral taking place at St Petri's Chapel, a first for them. The hearse and one car were booked so I took myself back to Cynthia's. I explained what arrangements I had made, albeit somewhat tentatively, but she was more than happy, indeed quite relieved that she had nothing more to do. Cynthia did say that she would organise some flowers, probably chrysanthemums, as they were Ernie's favourite. I asked if she wanted any particular hymn or music, but she wanted me to be responsible for anything to do with the service. I wrote a quick note regarding date and time and on my way home, popped it though Fr Blakeston's door.

It was Wednesday afternoon and I suddenly felt quite tired from all my walking. Tea and cake called but I first went to see Mavis. I had talked to her about Cynthia, told her about the suicide attempt but she was unsure whether she knew her at all, perhaps by sight. Mavis served the tea and cake and I settled to telling her about the visit of Joseph and Charles from Trumpingtons the previous week, the security collection of the book. I told her how I had received news about Ernie's death and Fr Blakeston's agreement to conduct the funeral at St Petri's Chapel. She told me that it was a lovely gesture on my part to relieve Cynthia of the worries of organising the funeral.

"Now, the auction of the book is for next spring, did you say? So, quite a sum of money perhaps to come from sale of 'The Hound of the Baskervilles'. Did Trumpingtons seem confident about their estimate?"

"Yes, indeed, in fact, they gave the impression that their top estimate could be exceeded. I think several factors impressed them: the overall condition of the book and the mysterious dust jacket, but the decision as to whether to repair it is still pending. The title is probably the most well-known of the Sherlock Holmes stories and consequently has very wide appeal. The inscriptions are unusual– so rare to have three related hand-written notes and two signatures. I explained that as well as thinking about the possible repair they were also going to see what might be discovered about George and Albert.

As I was drinking tea and munching my way through a large slice of a magnificent sponge and cream cake with a layer of homemade blackcurrant jelly, I let my gaze wander around the room for once. I had sat there on many occasions and yet for the first time, I noticed Mavis's framed pictures. They were quite varied: a print of the Cathedral, a watercolour – landscape which reminded me of the River Nene where people go rowing, there were photographs of who I presumed were her parents and there was also a small pastel sketch of her sister, Muriel and I wondered if Mavis had done it. More intriguing, in view of recent conversations, was an embroidery – very abstract in design in subtle shades of similar colours, pinks, purples and browns. I was tempted to say something but, in the end thought I would leave the matter alone.

"Monty, I'm glad you have called as I have an unusual invitation for you for Christmas, which, despite the unseasonably warm autumnal weather we have been enjoying of late, is only a couple of months away. Muriel's boss, Kenneth, has asked if she would like to ask me and you because she knows that occasionally in the past, we have joined forces, so to speak, at Christmas. Kenneth knows of you even though you haven't met and would be quite chuffed, his expression, if we stayed at his place in Kensington for a few days over the Christmas period. Muriel says she would be delighted to raid the food halls at Harrods for all that is necessary, and, more importantly, do all that is necessary. Does the idea appeal?"

"Yes, it does, wonderful idea, and something very different. Won't have to talk non-stop will I, as it's nice to curl up with a good book for an hour or so?"

"I expect we'll be able to do our own thing and rest assured that Muriel and me, we're not into endless party games! I'll tell Muriel then, that you're excited with the plan."

"I better away now as I expect I have a lot of book enquiries and sales to deal with. I feel I have been rushing around a lot today so I don't think I will make it to Compline this evening. When I got home, I caught up with some book work, ate a couple of sandwiches and listened to the news. Later I fancied a drink and a favourite film, a malt poured and the DVD of 'Tea with Mussolini' in its slot and I settled down for the rest of the evening.

I pottered away through the rest of the week, managed to get quite a number of books cleaned and repaired as well as allowing myself to be distracted by a lengthy read of a crime novel which I intended to hand on to Daniel. Because I read so much of it, I knew I would have to finish it or buy a Kindle copy for later. As much for the music as the service, I took myself off to the Choral Evensong at the Cathedral. I confess to not paying the closest of attention but did let the music stir my soul – always an uplifting experience.

7. PROMISE OF A SOUVENIR DUSTJACKET

On Friday morning I found a neatly written note which must have been hand-delivered quite early. It was from Fr Blakeston and I wondered who had delivered it for him.

Dear Monty,

Would it be possible for you to call on me mid-morning? I have some information for you regarding the funeral arrangements for Ernie Brownley. I think you will be pleased with what I tell you. Shall we say, 11.00am, I usually have coffee with a chocolate biscuit about then.

Fr Blakeston

I was just thinking how nice that would be and wondering what he had to tell me when the phone rang.

"Hello, Monty? Joseph Mallings here, from Trumpingtons, are you well?"

"Yes, fine."

"Look, a group of us were meeting at the end of last week and your book was one of the items under discussion. It was about the question of whether to repair the dust jacket or not and the strong opinion was that as it is a straightforward repair, it would be best to go ahead and get it done. The important point was that there was no need for any actual paper or surface restoration. We've shown it to our usual team who carry out this kind of work for us. They agree with the plan to repair and confirmed what we thought, that it would be a very straightforward task, reflected in the fee of about £75. The senior paper restorer was also of the opinion that the paper and the art materials were all contemporary with the book. If you are agreeable to this Monty, we'll go ahead. When finished, we are assured it will be difficult to see anything of the tears on the printed side and only just visible on the reverse. What's your thinking?"

"Go ahead. Excellent plan and I look forward to seeing the finished result. As a souvenir of the whole saga do you think it will be possible for me to receive a facsimile of the dustjacket? I wouldn't be trying to pretend otherwise, indeed I don't mind 'facsimile' being printed on the blank side."

"That sounds a lovely souvenir to have and I don't see any problem. So pleased that you agree with the plan to repair. I wish you well then Monty, we'll be in touch. Will you start looking out for an original copy of the book, one in poor condition, obviously no dust jacket, no autographs, shouldn't be too expensive.

"I did think that. Anyway, thanks for ringing Joseph."

"My pleasure."

It was time now for me to stroll down to join Fr Blakeston for coffee and the promised chocolate biscuits. It was a bright and sunny morning but decidedly chilly. Time to get winter coats out of the cupboard. I strolled along, nodding to one or two familiar faces, through Cathedral Square and into the grounds. Fr Blakeston's front door was ajar, I tapped lightly and walked in. "Hello Father, Monty here."

"Ah, dear boy, come in. The lady who helps me with this house, Susan, made the coffee just before she left. Sit down, biscuits are beside you so help yourself."

"This 'boy' as you call me, is looking forward to doing just that. Dark chocolate digestive biscuits are at the top of my 'must eat' list, thank you very much."

He handed me a mug of coffee and then sat down himself. "Now, about the funeral. I have been making some enquiries and I think you will be pleased with the results. After you left, Wednesday was it, I telephoned the Dean. He didn't recall the name Ernie Brownley, but he said he would call on one of the older, now retired, Canons, Fr John Evans, as he thought that he would remember him. It turns out he more than remembered him. Apparently, they were both in the RAF doing National Service at the same time and had known each other although not well. They had met again at the end of a morning service here and in conversation realised that their paths had crossed when they were both rather young, still in their teens. He has agreed to speak briefly at Ernie's Funeral Service. Fr John has also been in touch with another retiree who used to talk to them both over coffee, also after morning service. Fr Andrew, the fellow retiree, has also agreed to help at the service by leading some of the prayers. Fr Andrew is rather keen on music and was for a while Precentor and he has persuaded the assistant organist to 'borrow' four choristers from their school and between them they will lead the music of the service. How does that all sound?"

"You have been busy Father. I think Cynthia will be touched by all the effort being made for her Ernie. She has asked me to choose hymns etc., seemed most anxious to hand over the various responsibilities for the funeral although she is ordering flowers. It will be easier if we settle on choice of hymns now and psalm, if you have one in mind. By the way, is there an organ in the chapel, I've never noticed one."

"You are right Monty, no organ but David Jenkins is bringing his electric keyboard over. Tentatively we thought along the following lines: as we process in, the choir will sing the hymn 'Amazing Grace'. They will also sing the 23rd Psalm. We thought that two very traditional hymns would be right – 'O God, our help in ages past' and 'The day Thou Gavest, Lord, is Ended'. How does that seem to you?"

"You have been most kind and thoughtful and Cynthia, I am sure, will be particularly pleased with all that is planned. I certainly think a traditional style is the most appropriate. Now, you must let me know how much to pay the organist and the choir boys."

"They are giving their services free."

"That doesn't seem right to me, I won't argue with David Jenkins, but I'll get the boys a book token each, how will that be?"

"Monty, that will be fine, a sensible compromise. Time off school and a gift of a book token should go down all right. I'm glad you think the service for Ernie will please, it will be kindly to give him a devout send-off. A funeral here at St Petri's is 'first' as far as we know, I've asked about and nobody can recall it ever happening before."

I stayed chatting with Fr Blakeston for a while longer, managing to nibble a couple more biscuits. When I took the second one, he smiled at me and poured more coffee. Perhaps being addressed as 'Dear Boy' was appropriate after all.

When I got home, I just sat quietly for a while and thought over the various unexpected happenings of the last few weeks. It had certainly been an unusual Autumn and amazingly fruitful – nothing to do with giant marrows and cooking apples either. I couldn't imagine what else might befall me. I picked up the local paper which lay still unread. I usually looked at it for local advertisements as quite often people sold off unwanted books. I always made a note of small events, village fetes, jumble sales – not infrequently a source of minor treasures of just my sort. I turned over the first page and got no further.

LOCAL BOYS UNEXPECTED HEROES

'Two local boys whose names are not being released were involved in the rescue of an elderly lady, Cynthia Brownley, when she fell in the River Nene. This news only emerged at a Magistrate's Hearing last week when the same two boys pleaded guilty to shoplifting while truanting from school. It was noted by the Magistrate that the value of goods amounted to about £5 at each shop. Each boy was ordered to pay the shops involved, about £15, in all the sum of £75, and they were to take the money to each shop together with a hand-written letter of apology. The parents of the boys agreed to accompany them on each shop visit. The Magistrate congratulated the boys on the speed and success of the rescue of Cynthia Brownley especially as they must have realised that their truanting and shoplifting activities could not be kept from Police attention. They were told that no further action would be taken.'

That seemed a sensible kind of punishment to me; I just hoped that they will mend their ways. Given what I had heard about both mothers, I imagined that they would be taking action to ensure instant mending.

When the post arrived, I found a package from Trumpingtons, a letter confirming all that Joseph & I had discussed. As well, he had included three copies of previous sales catalogues which had featured large quantities of books, and also a list of forth coming sales. There was a sale scheduled for early December so I decided then that a day in London would be interesting. I could travel down the night before, stop over and go to the final day of viewing for the sale. Perhaps in the afternoon I would visit the V & A; I hadn't been there for years. I decided to mention it to Mavis as she might enjoy a pre-Christmas shopping day in London. I could take up the suggestion about 'The Williams Hotel' that Joseph mentioned.

Later, I had another phone call from Wendy. She wanted to tell me that she had been with Cynthia that morning when the Vicar called. Explaining herself, she said it was Anthony Blakeston, the one taking the funeral. She sounded a little flustered. Somebody had given him a lift but had stayed outside in his car. Mr Blakeston had introduced himself and enquired after Cynthia Brownley, wondered if it was convenient to have a few words with her. Cynthia called out at that moment so I darted back in, explained who it was as quickly as I could, went back and asked him in. He was ever so kindly and understanding, held her hand, didn't stay long, said it was a privilege for him to take the service for her, he mentioned the name of another vicar who remembered Ernie and that thrilled Cynthia, first time she'd smiled since before Ernie died. He went away soon after, said a quick prayer before going, told Cynthia not to worry, leave everything in God's hands. I thought he seemed most understanding, nice. Explaining that she was going back to Cynthia, Wendy rang off.

I only just a got a 'goodbye' in, not even sure that Wendy heard it. I was pleased to hear about the visit to Cynthia, how typical of Fr Blakeston; something else to tell Mavis. With Mavis in my mind again, I walked round to her cottage and fortunately found her in and very welcoming. She wasn't in the least surprised about all the efforts that Fr Blakeston was taking over the funeral arrangements.

"It will be lovely to have some music in the Chapel; I don't think I have ever heard choristers singing there. I imagine the acoustics will be beautiful."

"Well, it won't be for lack of musicianship, David Jenkins is a marvellous organist. I wonder what setting of the 23rd Psalm he will get the boys to sing, many to choose from. Now, Mavis, I've had an idea for a pre-Christmas trip to London. Joseph Mallings has invited me to an auction early December, and I thought I might go to one of the viewing days, so wondered if you might enjoy a pre-Christmas trip as well. What do you think? I'll be able to stay at a nearby hotel with which they have a nice little discount arrangement."

It didn't take Mavis long to consider this. "A shopping trip would be wonderful, could get my sister something for Christmas. You wouldn't mind my not joining you for the 'viewing' but we could meet for lunch. I could probably stay with my sister. Yes, a trip to London is a good idea, shall you book the train tickets?"

Yes, I'll get those booked, save some money when done in advance. Probably use the internet. Anyway, leave you now, some shopping to do, jobs to complete and there is always some outstanding 'book' work, a good job it never bores me. I've got to steam off some old labels and name plates as every so often you come across something more interesting underneath. See myself out now, bye."

8. ERNIE'S SEND-OFF

Saturday morning brought another somewhat breathless phone call from Wendy. She had had another visitor, Mrs Lucinda Ellerton, who had introduced herself as the wife of the Dean. She explained that she had decided to call about the funeral but didn't want to trouble Mrs Brownley so had hoped that she, Wendy, didn't mind her calling. She wanted to know whether any arrangements had been made for after the service and cremation, the reason, she explained, was that there were a number of rather elderly clergy involved and did she, Wendy, think that Mrs Brownley would like something very simple arranged at her house which was near St Petri's Chapel. I told her that I was a bit embarrassed to talk about it, but I had wondered myself because Cynthia herself hadn't said anything. At her suggestion we popped round next door to ask her. At first Cynthia looked quite startled but then as if she had only that moment thought about it, said she felt something close by the Chapel would be a lovely idea. Mrs Ellerton said that would be perfectly all right, that Cynthia needn't think about it again, said that she could easily organise a few sandwiches and some cakes, explaining that she thought everyone would have returned from the crematorium by about two o'clock and she would have everything ready.

Wendy went on, "I am a little worried about Cynthia as she seems to have closed her mind to everything. Often when there is a funeral in the family the bereaved rush about organising, if only to keep busy."

"I'm sure she will be all right and you will keep close to her. Perhaps she is still dazed by it all, especially with what nearly happened the day after Ernie had to go into care."

"You're probably right, I keep popping round and that seems to cheer her, and she has mentioned what she will wear so that's positive."

"Yes, indeed, just keep chatting to her, keeping her company." I hoped I had given enough reassurance.

The postman called soon after and this time Fr Blakeston had used a stamp to send me a note.

'Dear Monty, thank you for all you are doing. Just to keep you up to date, the following is the likely order of service for the Funeral next Wednesday.

Procession of myself, undertakers, pallbearers followed by Cynthia Brownley and mourners
Choir will sing Amazing Grace
Greeting and introduction – myself
Seated for Psalm 23 – sung by the choir
Lesson read by Fr Andrew Hutchinson
Hymn – O God our help in ages past
Short address – Fr John Evans
Prayers – led by me
Final Hymn – The Day Thou Gavest
Departure for Crematorium

Return to the Deanery

Monty, I know you are quite skilled with modern technology. Do you think you could turn this into a small printed sheet, or at least produce the words of the two hymns? It would be a little something for Cynthia to take away from the service.

With Blessings

Fr Blakeston

That didn't surprise me one bit, in fact I had thought to produce a simple 'Order of Service'. Single sheet of folded A4, Ernie's name and dates on the front, brief out-line of the service overleaf, words of the two hymns on pages 3 & 4. I had already put the words of the hymns into my documents' memory. At the time I had noticed the Dean and the author of 'The Day Thou Gavest' shared the same name, The Reverend John Ellerton. I made a mental note to ask him if they were related.

There seemed little else to plan as far as the Funeral Service was concerned. Mavis and I had already arranged to take a taxi and be at Cynthia's house for mid-day. The Service was to be at 12.30 followed by Cremation at 1.30pm and return to the Deanery by about 2.00pm.

I would tell Daniel all about it later this afternoon., unusually his regular Friday visit had moved to Saturday. Meanwhile other matters to attend to. Sometimes I forgot that my hobby was my business and source of income, somewhat small but useful, less than my teachers' pension but a little more than the old-age pension. I had inherited savings from both my parents, I had received a life assurance payout when I was fifty-five years old and I had also benefited from an elderly aunt who had died without any family. I wasn't wealthy by any means, but I certainly had enough, and I lived quite economically. I didn't smoke. Truth be told, I had smoked when I was at College, but had stopped by my mid-twenties. I had long since stopped running a car. I had only ever had a small mortgage, taken out so that I could fund repairs to the house and the alterations later; my mother couldn't afford to do that. This was paid off with some of the proceeds from the life assurance, but several thousand had built up from the 'with profits' element. I suppose I fell into that category of people referred to as being comfortable when talking about their money.

I was quite busy until I heard Daniel arrive, so time to pause and relax.

"Monty, I am very impressed with all you are doing for your acquaintance, Cynthia Brownley, I hope she appreciates it."

"That really doesn't matter, Daniel, it just seemed the right thing to do and if anything, it is Anthony Blakeston who has rushed around involving others in this event. I am very impressed to learn that the funeral tea is to be hosted at the Deanery; I wouldn't be surprised if somebody didn't just drop a small hint within the hearing of Mrs Dean, or am I being a little malicious! Anyway, how was your week and did I tell you that I read about those two boys involved in the shoplifting and the rescue of Cynthia. I thought the Magistrate's response struck a wonderful note of sound common sense."

"Yes, I agree. There is a sequel – two of my colleagues, one of whom attended the near drowning, both help with a local youth club and with parental approval the two boys have started to attend. Junaid Anwar is the colleague I know best, and he is also acquainted with the lad whose mother is Indian by birth. He thinks them a good pair of lads, enjoys their company and is pleased that they are enthusiastic with youth club activities such as the sport. Hearing this about these boys made me feel quite good for their future, strange reaction, but that was how I was.

An ordinary few days followed, during which time I produced some printed orders of service, remembered to buy the promised book tokens and after much thought I wrote a cheque for the usual sort of fee an organist would be paid for playing at a funeral and enclosed it with a thankyou card. I planned to tell David that the matter was not for discussion.

Wednesday was one of those early winter days, ground frost, bright sunshine, and a crispness in the air. I had already taken service sheets to the undertakers, I had four copies with me, the four envelopes for the choir boys and a letter for David Jenkins. I was at Mavis's house well before twelve, taxi having arrived very promptly, we were both at Cynthia's unnecessarily early; Wendy had already arrived. Cynthia was most pleased to see her copy of the service sheet, perhaps a little old-fashioned but Wendy thought it set the right tone. We all chatted somewhat inconsequentially, just passing time.

Nothing silences conversation more quickly than the arrival of a black hearse and accompanying car. As we went out the senior undertaker handed me an envelope, did so with quiet discretion. It was a short ride round to the Cathedral grounds and soon we were standing with Fr Blakeston watching the undertakers as they lifted out the coffin. A slight hand-movement from the senior undertaker and we started to process in. A sharp intake of breath from Cynthia caused me to look up; the Chapel was full. The candles were alight, the choirboys in red and white robes were standing and singing 'Amazing Grace' with David Jenkins providing only the lightest of accompaniments. The Dean attended but didn't participate in the service. The two retired Canons were standing on the Chancel step and they were resplendent in their former robes of office, gold and blue copes. Fr Blakeston, who led the procession, took a position between them, turned, and watched as the undertakers placed the coffin on the bier and the four of us were shown into the front row of chairs. He bowed to the chief undertaker and the service started just as the choir boys finished singing. It followed the printed service order exactly, with Fr Blakeston giving his words of welcome, a New Testament text and a short opening prayer of thanksgiving. We listened to the singing of the Psalm and the reading of the lesson. Fr Evans' address was something of a surprise, presented with the help of photographs. Clearly, he had been to see Cynthia and borrowed some of the photographs at which she was always looking. He also had one of his own. A group photograph of uniformed RAF Servicemen in which he and Ernie were both to be seen. He had a spare copy and as he spoke, he walked over and presented it to Cynthia. He didn't pretend to know Ernie other than as a passing acquaintance, but he spoke kindly and with feeling, drawing on the sense of expectation that the young men in his photograph all had when they first met at training camp. He also recalled talking with both Ernie and Cynthia occasionally after morning service at the Cathedral. His address was nicely done.

The concluding prayers were delivered by Fr Andrew & Fr Blakeston and ended with the congregation joining in the Lord's Prayer and the Grace. The final hymn was sung with great feeling, perhaps because it is such a beautiful hymn. In the last verse four boys' soprano voices soared heavenward with a glorious descant. David Jenkins continued to play while we walked down the aisle, and this was when I noticed that nearly all the regular members of the Compline congregation were in attendance. More surprising was a small group standing close to the back of the Chapel, two teenage boys with a smartly uniformed police constable.

The ceremony at the crematorium was quite short, conducted quietly by Fr Blakeston. Cynthia, Wendy, Mavis, Fr Evans, Fr Andrew, and I were the only mourners present and very soon we returned to the Deanery. I was pleased to see four choir boys stuffing themselves with cakes, so I was able to thank them and present them with a book token each. They hadn't got to return to school and David Jenkins was just shooing them away, to return their robes to the Cathedral and then off home. I gave David Jenkins my letter and enclosure and told him to do with the contents just as he wished, the matter was not for discussion. As I turned away, I came face to face with two young felonious heroes. I decided not to tell them that I had witnessed one of their escapes, instead congratulated them on their life-saving skills. They looked slightly abashed and Junaid Anwar spoke up for them, telling me that it had been the boys' idea to come to the funeral. I mentioned to him that Daniel Harrison was a good friend of mine. I urged the boys to eat plenty. Seeing the Dean hovering nearby I asked him about a possible forebear in the author of 'The Day Thou Gavest.'?

"Yes, I believe John Ellerton was a great, great, uncle of mine. One of my cousins did the research and found the connection.

I mentioned the kindness of his wife in providing tea and that I thought it nice that St Petri's Chapel had been used for the funeral, it had been a moving occasion.

I spoke quite quickly to most of those at the Deanery gathering, and then I noticed that Cynthia and Wendy were being approached by the Undertaker. I expected this was for their journey home, so I waved to Mavis and we joined them. Fr Blakeston appeared just at that moment to tell Cynthia that if she were agreeable, he would visit in a few days.

As well as returning Cynthia and Wendy, the Undertaker also gave Mavis and me a lift home. My first task on getting in was to write a short letter of thanks to the Undertakers, enclosing their account together with a cheque. I also wrote, but at much greater length, to Fr Blakeston.

9. TRUMPINGTONS AND FOYLES

A week or so later, Mavis and I felt like a pair of seasoned commuters as we stood waiting for the 0800 nonstop train to Kings Cross. Travelling first class gave us just that little bit more comfort and when the coffee trolley arrived a sense of luxury was added to the feelings of our well-being. As I have my computer on every morning, I have got out of the habit of reading a daily newspaper, but I had picked up a copy of The Times for this journey, if nothing else, I could have a go at the various puzzles.

However, it was a short article on page five which first caught my attention. A report about the conference which Daniel had told me he was attending. Clearly it had been a high-powered gathering attended by very senior police officers, anti-terrorism personnel, representatives from the security services, several MPs, members of the House of Lords and representatives from the Ministry of Defence. The Times' report was quite brief, information seemed secondhand, but topics had included techniques which could be used to cripple, if only temporarily, nation-wide systems, digital systems and procedures vital to national security – any disruption if only for a short time could be disastrous. Examples given were component failures within the National Grid, sabotage of Air Traffic Control, hacking of computer controls to major city traffic light systems. Concern was being expressed about the relative ease with which only a small amount of component malfunction could bring to a standstill an enormous amount of the system of which it was a part. A recent power cut was cited as an example, where two generator failures rendered several million households without power and the ensuing transport chaos lasting several days.

Perhaps Daniel would be prepared to tell me more, I'll try and wheedle that out of him when he is next round for a Friday afternoon malt. I spent the last few minutes of the journey with the easier cryptic crossword and the sudoku puzzles. I noticed Mavis was watching me as I completed these, so I asked her what she had planned once we had arrived at Kings Cross.

"I'm going to Muriel's apartment and then we're off for a splendid 'Harrods' day.

That didn't surprise me one bit so I suggested a shared taxi to Muriel's address and then I would carry on to Trumpingtons where I was going to look at various lots and probably meet up with Joseph. "I don't know how long I will stay there as I'm not really sure how much I can look at. I'm hoping Joseph will be able to update me on any progress with the repairs to the dust jacket – it may even be finished.

We agreed a telephone call for late afternoon to decide on any plan for the evening. We returned to our reading material. Not long before we pulled into Kings Cross, Mavis surprised me with a question.

"Monty, I hope you don't mind my asking, but have you any plans for when you suddenly acquire what might be a considerable sum of money this summer?"

"No, I don't mind talking about it, and it would be hopelessly dishonest to pretend I haven't given the matter some thought. I've never been wealthy as you may have realised, but I've always had enough, never had to worry. This will be the first time in my life that such a grand sum of money has come my way. I haven't yet asked about capital gains liability; I hope Joseph might have some general knowledge on the matter, given he must have dealt with many people over the years who have been in a similar position to mine. I have no immediate plans, but I do fancy something of a holiday."

"A giant book trawl?" Mavis was being a little 'tongue in cheek.'

"Well, nothing like that, although I would enjoy a 'giant trawl' as you put it. No, I've never been to Italy and I have enjoyed watching Francesco da Mosto touring Venice; I fancy a little of that. Not far from there is Verona and the Arena for the open-air opera and I have already noticed that Aida is scheduled for several performances in the next season. After that, perhaps a period of 'do nothing' at a classy hotel."

"Good gracious, you amaze me Monty. Two or three weeks with no old books to renovate, won't you suffer some withdrawal symptoms? I tease; a holiday like that? A dream, so go for it."

"I haven't booked anything but I'm putting out some feelers."

Just then the train started to slow and cross several sets of points and it wasn't long before the platform ends came into view. Just overnight luggage for each of us didn't slow us down and we were soon in a short taxi queue. First drop, somewhere in Knightsbridge and when Mavis had finished giving that address, I mentioned` going straight onto Trumpingtons, just off Regents Street.

"Give my regards to Muriel, enjoy yourselves, but you're going to be in Harrods, so better keep a firm grip on all those credit cards! No, no, close your handbag, please, I can pay off the taxi when I get to Trumpingtons. We'll speak later this afternoon. Have a great day."

Mavis hopped out and made for what looked like an impressive entry way. The taxi did one of those 'turns on a penny', of which they seem capable and I was soon being dropped outside the main doors to Trumpingtons. This entrance had all the majesty of an elegant and traditional hotel, except there was no portly doorman in a uniform-style great coat and encrusted with medals. Splendidly large and traditional looking doors opened automatically, and I moved into a spacious foyer; Joseph Mallings was soon found.

"Monty, I'm so pleased you're here, perfect timing, as we received the repaired dust jacket two days ago. Let me show you that before you do anything else. Perhaps a coffee, but not too near the dust jacket!" Off we went, at some speed too; clearly Joseph was one never to stroll or amble around his place of work. Finally, in to a spacious and well-appointed office. "Come in, Monty, this is where I hang out and where I was that evening when your email arrived with such memorable news."

"Surely you often receive emails like that, what makes mine so special?"

"Oh, no, not so, Monty. Yes, we are often hearing about valuable things which people want us to sell. An old family painting, some jewellery, silver, pieces of furniture etc but such pieces are not surprises to the owners and generally not to us as such items are always coming up for auction, essential bread and butter you might say, and without them and in goodly numbers we wouldn't survive. They are the items which owners feel are too good for smaller local auction houses, they think they need a greater international exposure and perhaps they're right. From time to time the contents of an old family house are being auctioned in their entirety and here again these situations are known about, although interesting finds appear from the attics, old garden sheds, kitchen sculleries and other nooks and crannies.

No, your particular find Monty, is different: you were not looking for it and didn't expect anything much beyond the usual kinds of books that such boxes yield, an old diary, a valuable atlas, something containing beautiful prints or hand-tinted illustrations. 'The Hound of the Baskervilles' is a book most people have heard of and many will have read and watched the films; what most people won't know is the significance of the first edition and with a dust jacket, a dustjacket which in its own right is most unusual, indeed, unique. Most people know about authors signing copies of their books but never more than something on the main title page; your copy has an inscription in three parts and carries two signatures – so very unusual. It is a treasure trove, perhaps not gold ingots or even pieces of eight, but a very well-known book in very unusual form. That's why I am so excited and can't wait to see the degree of interest it causes when it becomes public knowledge."

"Anyway, enough of me getting carried away, here's the dust jacket. I keep having to remind myself that it shouldn't exist, indeed it is an original piece of artwork completed for a particular purpose. At present we have it lying flat, and in a protective sleeve but both sides are visible. At the auction we may have it displayed between two panes of glass, something like a double-sided picture frame; special permission will be required to handle the actual paper."

"Joseph, it is magnificent, I can see nothing of the joins. Gosh, I wish I could repair tears like that."

"Here, use this." Joseph passed his magnifying glass over.

"Ah, that makes a difference, I can just make out the ragged but feathered edge but still with much difficulty. A bit easier, as they said it would be, on the reverse. Even so, I never realised how good the repair would be.

"We have made two facsimile copies at present, one I have packed for you to take away but on the reverse, it is signed by two of our directors and certified as being a facsimile copy; the second copy (also certified as a copy) we will use during the preview days, placing it on the book. We will not be using the original."

"I have to say Joseph it really is quite superb and more than exceeded anything I expected. I should love to meet the restorer."

"I'll ask around Monty, as he does sometimes come in on preview days to check work for us, and also to talk to interested clients who are thinking of bidding on a lot, but know that extensive restoration will be needed if the purchase is to be worthwhile."

"Thank you, Joseph, I'd certainly love a quick chat. Now, I mustn't hold you up anymore, I imagine you are much in demand on preview days. If you care to point me in the direction of documents and books and supply me with a catalogue, I shall happily lose myself for a few hours.

True to my word I soon found myself engrossed in looking at many magnificent volumes. There were some C20th Children's books with wonderful illustrations by Arthur Rackham, Shirley Hughes (a modern favourite of mine) Edmond du Lac – signed copy of Treasure Island. Another modern one, Edward Ardizzone, was represented. You could spend a fortune here and only scratch the surface in making a collection of illustrated children's books.

I was looking at some old documents which were fascinating. I have little knowledge of documents and only acquire them in mixed lots. Large collections such as these, connected with one individual or family, and legal documents exquisitely written. Engrossed in these, I felt a tap on the shoulder and there was Joseph. "Monty, this is Henry Tay, he completed the repair to the dust jacket. Perhaps we can grab a coffee and chat?" Off at speed again and back to the office where someone was just placing a tray of coffee. "I can only stay a few minutes but perhaps I can leave you two for a little linger?"

Joseph must have scalded himself as he swallowed his coffee so quickly and was off with a wave. "Henry, the dust jacket is superb. Now, I occasionally undertake repairs such as that, but nothing valuable, although no matter the care I take it is rare that I finish with an invisible repair."

"Well, I'm doing such work every day, and it comes with great patience and practice. Do you use a magnifying stand so that you have both hands free and obtain close-up views of the work? It is important to obtain the right materials and tools. You ought to come a spend a day or so at the workshops and watch – we back-room boys and girls always enjoy explaining our skills and materials, gives us a chance to show off. Here's my card, give me a ring sometime."

"Henry, that's most kind of you, I may well take up your offer. By the way, what about the date of the paper and the colours etc?"

"We're quite sure both are contemporary with the book."

"Look, I need to move on now. Are you likely to see Joseph again, give him my thanks and tell him I will be in touch? I'll also be in touch with you."

"That's fine Monty, he's giving me lunch. Am I to tell him that you have placed a number of bids for the items that you have been looking at this morning?"

"It's a good job I spotted a twinkle in your eye. Yes, you can, mention that I will need extensive credit!"

"Goodbye Monty and I hope the Conan Doyle brings you a great result next year."

We shook hands and I was on my way. Charing Cross Road and Foyles was on my itinerary next. I had read that there was a café there so that's where I planned to have a bit of lunch. I set out to walk there via Piccadilly Circus as I knew it wasn't far.

Strolling into Foyles café, I was pleased to find it not busy. Turning towards the servery, my attention was caught by a wave and a distant voice: "Over here Monty, bring a coffee with you." Surprise, surprise, there was my good friend Daniel Harrison with two other men, one of whom I knew from newspapers and television.

Coffee in hand I took the remaining place at the table. "Monty, I didn't expect to bump into you here. What brings….no sorry, let me introduce you to…."

"Jon Mostang?" I said, interrupting Daniel. "We've not met but I have read about you and have encountered your image taking part in late night television discussions."

"And if I have remembered correctly about what Daniel has been chatting, you must be the Monty who is his book collecting friend, and is there something about a significant find of late, am I right?" Jon Mostang seemed rather pleased with this reply.

"Yes, perhaps more of that later. And your friend is….?

"Sorry, this is one of my Parliamentary colleagues, Nat Lawton. Jon quickly made the introduction.

I sat down and started to drink my coffee. Unexpectedly Nat Lawton was quick to start speaking. "I presume you, like Daniel here, live in Peterborough, not my favourite City although it is only an hour or so away from my base in Lincolnshire."

"That's sad, perhaps you haven't spent enough time exploring all its interesting nooks and crannies. I've lived there the best part of sixty years, so I know it incredibly well and I have seen an amazing range of change. It's a vibrant City, full of life and very cosmopolitan and I enjoy all that, the mix of languages and cultures. Like most large cities, Peterborough is not without difficulties, but I still see it as looking to the future with confidence."

Perhaps Mr Lawton sensed I was prepared to defend Peterborough vigorously and he lapsed back into silence. I turned to Daniel and explained that I was in London for a couple of days, visiting Trumpingtons, looking at various items on their current preview day. I was also shown the finished dust jacket and I showed them the facsimile. Daniel was impressed because he had seen the original, creased and in three pieces. Nat showed virtually no interest; Jon, more so because he had heard something about it from Daniel. I quickly told Daniel that I had travelled down with Mavis but that she was spending the day with her sister, Muriel, over in Knightsbridge,

"I know those two names, sisters did you say, and does Muriel have anything to do with Ken Peterson.?"

I just nodded; Jon continued, "Yes, Mavis and Muriel Missily. I've met them both, Muriel on a few more occasions as I see Ken on business now and then. She is an outstandingly good cook."

"Indeed, she is," I replied, with equal enthusiasm. "In fact, Ken has asked her to invite Mavis and me down for Christmas; food from Harrods and cooking from Muriel – I don't think it can go wrong." Still sensing some hostility from Mr Lawton, I decided to get going.

Turning to Daniel, "I'll be moving along now, I only popped up for a coffee. I'm planning on spending the afternoon exploring the many secondhand bookshops in the area and I'm meeting up with Mavis late afternoon. I'll see you Friday, back in Peterborough, or perhaps you can give me a ring." Looking to the pair of politicians, "Nice to have met you both."

Quick handshakes all round and I was away. I didn't want to worry about food here with them obviously having a rather quiet meeting and somewhat off the beaten track; there were plenty of sandwich bars around. I certainly didn't want to get into any argument with the man from Lincolnshire.

I wandered off along a side street, found a small snack bar where they made sandwiches to order. Their rare beef and mustard on a crusty seeded bread was excellent and I finished with a Danish apricot pastry. Spending some time over a coffee and after a while, a refill, I wondered what brought Daniel together with the two MPs. Quite possibly he had met up with Jon Mostang at the conference I had read about in the press. I had never heard of Nat Lawton, so I looked him up via a google search. He represented a Lincolnshire constituency, had done so for about 20 years; had been active in Middle East affairs which probably explained his being with Jon Mostang; now no longer on the Select Committee but no reason given. Being a Lincolnshire MP, it was hardly surprising that he was very keen on Brexit, at least that was the impression he had given me. He was active in agricultural affairs which was logical. Made a mental note to ask Daniel about them, couldn't put my finger on a reason, but didn't get the impression that he and Jon were bosom friends and I doubt Nat ever becoming a bosom pal of mine. When I looked up internet information for Jon Mostang, I found enough material to write a book – seemed to have been 'high profile' since the day he was born! – rather made Mr Lawton's entries seem very inferior.

10. JON MOSTANG, M.P.

You would have to describe Jon Mostang as one of those 'larger than life' individuals. Wherever he went he always made his presence felt: perhaps making comment on something in the news or appearing as a guest in a political discussion on late night television. He would be described as exceedingly photogenic and televisual; he came over with confidence and charm and never seemed to be wrong footed. He contributed articles in the more serious press for which he received favourable comment. He gave the impression of being well connected in all matters 'Conservative'. From what gets mentioned in media comment and published via internet, a fascinating picture of him and his forebears emerges.

Jon Mostang has been the Conservative Member of Parliament since 2010 for a very safe seat in Kent. He gives every impression of being a successful MP and he increased his majority at the last election, contradicting the national trend. He frequently speaks on Middle Eastern affairs, generally agreeing with government policy; he adds his own insights, and always appears well informed whenever he appears in public discussions. He sits on the Foreign Affairs Select Committee although it is no secret that his Iranian background has caused some columnists and indeed some fellow MPs to view him with suspicion. He doesn't attempt to counter or deflect this in anyway. He presents with great confidence.

His Grandmother, Mosseema, was Iranian by birth, came to the UK in her teens after her mother was widowed although she stayed in Iran. It is not quite clear how Mosseema managed on first arriving, but she was soon eighteen, earning and living quite independently. She appears to have been able to move among quite influential people and in her early twenties she married a banker, Johnson Heverstone. He was wealthy in his own right as well as holding a senior post in one of the Merchant Banks. Mosseema had been adopting a rather western style of life and after her marriage she continued this. Their one child, Selina, was also brought up in a very western style and she of course was a British Citizen which ensured that when her son, Jon Mostang (Heverstone as he was then) was born he too would hold British Citizenship. Selina didn't exactly keep to the path that her parents thought that they had carved out for her.

Towards the end of her boarding school education there was considerable tension between Selina and the school authorities. However, she achieved sufficiently good results there to take up a place at Durham University but by the time she gained a 2.1 degree in history she was already pregnant with Jon. It was rumoured that she had come close to being sent down on more than one occasion – disorderly parties, inappropriate visitors on campus, strong disagreements with some tutors – so actually gaining a good degree was remarkable and must have reflected her considerable academic abilities. She either didn't know who the father of her child was, or she chose not to name him on the birth certificate. Selina certainly called her son Jon, Jon Heverstone, grandson of

Johnson Heverstone, the wealthy banker and Mosseema, his wife and Jon's grandmother. Jon's father may well have been Middle Eastern because Jon's complexion would suggest both parents had Middle Eastern origins.

By the time of the birth, Selina's behaviour had become so wayward that the grandparents felt compelled to take over the child's upbringing. His grandmother, Mosseema, brought him up bi-lingually and from an early age, Jon was showing outstanding linguistic gifts. Indeed, the various schools he attended had to buy in specialist tuition to keep up with him; no doubt Johnson Heverstone contributed to these costs in addition to fees. His education finished at Oxford where he distinguished himself by achieving a double first in Middle Eastern languages: by his mid-twenties he was fluent in Persian, Arabic, Turkish and Egyptian Arabic; he also had excellent command of French, Spanish and German as well as a number of Middle Eastern dialects. There must have been very few areas in Mediterranean countries where he wouldn't be perfectly understood. It was these skills which, together with his UK political base, enabled him to possess an amazing array of international contacts. Consequently, any security organisation that came remotely near was always going to have more than a passing interest in Jon Heverstone. It was possible to assemble much information about him because hardly a week passed without at least one newspaper or magazine running an 'in-depth' article about him; many overseas newspapers may have had a similar degree of interest.

While Jon was still in his teens his mother died from a drug overdose. Her life had just spiralled out of control and her parents had been unable to help, had they even been allowed. Because he demonstrated to his grandparents a high level of personal responsibility, Jon was given a considerable allowance from the time he went up to Oxford. The nature of his studies was such that he made many lengthy visits to different parts of the Middle East, indeed, it was five years before he completed his degree. Some of these overseas visits were arranged by his college, others by the British Council, international educational organisations, and various language study groups. Jon was occasionally required to teach English at university level, accept employment in different government departments, international companies and these requirements varied depending on the country he was visiting and his associated language skills. What doesn't get mentioned in the various articles are the many social contacts he must have made and, more importantly, whether he ever contacted his grandmother's Iranian family. This question was raised when he was interviewed by the Constituency Selection Committee and he explained that he had met some distant relatives once, and one who he spoke to at length had a name not dissimilar to 'Mostang'; it was as a kind of memorial to his grandmother and great grandmother that he decided to change his name. That, it seems, has been the only public comment about his name that he has made.

He was in Iran for a few months immediately after taking his degree and was there when his grandparents were both killed in an appalling head-on car collision; also killed were the three adults in the only other car involved. The subsequent inquest ruled death by manslaughter; alcohol was deemed to have been a major factor because the driver of the other car was well over the permitted blood alcohol level, as were the two passengers. There were also two independent eye-witnesses who testified that the Heverstones' car was being driven at a moderate speed whereas the other car was travelling very fast and had been seen on the wrong side of the road immediately prior to the accident. All three mobile phones recovered from the car showed that they had been in use at the time of the collision. Eventually, the inquest verdict led to a high compensation award paid by the insurance company of the guilty driver – the actual amount has never been revealed. As Jon Heverstone was the sole beneficiary of his grandparents' will, he became an extremely wealthy individual. His family's solicitor, Peter Prendle, was much younger than his grandparents, only ten or so years older than Jon and a former student of the same Oxford college, consequently Jon felt able to continue to entrust his affairs with the same company. He and Peter Prendle became good friends and have been together occasionally with Peter's wife and two children at some family celebrations.

Initially, Jon arranged for the sale of his grandparents' properties, a house in the country and another, closer to central London. Jon took a lease on an expensive and very exclusive apartment, overlooking the Thames and close to the City. After he became an MP, he purchased a small apartment in the main town of the constituency. His solicitor, together with his grandfather's former bank, took on the responsibility for his extensive investment portfolio and from which he has been able to draw a substantial income, as well as see his overall level of wealth increase. Jon Mostang does admit that his financial security owes much to his grandfather's very shrewd investments.

Jon Heverstone continued to travel to different countries in the Middle East although the details are a little vague. It was on his return from one of these journeys, soon after the death of his grandparents, when he contacted Peter Prendle and asked him to make the necessary moves so that he could change his name to Jon Mostang.

For a relatively young man he has already led a remarkably full life, coped with several difficult experiences and from which he appears to have emerged unscathed. It is the kind of life that is always going to lead journalists, and most likely some colleagues, to want to know more and inevitably, where clear and precise answers are not forth-coming, rumours abound.

11. KENNETH PETERSON

I must have been pondering 'The Life and Works of Jon Mostang' for some time, as glancing at my watch I discovered it was late afternoon and time for me to ring Mavis.

"Hello Monty, I was wondering if you would be ringing soon?" Mavis sounded particularly pleased with herself, so I presumed a good day enjoyed by the sisters.

"You seem to be in good spirits, spent a lot?"

"Now, you know me Monty, never extravagant, especially for myself. Did you mention eating tonight at the 'Wellington'? I only ask, because Muriel would love us both to eat here and she is the only one at the apartment tonight; Ken has gone away for three days and his chauffeur, Tony, is with him."

"Excellent suggestion which could well save us £100 and we haven't reserved a table either. I've had a strange afternoon so looking forward to telling you both about it – involves Muriel in an unexpected way. Where are you now because I can meet you with a taxi if that would help?"

"You sound very mysterious, Monty. We are both back at Muriel's now, so whenever is convenient, come straight here. I don't expect we'll eat until about seven o'clock but there is plenty of wine to keep us occupied."

"Fine." I told Mavis I expected to be over in about half an hour and true to my word I was paying off the taxi precisely thirty minutes later. Mavis let me in, ostentatiously large glass containing a small amount of red wine in hand, and with which she toasted my arrival. Muriel appeared at the kitchen door and greeted me in like manner; I wondered how many glasses had already been consumed? Not to be out done, I accepted a similar glass but with a larger measure. It tasted divine, glanced at the bottle to discover it was a rather old 'Nuits St George' and of, or was, considerable value.

"My, this is good, Does Kenneth maintain a cellar or just buy what he likes and when he needs? No, forget that, how rude of me, sorry Muriel, is this your treat?"

"Worry not Monty, I'm not that sensitive. Ken opened this the other evening for a guest and they only had one small glass each. It is understood that whatever wine is left unconsumed, will be used by me – perhaps in some cooking, or more likely, for dinking. Actually, this tastes better now than it did two nights ago, and it is only still around because I knew that you were both coming. Ken buys most of his wine at Harrods, keeps an eye open for good prices and I think he bought half a case of these a while back. 1974 was said to be a good vintage year but I think he only paid £30/£40 per bottle. He doesn't drink much wine, but he always likes to have available a choice of several good vintages. His more favourite drink is Laphroaig."

"Thank you, Muriel, that answers the question of 'what I can give him for Christmas'; two down and one to go." As I had hinted earlier to Mavis, I had a little mystery to tell, so I thought that slightly cryptic remark would create a second. "Are you cooking at this moment Muriel, or can you just listen to my odd encounter of the afternoon?"

"Sit in here both of you, this kitchen is quite multi-purpose and what preparation I'm doing can be completed with only half an eye and no brain!"

"Well, up until about mid-day my plans had worked out all right. I had an interesting time at Trumpingtons, and they gave me a facsimile copy of the repaired dust jacket, I'll show you that later. Before I went off exploring secondhand bookshops in Charing Cross Road I decided I would visit the café in Foyles so imagine my surprise to find my good friend Daniel Harrison sitting there with two other men. They turned out to be MPs, one I recognised from television and newspapers, Jon Mostang; the other I didn't know and actually took quite a dislike to."

Mavis looked up in surprise. "That's not like you, Monty, you always seem quite affable with whoever you meet."

"Yes, that's the normal me. This guy was one Nat Lawton, a Lincolnshire MP who was immediately critical of Peterborough. Not in so many words, but I formed the impression that his dislike of our home City, as we might say Mavis, was partly, if not wholly, racist."

"Yes, it would have been." Muriel made this sharp comment and went on, "He, and the other one you mentioned, Mostang, were both here a week or so back and whenever I went in with food or to collect empty plates he was always making some unpleasant remark about foreigners or 'coloureds' as he termed them. Horrible man, I thought, and he seemed to cause Ken to lose his usual amiable persona. I have no idea why they were here. Jon Mostang has visited before as I believe he helps Ken with aspects of charitable work. They arrived and left together, but that might have been convenience of taxis if they left Westminster together. They may be colleagues, in a Parliamentary sense; friends, I doubt. Now, change of subject. Monty, are you happy with fish pie this evening? I'll take that smile as a 'yes', and as I have the oven on there will be an autumn fruits crumble to follow."

I provided a second smile. "As we're changing subjects let me show you the dust jacket I mentioned earlier. This will mean more to Mavis as she discovered the rolled-up wreck that it once was. The restorers made a superb job and you really can't spot the repairs unless you take a glass to the printed side."

As I unfolded it from my brief case Mavis gave instant approval. "Monty, that is so impressive, and have they cleaned it as well, it seems just that little brighter? Of course, that might be because this is a facsimile copy. Never-the-less, I am pleased for you. Have they anymore knowledge about its date?"

"Just that they think it contemporary with the book. I'm going to start searching for a badly damaged, unsigned copy of a first edition so that I can make good use of this dust jacket."

"I am amazed Mavis, you, in at such a discovery, on your hands and knees. I always see you as the calm sort, not in at the 'breaking of news' kind of person."

"Well, thank you for that personality analysis Muriel."

I thought Mavis looked a shade peaked at that comment. I folded the dust jacket carefully and slipped it away. "Do you know where Ken has gone, or doesn't one ask questions like that."

"No, just away for two or three nights and he'll return when he returns. Sometimes he tells me where he'll be, perhaps give me a phone number in case he is out of mobile signal range, occasionally he asks me to accompany him in a kind of p.a. role – make notes, keep papers, even iron a shirt in an emergency. I'm likely to travel with him more often when the journey is overseas and expected to last more than a few days."

"Living in one of the best postcode areas of London, on the doorstep of Harrods with an account, international travel – you lead an exciting life Muriel."

"Look, Monty, Mavis tells me you're discretion personified so I think I can tell you about Ken. Kenneth Peterson has been my boss for over twenty-five years. Now, his surname is something of a joke as he is a former convict, although I think all his crimes were in the fields of high finance, never blowing safes. Anyway, he did two years, released well over twenty years ago but even when he was released, he was still a very wealthy man, 'didn't need to work' kind of wealthy. He owns this pair of apartments and I share this one with Tony (he's got one large room with a kitchenette at one end, also a shower-room/toilet. When he's not required to drive, he paints, oils mainly, his work sells quite well. I have the rest of the apartment. Going back in time a bit, Ken was left very wealthy by elderly parents, he was in his early twenties I believe. He worked for some investment company and it was there he got into trouble. Not an original set of circumstances, many have done it before him, and no doubt others still are. He invested client funds having found ways to avoid the company's accounting procedures. When it all came out (he had suddenly made some big losses) the Managers got severely criticised for their rather old fashioned and lax procedures so Ken's one major foray into crime took down quite a few people in addition to the clients he swindled. Apparently, and very naively, he thought all these investors were very wealthy and could afford to be swindled but in fact, some of them were cleaned out of life savings – not nice. He got four years but was out after two. As I said earlier, this was all when he was in his twenties and he is in his early fifties now. I'll speed this up. When he was in prison, he met several prisoners who had been victims of his kind of crime but because they had ended up so impoverished, they had resorted to crime just to survive. This wasn't just financial crime, anything that would produce money – pimping, extortion, receiving, holding goods for other racketeers – you name it and they tried it – frequently failed and ended up inside. This all led to a kind of 'Damascus Road' moment for our Ken, so some of that bible work did get remembered Mavis. He started to tell some of these fellow inmates to get in touch when they got their release. He has been doing something like that ever since. He has others to help him now, act as intermediaries, supports ex-prisoner charities, even has contact with Salvation Army. I'm not sure that some people who have been responsible or partly caused some imprisonments haven't perhaps felt the heat from time to time. He keeps a very low profile about most of it. He leads a rather quiet life and really the only people who call are involved in his 'charitable' work. He has got quite well known in a very quiet sort of way but from addresses I hear him give the chauffeur, it is high places where he is known - The House of Lords, The Athenaeum Club, Twickenham, and many of the most well-known hotels. I don't know who he goes to meet but some of the visitors to the apartment are sort of familiar, faces seen in newspapers etc. I did recognise that MP who is always in the news, the one you met earlier. I'm not sure what they do together. Some of the other addresses I have heard him give to the Tony are quite 'down market'. Occasionally Tony drives him to some provincial crematorium. I think he looks out for folk who have really fallen on hard times. He does occasional hospital visits too."

"Sounds as if his 'Damascus Road' moment was extremely dramatic and long lasting. Still, certainly strange is our 'Kencon' as I feel tempted to call him."

"Hard to avoid thinking like that, Monty. Mind you I also get the feeling that some activities are conducted very quietly or even in secret. I feel this most when he goes overseas for short trips, especially by himself. I can't put my finger on anything precise. When he travels overseas alone, he must be meeting people. Anyway, that's about all I can tell you. " I like to think his work is wholly honest now, or at least with very honest intentions.

"Thank you, Muriel, for that, and I look forward to meeting him at Christmas as he sounds most interesting. I'll let Mavis get details off you – you know, arrival times, when we leave etc Not likely to require a dinner suit am I?

"Ah, not sure about that, because if you are still here at New Year, we might all be somewhere posh, so better pack one to be on the safe side. Now, you finish the wine, nearly an empty bottle anyway; I'll open something white for the meal. Let me get on now for half an hour and then we can eat. We'll be in here.

A copy of The Times and still hardly read, so 30 minutes passed with speed. We both returned to the kitchen at the same time, just as Muriel was serving the fish pie with roasted baby tomatoes and some tender stemmed broccoli. All cooked to perfection and it was delicious. The bottle of Pouilly Fouisse which Muriel served, went very well with the fish pie. Now, to an elderly man who looks back with some nostalgia to school puddings, the thought of a fruit crumble with thick custard was divine and the reality was just as holy.

"I have a coffee tray already now, so let's go into the lounge."

At Muriel's bidding we did just that and was where we found some specialist chocolates, Harrods again, and a rather fine-looking bottle of brandy; with the thought of dozing in the back of a taxi, I could see the evening slipping to a most pleasant end.

12. ADVENT AND DANIEL'S PAST

The Wellington Hotel served the kind of breakfast that was normally found exclusively in one's imagination. I ate my first kipper in years – stunning. Thereafter I stayed with the cold selection, cheese, hotel baked breads, fruit, a slice of very moist lemon cake and all was accompanied by a never-ending large pot of coffee. I wondered what Muriel was serving for Mavis, probably quite traditional with an equally large pot of tea, which I knew she would enjoy. After checking out I returned to Muriel's and left my luggage there. A taxi dropped the sisters at Oxford Street for some serious window gazing and I went on to Charing Cross Road to browse the secondhand book shops which I missed the day before.

The rest of the day went according to plan, back at Muriel's for some tea mid-afternoon, taxi to Kings Cross Station for a late afternoon train to Peterborough. I noticed Mavis was clutching several expensive looking carrier bags, never mind the cost of the contents; my very modest purchases were slotted in my briefcase. A gentle snooze seemed to be accompanying me most of the way, but I came too for the last 15 minutes or so and found Mavis tapping away on her Iphone.

"Monty, you're back with us. I've been looking at the news, nothing unexpected. More mention of security risks but nothing actually specific.

"There have been several mentions of such risks lately, perhaps Christmas being so close has something to do with it. I wonder if Daniel has heard anything, but I never like to ask about matters which from his point of view may well be confidential. Let me show you my modest half dozen treasures from this afternoon's trip down Charing Cross Road." I pulled out the leaflets/booklets which I had found, all pre-war and all small guides to little known villages and which appeared to be first editions.

"What makes those special, Monty?"

"Nothing really, except that there is always a market from people who move to villages and other small places, wanting to find out something of the place's history and these days their first 'port of call' is often via a 'Google-search'. Without the widespread availability of the internet, I would struggle to find buyers for this kind of material, but now a days, almost a certain sale, a good sale too, if more than one person wants it."

Just then I noticed Huntingdon Station flash past the windows, so I got up to lift down our various bits of luggage; I noted that Mavis had nearly doubled her quantity. "That was Huntingdon Mavis, so we should be...." Action took the words out of my mouth, as the train started to slow and rattle across various sets of points. Another taxi and our two days in London came to an end.

Children often feel that the wait for Christmas to arrive is endless; adults generally feel the days speed by with too much to do. Being retired, I could plan my use of time carefully but even so, I had several events to fit in. Back in the early Autumn I had been contacted several times about my willingness to play the organ for an organisation's Christmas Carol Service and looking at the calendar now I saw that I had agreed to four, two junior schools in the City, a Guides and Brownies' Group Carol Service over in Whittlesea and a mid-week Church Carol Service in the village of Southwick, near Oundle.

There were a few recorded telephone messages and one of these was a request to play the organ for a funeral the following week in Bulwick, a village in the Corby direction. At present none of these events clashed. Need to think about booking a taxi or hiring a car. I know some may see this as a terrible waste of money but I wouldn't think twice about saying yes if I owned a car; by not doing so I save hundreds of pounds so hiring cars or taking taxis for longish journeys was still cheap in comparison. I also wanted to get to one or two Christmas Concerts taking place in the Cathedral. Another of the recorded messages was from Daniel, he was hoping to call on Friday and he would assume it was OK if he didn't hear otherwise. I was pleased about that as I hoped to ask him about his MP friends.

I hadn't forgotten about Cynthia Brownley and I wondered how she was keeping. I had a little plan in mind – to take some flowers as a Christmas present and to take her out to afternoon tea which many restaurants in the City now served, I would invite her friend and neighbour, Wendy. Thinking of Christmas presents I realised that although I only gave a few, they still needed choosing, wrapping, and giving. The final thought of Christmas tasks took me to cards – I usually sent about fifty or so and I only ever could manage to write half a dozen at a time. I hated the 'round robin printed letter' that so many people sent these days, preferring to write a shortish letter to each relative or friend as the case maybe. I had the cards so could start those now. I didn't even like using printed address labels so must look up and write each address longhand. Somehow, I felt it made them seem just that little bit more personal and individual.

Opening all the accumulated post I found a letter from Trumpingtons, they wanted my approval for the description to go in the catalogue regarding, 'The Hound of the Baskervilles' together with a promise of an email with possible photographs to be used. That was a nice but unexpected gesture, yet I couldn't see my having any objections. They also told me about some advance publicity they would be mailing to their branch and agents' offices in the UK and overseas. This was something they always did for the more significant items in any forthcoming sale. They expected to have the catalogue ready for posting by the end of January. The sale was scheduled for the second Thursday and Friday in May. Glancing quickly at the emails I found the one from Trumpingtons. The photographs were excellent, and I was delighted to see that they were thinking of placing one of them on the top half of the inside of the front cover – how prestigious.

My ebay site was showing several books with opening bids – people bought more in the run up to Christmas, favourite books with a publication date which coincided with a family anniversary were popular as Christmas presents, as were copies of childhood favourites, old annuals of famous comics suddenly became very saleable. I kept copies of Whittaker's Almanacs whenever I found them for sale, these 'year' books made good gifts as did specialist diaries. I also noted that I had three items to pack and post. So, even by my leisured standards, I had plenty to do in the next twenty days.

I made an early start on Friday morning and brought the ebay site up to date and got three parcels ready for the post and I took down from bookshelves the items which has received a starting bid. I checked all the listings as I needed a break over some of the Christmas period if I was to be away, a pity as a lot of bored people tended to use their computers more. With Christmas still in mind, I made a list, last year's updated, of people who needed to receive a gift. I went online and made a search for quality bottles of Laphroag and found one which I could purchase locally. Muriel was easy as I had an early edition of Mrs Beeton and I thought she would be amused with the recipes requiring a dozen eggs, one pint of double cream and so on. Mavis was difficult because although I knew her well, I didn't know her at all when it came to things like perfume, jewellery, and gifts of that style. Then I remembered a forthcoming exhibition of the work of local artists and decided that might provide the answer. Fr Blakeston was usually happy to have a bag of luxury eatables because he would never buy them himself.

Fortunately, or sadly, I didn't have a long list of nephews and nieces requiring varying sums of money. On the other hand, there were several charities which required extra money at Christmas. By early afternoon, I had started on the Christmas card writing, posted the ebay parcels, visited Cynthia who seemed delighted with the idea of afternoon tea and she promised to ask Wendy and get her to ring me with possible dates. On impulse I called on Fr Blakeston to ask if he would like to go out to dinner one evening before Christmas, and on my way back had purchased a bottle of Triple Wood Laphroag. I celebrated these initial achievements with some sandwiches, a glass of wine and an hour or so searching the sites of various book dealers; I never got bored at looking at what other dealers had to offer.

I knew that Daniel would call about 4 o'clock so got glasses and the current bottle of malt ready and set out my copy of the facsimile dust jacket. True to expectation Daniel was tapping on the door on the hour and he poured himself glass number one. He was clearly impressed with the restored dust jacket, being one of only three of us who had seen it in its dishevelled state. He was silent for a few moments and then started to speak and very quickly it became obvious he had been planning with care what he needed to say. "Monty, your meeting me unexpectedly earlier in the week makes it necessary that I should tell you something of my personal history. These are all matters which I have kept to myself since living in

Peterborough. You know that I am a widower, but what you don't know is that my wife, Noura, was Egyptian, and she was murdered thirteen years ago. Officers who investigated the death became confident about who was responsible but because of my work at the time no satisfactory action could be taken, certainly not an arrest. It was thought that the killing had been as a warning to me because of work that I was involved in, which for several years had covered aspects of VIP protection and international terrorism and all of this involved important liaison with the Home Office and the Security Services. At the time I was holding the rank of Commander. After my wife's death I needed time off; I was suffering from a terrible sense of guilt, felt that I had brought about her death.

I didn't get over her death for a long time and I suffered from recurring bouts of depression. The other senior officers with whom I worked were concerned to get my expertise back within their operations but it was also clear that I couldn't face the conflict between knowing that my work may have caused her death and that if I returned to active duties there would inevitably be a greater risk for all working in the field. I wasn't old enough for early retirement and I couldn't retain my rank if I moved from London. A unique solution presented itself: I would relinquish my rank and move to another force at a less senior level; my London colleagues would keep me abreast of what was happening, particularly with what I was doing at the time of Noura's death. From time to time I would meet various people in London for discussions and briefings. As far as the local force was concerned my circumstances would be fully explained to the Chief

Constable, and with one or two other officers on a 'need to know' basis. So far, the arrangement has worked well and there have been no conflicts over duties. During the last few years there have been some similar initiatives with senior London based officers working on a more local basis, and this has proved useful as elements of terrorist networks have moved out of London."

During this long explanation I had said nothing and only moved once to top up his glass. I was amazed to hear what Daniel had to tell me as well as saddened to hear the details of his wife's death. "Daniel, I don't know what to say; that must have been a terrible time when you carried such a guilt as well as bearing the loss of your wife. You've never said but were there no children? Did Noura have relatives you knew well?

"That's more of the sadness. She had been, we'll say, 'damaged' as a child, involved close members of her family; she could never have children. When she was old enough to be a little more independent, she made friends with some members of the Coptic Church who helped her immensely. She adopted their faith, became a Christian and it was then that I met her. I was visiting Egypt on diplomatic service and had to accompany a member of our party to the church. I suppose it was a 'whirlwind' romance; it was terrible when I had to travel home after the official visit ended. Some members of the party had gathered knowledge of my romance, and they were very helpful in covering aspects of my work, so this gave us more time to be together. We kept in touch constantly and as soon as I could take enough leave, I went back out to Egypt and we married. Her immediate safety depended on her coming back to the UK with me. That was an awful idea as she was dead within eighteen months. We never knew whether her family had heard about our wedding and the enquiries into her killing never revealed anything to suggest their involvement. Noura kept in close touch with one friend from the church and I've maintained a loose link ever since as I feel I owe that to her memory."

"What about your family?"

"I suppose you must think that I have kept myself very private, that partly reflects my work when I was in London. My parents died many years back. I have a younger brother, Stephen, who is married with a family. He lives in America. He was at University in this country, then took a second degree in New York which is where he met Cleo, his wife. They live in Boston where he lectures in International Law, his wife is employed in fields associated with ecology and related research and they have two teenage boys, Rowley and Den and who keep them very busy. All being well, I'll be with them for part of the Christmas period. I usually do, although I stay at a hotel nearby, gives them a break from the 'uncle'. It also enables me to keep in touch with work, without them having to know. Sadly, they never met Noura. We skyped, and plans were made to visit Boston but…."

"That's an awful lot of personal history Daniel, but thanks for taking me into your confidence; it goes without saying that you can trust in my discretion absolutely."

"I have never doubted that." Daniel smiled, the first time that afternoon. He relaxed back into the armchair, broke with custom and accepted the offer of a third glass of malt.

13. NAT LAWTON AND OTHER MATTERS

"Let me have another look at that dust jacket, I did no more than glance at it just now and I didn't give it full attention when you showed it to us in London when I was a bit preoccupied, as you might have noticed."

I passed Daniel the dust jacket. "Here you are, admire at your leisure. What I did notice was that your two guests seemed an awkward and uncomfortable pair. I also took quite a dislike to Nat Lawton, seemed something of a right-wing nasty, bit of a racist?

"This dust jacket is quite superb; I know it's a facsimile, but the original has to be wonderful for this to be produced. What do you intend to do with it?"

"My plan is to find a thoroughly battered original first edition of 'The Hound of the Baskervilles' and then make it look rather good by placing this dust jacket around it. I must keep reminding myself that this dust jacket was not published with the book. Now, tell me, what were you doing with Nat Lawton?"

"Strictly between the two of us, I was making my own assessment of his particular charms. We have an eye on him, he holds views which might be far more unpleasant than racist, and he has some very questionable associates."

"Why was he with Jon Mostang? There was clearly little friendship between the two of them. I've been reading about him, amazingly talented, not to mention wealthy."

"That's certainly true, Monty. One of their problems is that Nat Lawton was a member of the Foreign Affairs Committee, where he took to expressing some rather non p.c. views. Not long after Jon Mostang was elected M.P., he effectively replaced him on the committee."

"Later in the afternoon when I met up with the 'girls', I mentioned having bumped into you with Messrs Lawton and Mostang. It caused Muriel to pipe up with some equally unflattering opinions of Mr Lawton. Both had been with Kenneth Peterson recently; she had served dinner to them all. With her going in and out she heard several unpleasant remarks from Nat Lawton, and she could tell by just glancing at Ken that he didn't like what he was hearing. I know he is only saying what plenty of people say quite casually in the pub, so to speak, but one would have expected an M.P. to be a little more discreet. Jon Mostang having been present makes it more surprising given his background and holding what appear to be views of a very international flavour. I imagine they hold sharply differing opinions over Brexit and probably on immigration as well."

"I haven't had an opportunity to meet Kenneth Peterson, but I know of him 'officially', and I am aware of the kind of work he undertakes. I think their meeting may have been to do with how some temporary immigrant workers have been treated in parts of East Anglia; some concern about how they even arrived in this country. Ken's philanthropy is known to be very wide ranging these days and involves many people on what could be termed the 'q.t.'.

"Well. I'm staying with him this Christmas together with Mavis and Muriel, so I look forward with interest to getting to know him."

"You're very honoured," was Daniel's somewhat enigmatic response. "Now a change of subject, Monty. When you first told me about the find of the Conan Doyle volume you mentioned that you would have to explore the tax position. Did you do that?"

"Yes and no. Although my affairs are relatively straight forward, I have used the expertise of an accountant for a few years. He always saves me more than the cost of his services. My two pensions look after themselves but my book buying and selling activities are a bit complicated. As far as tax is concerned, I'm running a small business and the accountant keeps all that sorted. Each month I give him all my accumulated receipts for books purchased, notes of any journeys I have made, receipts for petrol if I have hired a car and the cost of the car, related taxi journeys, accommodation. I also keep a running total of books sold and the profit made after taking account of the original cost to me and commission paid. I don't seem to end up paying too much tax. I think he puts in costs to offset tax such as time I might spend on repairing, equipment and costs to do with working from home. I'll give him all the details about this lucky find and let him sort it out. There may well be different ways to approach the matter, if indeed, tax is payable. Perhaps I'm a bit odd regarding these affairs, but it's not my intention to try and defraud the Inland Revenue."

"I hope he does find some method of reducing any tax demands that may come your way. Incidentally, what are your plans now for the run up to Christmas?"

"As I just said, spending Christmas in London, don't know for how long. Muriel did mention events to attend over the New Year. I will check with Mavis as I don't know how long she wants to be away. I have invited Cynthia and her friend Wendy out to an afternoon Christmas Tea, Cynthia seemed quite thrilled by the idea. If I can persuade him, I'll take Fr Blakeston out for dinner. I want to get to one of the concerts at the Cathedral in the run up to Christmas and I have some Carol Services to play for – enough to keep me busy. Are you crossing the Atlantic this year?"

"I'll be going 23rd and away for about a week; I'm booked for the usual hotel in Boston and no doubt a little work will be sent my way. I'll be in touch before I go though, give you a ring."

Daniel got up to go and as he opened the door, I was able to hand over a card and present; a bottle of malt whisky in a wooden gift box makes a lovely shape to wrap and he looked quite pleased as he went on his way.

After he had gone, I reflected on one aspect of living alone, especially at Christmas. The first time I experienced this after my mother died, I made a conscious decision not to ignore the celebrations: I took to having a small Christmas Tree, for the last few years, artificial, and I would place this in the corner of the lounge area where I sat watching television, hang some lights nearby and arrange some of the old decorations which my parents used to get out every year – a good dose of nostalgia, one might say. I concentrated it all to one corner, more effective visually I thought, but I would stand cards anywhere there was a convenient flat surface.

When I was born my mother had bought a Nativity Scene, made from cardboard and in the form of a double page from a pop-up book. I still have it and I place it near the television. It used to rest on the top when I was a child, as televisions in those days were very stout. I had an outdoor electrical socket fitted near the front door, so I arrange a rope of lights outside. My immediate neighbours usually comment when I put them up and we will arrange a time to share a Christmas drink. Mavis joins us for this, along with a few other folks from nearby; we take it in turns to host this little Christmas Jolly. It had been my turn last year and I had yet to learn who was cooking the mince pies this year. Dare one say that in that little matter we are not all equally talented. I smiled at myself then, my thinking had been as if I was telling somebody all about it, another consequence, but harmless, of living on one's own.

14. CHRISTMAS EVE

Our Christmas trip to London started with a taxi in time to catch a mid- morning train, 1st class to Kings Cross. A copy of 'The Times, and a cup of coffee resting on the table in front of us made for a relaxing way to get going. Mavis was engrossed in a sudoku puzzle and I was reading the odd article, not too seriously, wanted to maintain this gentle start. Suddenly my eye caught a short headline: 'Lincolnshire MP to be Investigated'. There was only a couple of brief paragraphs which explained that the MP, Nat Lawton, was being investigated by party officials following an accusation that he had been seen associating with some known right-wing extremists and that he had attended a meeting of a banned group which had links with European Nazi Sympathisers.

The article said that Mr Lawton had denied all the accusations and that he was happy to co-operate with any investigation by the Whips Office. The Chairman of his local party had put out a statement of support. It occurred to me that the timing of this was very convenient for the MP, probably hoping that with the Christmas recess, all would be forgotten by the time Parliament reconvened in January. I couldn't help but wonder if Daniel had some inkling of the matter. If what the MP was being accused of was true it didn't surprise me one bit. I nudged Mavis. "Here, look at this small article, tucked away on an inner page."

"Keep the paper and we can show it to Muriel later; she may not have heard about it. I imagine you feel quite vindicated with your original opinion of Mr Lawton."

"I certainly do. He seemed a nasty piece of work to me and I expect there is some truth behind the accusations mentioned in this article. Of course, what it will come to is quite another matter."

"By the way, Monty, how did all your pre-Christmas events of the last week or so go? We haven't had a chance to catch up since our annual mince pie evening."

"All went well I think, Mavis. Cynthia and Wendy came with me over to a little upstairs café at the village shop at Alwalton. I know it because occasionally I go that way and use the post-office which doesn't close at lunchtime, rather handy. They set out a spectacularly good tea and we came away quite stuffed. Fr Blakeston permitted himself an evening visit to a City centre hotel, just a stroll away from his house, as well as dinner he accepted a bottle of vintage port. I got all my cards and letters off, some of the cards were reproductions of the very first ones ever sent back in the 1850s, quite attractive. Of course, you were with me for the mince pie eating at our end of the Avenue, good quality pie-making I thought. Did I tell you I was playing the organ for some carol services, one was candle-lit – something of a problem for me, couldn't see my music. And now? Knightsbridge, here we come."

We planned to meet at Muriel's place round about 1.00pm and the arrival time of our train followed by a taxi got us there not too late; one can't be that precise with travel times on Christmas Eve. Muriel had some lunch ready, the sort that could be eaten at once or kept nicely for an hour or so. Somebody had been very busy with Christmas decorations, probably Muriel, with the entrance way to the two apartments fairly dripping with very tastefully arranged lights, baubles, dried evergreens with flashes of reds although the overall effect for the whole area was mainly green and blue. Here and there were white ornaments made from carefully cut card. It occurred to me that the chauffeur, Tony, was an artist, so perhaps he had had a hand with the decorations and the thought cautioned me about what I might say. Red wine and sandwiches in hand we wandered around the flat with Muriel.

"I hope you like all the decorations; Tony has been responsible for most of it. I have just provided the extra pair of hands and I did quite a lot with the tree which is in Ken's main room. Leave your wine here and come and look."

If I thought the entrance way looked splendid, then there were insufficient superlatives to describe this room – 'breath-taking' would have to do. In addition to a magnificent tree in one corner, predominantly red and gold, there was an exquisite crib set in the opposite corner. The figures were probably about twelve inches high, beautifully modelled with colouring which was very gentle. Muriel noticed my gaze. "Ken is not one for great possessions, but that crib set came from his grandparents. I believe it is Italian and very old. Even if Ken is away for Christmas as has happened some years, the crib set is always out on display. I think it takes him to a happy time in his childhood memories.

I nodded my sense of understanding; it was a sentiment I could identify with. Looking round the rest of the room it was clear that Tony had made sure that the crib set retained centre stage effect – nothing out-shone it but there was still plenty to see including more of the cut card models – several rather stylised angels and other figures. There were strings of lights, mainly golds, blue and whites. It was still 'breath-taking' but because of the artistry and craftsmanship behind it all, there was a peacefulness to it. I realised Mavis had been rather quiet, of course she had no doubt seen much of it before. It was Muriel who spoke again. "Mavis, dear, are you all right?"

"Yes, yes, Muriel, I'm fine. I'm perhaps a little over-whelmed by the… what do I……I know, I just hadn't realised how good an artist Tony is and how wonderful it is that he can still…….. you know, still use all his talents so creatively. It makes me feel rather tearful and I don't understand why. I'll be all right in a few moments. Let's go and finish the wine." Mavis was quick to lead the way through to the kitchen.

I had rarely seen Mavis upset in this way as she was always calm, thoughtful, seemingly well controlled. This outburst was very out of character and it reminded me of the conversation when I first met Joseph and Charles from Trumpingtons. They had spoken of Mavis Missily as having been a talented artist and I had not followed this up, truth be told there hadn't been an obvious opportunity; perhaps one had just arrived.

We sat quietly for a few minutes, sipped the wine, and ate some salmon sandwiches. Just then, Muriel spoke up, perhaps a little over cheerfully. "Hot mince pies anyone? Cornish cream if you're feeling really greedy!"

Two or three minutes later, a hot gas oven soon caused a lovely aroma to assault our senses. Just a few more minutes and we could savour that exquisite seasonal taste that never disappoints from a perfectly cooked, home-made mince pie.

For a while Mavis and I wandered about looking at the delightful decorations – far more than we had anticipated and all rather lovely. We placed our few gifts under the tree, joining those already there and fortunately neither of us caused any clash in the colour scheme. Muriel called us after a while to ask if we wanted to go and hear the Carol Singers who were out and about in the area. She also mentioned that there was a short Nativity Service taking place at St Paul's Church, Wilton Place. All three of us strolled out; it wasn't particularly cold so there was no need to look extra Dickensian with mufflers and scarves. There was certainly some very classy Christmas music to hear, unaccompanied part-singing on one corner, a string quartet at another. Some distance away there was a Salvation Army Brass Band with a chorus of singers – they were loud but excellent; the Salvation Army always train great musicians.

After a while Mavis and Muriel went back, no doubt to gossip and catch up on each other's news. I strolled on to St Paul's Church where the Nativity Service was just about to start. This was charming and involved several children who all carried figures for the crib. Passing close to me I could see that in previous years there had been the odd accident as there were some repairs, a bit of sellotape for one and a large amount of glue holding an arm in place. Two of the older children sang solo verses in the carols. We may have been in the centre of London but there was a very homely feel to the whole event. As I came away, I noticed that a mid-night service starting at 11.30pm was advertised so I decided to attend that.

Back at the flat I found Muriel explaining why neither Ken nor Tony were home. Apparently, Ken had been called away unexpectedly first thing that morning, but he was confident that he would return in time for the evening meal. Tony was manning a stall at a Christmas Street Market, where, according to Muriel, he would sell quite a number of his paintings – he always builds up a stock of small items for this particular market as he finds that people are more confident about a gift's suitability if only a small amount of wall space is required. Muriel had opened another bottle of red wine and we sat round her kitchen table enjoying this and watching her prepare what was clearly going to be a quite sumptuous evening meal – roast pheasant would be the main item.

True to expectation, Ken turned up about six o'clock and quickly became the genial host. Not long after, Tony arrived looking very pleased with himself. He explained that he had broken his record, selling thirty-five items, half a dozen more than the previous year. He disappeared to shower and change, and Muriel took the opportunity to explain that he certainly ought to have been looking pleased as he sold those items for between twenty and fifty pounds. That left my book selling way behind.

Ken was keen to hear the story of my discovery of the Arthur Conan Doyle, a story I was yet to tire of relating. I was able to show him the dust jacket facsimile and I could see he was quite impressed. Mention of 'The Hound of the Baskervilles' prompted Mavis to ask if I had thought more about my planned trip to Italy.

"Well, yes, as it happens, I have. I have spoken to a self-employed travel expert, you might know him Mavis as he is an occasional member of the Compline congregation, Anthony Breakspeare. He used to work full-time for one of the large travel companies, but a few years back set up on his own. He also acts as a courier on some pre-arranged European city tours"

"That's a great name for an expert on travel in Italy," remarked Ken suddenly. "Nicholas Breakspeare was the only Englishman to be elected Pope, twelfth century I believe."

"I didn't know that Ken. I must ask Anthony if he is aware of the prestigious nature of his surname. Anyway, just as soon as I tell him where I might like to go after Venice and Verona, he'll put together some hotels for me."

"What kind of place do you want for your last port of call?" asked Ken. "If it is to relax and admire magnificent scenery and stay at an impressively historic hotel, then look no further than The King's Tower, Gardone. It is right on the shoreline of Lake Garda, towards the south-west and about an hour's taxi ride from Verona. You'll find plenty of information on the internet. It is quite idyllic. I stayed there for a couple of nights three or four years back. I was on my own, otherwise Muriel would have been able to vouch for my opinion."

"Obviously, I missed out then," commented Muriel. "Anyway, it is time for you all to vouch for the quality of these pheasants. I believe you have some wine to open Ken; Monty, shall you give Tony a shout and Mavis & I will 'dish up' to use a traditional phrase."

Not just the pheasants, we could also vouch for the mouth-watering quality of everything that Muriel had prepared. We ate a starter of mixed shellfish, the pheasants followed, accompanied by some very subtle stuffing, roast vegetables, and various sauces. The one sweet was a wonderfully rich trifle; finally, there was a board of cheeses and biscuits and for which Ken produced a decanter of port.

We spent the rest of the evening sitting in the main lounge where the crib-set was on display. Conversation flowed quite happily, nothing too serious. At one point, Tony showed how some of his small white card models has been constructed and I noticed that Mavis showed considerable interest in this and it was as if none of the upset that beset her earlier had ever occurred. Ken hadn't seen the Times that day, so I showed him the short article about Nat Lawton. He hadn't heard about it but like me he was not in the least surprised. Muriel served coffee at one point and Ken produced a selection of liqueurs. At about 11.00pm I mentioned that I intended to go to St Paul's Church for the mid-night service. Muriel was able to assure me that she, at least, would still be up, and that the main entrance on the ground floor would still be unlocked.

15. CHRISTMAS DAY

Entering St Paul's Church for the midnight service was like stepping back over fifty years. The whole atmosphere was just as I remembered such services when I was a choirboy. This was a giant dose of nostalgia and more so when we stood to sing the first hymn, 'Wake, O wake! with tidings thrilling. The watchmen all the air are filling, Arise, Jerusalem, arise!' When I was a choirboy, we only ever sang this wonderful old Advent hymn on Christmas Eve, rarely sung these days, indeed, I can't remember when I last sang it. The tune, 'Wachet Auf' and harmonized by J. S..Bach, was glorious and I recalled as a teenager learning to sing the bass part with its ornamentation of passing notes.

So much of this service was just as I remembered, the prayers, the robes, the incense, and the traditional readings from the Book of Common Prayer, including the first fourteen verses of St John's Gospel. The service was very well attended and during the Communion the choir sang several short carols. It ended as I expected with the carol, 'O come all ye faithful.' The choir sang a descant for the 'Choirs of Angels' and another descant for the last verse, 'Yea, Lord, we greet Thee, born this happy morning; Jesu, to Thee be glory given.' The choir and clergy processed out as the organist continued playing with a truly triumphant voluntary. Gradually, the congregation dispersed, some small groups of friends stood chatting quietly, but I suspect there were a number of folks, who like me, were on their own.

I was still very absorbed in the service as I strolled back along Wilton Place, quietly singing again odd verses of the carols, and reflecting on my seeming to go back in time. There were still cars and taxis about, people crossing the road, so I hardly noticed the sound of running feet and raised voices. It was just as my mind started to alert me that all was not quite right, that I felt a terrible shove from one side and a sharp and blistering pain to the back of my head. Actually, I may not have remembered that, but understood sometime later that that was what must have occurred, because 'sometime later' turned out to be tea-time, Christmas Day. I woke up to find Mavis sitting to one side and Ken the other; I had been hospitalised!

"O Monty, O good, you have come round at last. I'll call the nurse." As Mavis stood up to do this, Ken reached to shake my hand.

"Welcome back, you have had us all very worried."

The nurse came in them, checked readings on various monitors and then shone a pinprick of light into my eyes. "Well, I think you're going to be all right and more quickly than we first thought. The doctor will be here in a few minutes and if he's agreeable you'll probably be able to go home. These two visitors have been most kind and have sat with you for several hours. I'm sure they will continue to care for you, mind you, it will have to be alcohol free care. Ah, here's the doctor."

"Mr Warnock, very pleased you are back with us. I'm afraid you have had quite nasty experience although I imagine you don't recall much. You were attacked along Wilton Place, but people came to your rescue almost at once. Someone seemed to have known where you were staying, and a policeman went and fetched Mr Peterson here. Of course, the police will want to speak to you again. But from our point of view and given what the monitors are recording about you we don't need to keep you in. I'll just take your pulse and check your eyes again. You won't feel like doing much, drink plenty of fluids, non-alcoholic though. Rest and relax. If headaches get worse or you become dizzy call your doctor."

"Excuse me doctor," interrupted Ken. "I wonder if you know my neighbour and friend, Mathias Poynton, he lives in the apartment below mine?"

"Good gracious, yes, he's very well known, and works at this hospital, Neurology, am I right?"

"Yes, you are. Mathias and I have done the odd good turn for each other and I know he won't mind looking in on Monty and making sure we're doing all the right things."

"Well, if you can speak for him, we won't have any worries in organising Mr Warnock's discharge, just as soon as I can get a letter finished and signed."

"Mavis, you stay here with Monty and I'll go and call Tony to bring the car and by the time he's here, no doubt we'll all be able to go. I'll get him to bring a pair of pyjamas, slippers and a dressing gown."

"I'll leave you all to it then and go and organise the letter. I'll also get the nurse back to help you get up, you might be just a shade wobbly when you stand up. She'll bring a wheel-chair in as well." With that my doctor disappeared. I realised then that I didn't even know his name. As it happened, I didn't need to worry about that as I wouldn't have to see him again. I lay back, waited for it all to happen and asked if a cup of tea might be a possibility.

In the end it was nearly two hours before I was helped into Ken's car by Tony. And what a car! A Humber Super Snipe, and I hadn't been in one since I was a boy. Ken was on hand to witness my pleasure, explaining that he didn't use this car very often, but thought it would provide a greater degree of comfort for the short ride to 'Leopold Mansions'. We just seemed to glide round to the main entrance and there were Muriel and Mavis waiting to assist me into the wheelchair and get me up to the apartment. They established me in the main room where I could gaze at the Crib. At my request I sipped a well iced tonic water and it was at that point that my Christmas Memory activated itself.

"Good gracious, I've only just remembered, what happened to your Christmas Dinner, did I cause a disaster? Happy Christmas to you all."

"Don't be concerned," soothed Muriel. "I don't allow disasters in the kitchen and just as soon as we knew of your attack and admission to hospital, we decided that the meal should be postponed to the evening, in fact we'll be serving it in about half an hour."

At that point, Ken came in, accompanied by a stranger who I realised must be the friend from downstairs, Mathias Poynton, so no trouble with my current memory, I realised.)

"Here we are Monty: this is my good friend Mathias who has come to give you a very speedy and professional once over."

Mathias was introduced and in a matter of a few seconds he was quite confident in agreeing with the hospital doctor's decision to let me out.

"As they instructed, sorry, but no alcohol for 24 hours, plenty of other drinks, normal diet and just take things easy for a few days. If headaches return or you feel nauseous let me know, and we can get you back into hospital for a more detailed check, but I don't think that is likely. Sorry about your Christmas Day."

Matthias sat and joined Ken in a whisky, didn't bother me as the brand was my least favourite. I allowed them to propose a toast to my future good health. Very quickly Mathias was on his way with a promise that he would call in the morning. Ken saw him off and then returned and sat down beside me looking somewhat more serious.

"Now, Monty, so far you have asked no questions and nor have we, but the police will be calling tomorrow to take a statement and you need to think about that. It seems highly likely that this was not a random mugging, rather you appear to have been targeted. Furthermore, you were being follow by at least one other person who both knew you and knew where you were staying. He gave this information to the policeman who was there by chance having witnessed the event from the other side of the road. How does that analysis seem to you?"

"My, you have got it worked out. I must admit I hadn't got beyond thinking that I was attacked by someone who wanted to rob me. Your interpretation seems to suggest a much more organised incident and consequently far more serious. But who could know about me here in London, and know my address?

"Mavis is going to bring a small helping of Christmas dinner through to you in a moment. She's staying and eating hers with you. Perhaps you ought to consider what I have said, ask her opinion. One final thought: I believe Daniel Harrison is a close friend of yours, never mind how I know but if that is so I think we ought to give him a call as I think he might want to know what has happened. Have you his mobile number as it will be mid-afternoon on the east coast so now's a good time? He and I know of each other but haven't actually met."

"With my wallet, in the bedroom, is a small address book and his number is in that. I take it you'll ring him now?"

"Yes. Now, a change of subject and action; here is a laden tray for you, well, not too laden, just small quantities of all the right bits. There is a small table just here that should be all right for you Mavis. I'll leave you both to it. Bon appetite!"

Tray to my lap and the rising aroma was delicious and there was one of my Christmas favourites, bread sauce, O joy! Mavis came back very quickly with her tray and we both tucked in. Any delay that might have occurred in the kitchen could only have enhanced this meal, it was wonderful, and in all ways would prove a most memorable Christmas dinner.

I spoke first. "Mavis, Ken has been making one or two rather amazing yet very plausible suggestions, that my attack was not some random affair but part of an organised attack and that it failed because someone, who knew all about me, was around to intervene and then sent police here to fetch help. The question is, how can that be?"

Mavis rested her cutlery for a moment although I noticed she had nearly finished. "Actually, I have been thinking along similar lines because that is the only way I can make sense of your having been protected. Someone, who didn't want to be identified, knew you and where you were staying, was strong enough to see off the attacker and sharp enough to get the policeman to come here while he disappeared, leaving you in the care of one or two bi-standers. Why it should all have happened I simply can't imagine.

Given that you didn't announce your intention of going to church until late yesterday evening, the attacker or attackers were organised to strike at any opportune moment and by the same thinking any protection must have been organised in a similar way."

With that clear analysis in place we sat quietly and thought. If I were about to say anything I didn't because Muriel came in at that precise moment bearing a small drinks tray. It was a good job that I was very fond of tonic-water as that was my Christmas tipple for the next couple of days as evidenced by what Muriel handed to me. Gradually everybody came in from the dining room, all bearing that wonderful expression which simply radiates the pleasure of having consumed an enormous and wonderful feast. I was pleased that nobody seemed anxious to talk about my bang on the head, in fact Tony was the first to speak. "I gather Monty, you enjoyed the ride in the Humber, something of a Christmas treat, and talking of treats, thank you very much for the present, where did you find such a beautiful frame?"

"Ah, now that was in the way of being like the discovery of the Arthur Conan Doyle. Occasionally I'll see the odd box of bits and pieces at an auction and something will catch my attention. On this occasion it was an old ink well, nothing else I wanted, but lying across the bottom of the box was the picture frame. Can you date it?"

"Yes, I think so, probably early nineteenth century. The date doesn't matter to me as much as its size and appearance does. It won't require a large painting and with the right mount, it would set off beautifully a small work. It's lovely, thank you so much."

Ken was next, telling me that he had already opened the Laphroag and treated Mathias to the first measure. He apologised for having started it before he had given thanks for it. I just laughed and waved away his apology. Muriel threatened me with a rabbit and tripe stew from the Mrs Beeton volume, but I could see she was pleased with the book. Mavis rustled some paper beside her chair and showed (with all the enthusiasm of a child at school) the sculpture of the Red Kite. I had found this at an exhibition of local artists in Peterborough and thought she would like it; without doubt I was right and Ken asked if it could stand on his side table for a few days suggesting it would keep it safe, a little cheeky, I couldn't help thinking. At that point Muriel got up and placed a neat sack tied with beautiful ribbon in front of me, so now it was my turn.

This was real Christmas fun except this sack ought to be a stocking and it should be 6.00am! First out of the sack was something quite small, narrow oblong box perhaps – off came the gold foil paper and revealed what was a beautiful old fountain pen still mounted in its presentation box and with the original presentation slip now completed with Mavis's name. "How absolutely lovely, Mavis." And I blew her a kiss. Next out was a flattish oblong about nine by six inches, no guesses for what was inside: a delightful oil painting in a very gentle style, of a robin sitting on an old post-mounted letterbox. I didn't have to blow

Tony a kiss; he could see pleasure written all over my face. Next out was a silver paper covered box and inside – twenty-four absolutely scrumptious-looking hand-crafted chocolates from Muriel's fair hand. She was sitting next to me, so the kiss was real. "Muriel, these must have taken you ages and did you have to try many along the way?"

"A cook never reveals her secrets and that box of chocolates is not to be started until you are home. For now, I have a few to hand." So saying, she reached under her chair and brought out a crystal glass bowl to hand round, laden sufficiently for three or four circuits of the room.

Last to make its entry on the stage was the largest and heaviest and given its shape no guesses were required. Unwrapping some very thick and colourful paper was to reveal a wooden single bottle wine box. Mounted on the sliding lid was a neat card with a carefully written inscription: 'I believe you tasted something like this a few days ago' Wishing Monty a very joyous Christmas, Ken' Sliding the lid was to uncover a bottle of Nuit St George, and of the same vintage which Muriel had caused us to finish up early in December. "Ken, you couldn't have chosen better, and no kiss is needed to show my appreciation. Remembering the divine tasting a few days ago I shall make sure I open this bottle well before drinking and that also means it must be saved for a special occasion. Thank you so much, Ken."

16. BOXING DAY

The following morning, I awoke quite early but having slept so much in the previous forty-eight hours I wasn't surprised. I was very thirsty and appreciated the presence of a large jug of water nearby. I must have dozed on for a while and was surprised to find it was nearly ten o'clock when the door opening woke me again, and Ken came in with coffee and a warm mince pie – something I could eat anytime of the day.

"Good morning Monty, you look well rested, and I hope, feeling better. Mathias rang to say he would pop up just before lunch and give you a check over, timed his visit for something else I wouldn't be surprised. I didn't mention it last night as you were beginning to look rather tired, but Daniel Harrison rang me rather late; he had been out when I rang him earlier. He was very concerned to hear about the attack. He explained that he will meet up with you as soon as he gets back. He made one or two aspects clear but wants you to keep matters to yourself as far as is possible. Through his occasional work in London (you know about this I believe) he had been warned that he was likely to be targeted. Because of how his wife died, seen as a way of targeting him, he wanted to make sure all his family and friends were safe. His brother and family have taken advice and are following some precautions. In this country he doesn't feel any colleagues are at danger, but he is concerned about you so that is why he organised some protection. He thought it better not to tell you as he didn't want to cause unnecessary worry. It seems the organising of protection was a good move and he is more than pleased that it saved you. He hopes, Monty, it hasn't shaken you up too much; I assured him you were fine. Was I right to say that?"

Goodness, I did know he was involved in some important work, but I had no idea about any danger. But it was only very recently that he told me about some aspects of his work and what had happened to his wife. I think I'm OK now, a bit shaken up, but not suffering any lasting ill effects. At least, I think so."

"Unless I'm mistaken the man to make a definitive statement on any lasting effects has just arrived; I recognise the sound of the door. Good morning, Mathias. Monty here would like to be reassured as to suffering no lasting ill effects from his experience on Christmas Eve?"

Matthias reached to shake hands with me: "Good morning Monty, you certainly look to have a better colour than when we last met. Let me just shine this torch around your eyes, just follow the pinprick of light as it moves. How are the headaches now?

"Hello Mathias, sorry to interrupt your Christmas again. At this moment I have no headache which I suppose it good news."

"Yes indeed. I have a little kit with me this morning so let me take your blood pressure, just relax and Ken, don't start chatting with him. Well, that's all right, one hundred and thirty over seventy-five, can't complain about that and your pulse is steady at one hundred and fifteen. Plenty of men your age would not have readings as good as those without having been hit over the head. Now, can you just stand up for me. Turn to your left and look straight ahead. Now turn and face the opposite direction. Good, if I tell you that you are now facing north, please turn and face to the west. Yes, and you're looking at me again. Hold your left hand out, now reach round and touch your right ear. Good, with your right-hand, bend and touch your left knee. Close your left eye, reach out with either hand, then touch my right shoulder. Excellent. Look, I really don't think you have anything to worry about. Give it another forty-eight hours and if no headaches, then really, all's well. "

"That really is good news, thank you so much, most reassuring. I think on the strength of that Ken will treat you to a little something and there is no knowing what Muriel might produce."

Smiles all round and Ken and Mathias wandered out to the kitchen and Mavis came and replaced them. "Pleased with your recovery, was he?"

"Oh yes, Mavis. Matthias seems to think I'm quite well for my age, let alone having been banged on the head. You've heard that Daniel has been in touch? I suppose there will be a visit from the police today, I think that was mentioned yesterday."

"Yes, didn't Ken tell you, apparently they telephoned about nine o'clock and said that one of their officers would be calling early this afternoon if that was all right."

"I shall look forward to that Mavis. I wonder if they know about Daniel's involvement?" It'll be slightly complicated if they don't. Perhaps I must get Ken to tell me if Daniel said anything about that."

"Now Monty, if you don't mind my saying, stop worrying."

"Yes, of course, I'll give lunch some thought, any idea what your dear sister has in mind?"

"I do as it happens, some extra special vintage chutney of her own making, together with slices of turkey, pheasant and ham with 'bubble and squeak' though I doubt she'll call it that; at a quick tasting about fifteen minutes ago, never mind what she calls it, the finished dish has a magnificent flavour. There's Christmas pudding if you have room for it, alternatively a delicate mince pie."

"Sad to say, it still might be a mice pie, perhaps not too delicate."

An hour or so later and well after I had finished the glass of red wine which I had been allowed (my first that Christmas) two police officers were shown in.

"Good afternoon, Sir, recovering well, we hear; that was a very nasty experience and the circumstances, as we understand them, seemed to have brought you through remarkably unscathed. I'm Chief Inspector John Prentice, and this is Sergeant Jones and we're both from the Special Branch. Now, we know where this attack occurred and almost to the minute when it occurred. Perhaps you would just describe what happened from your point of view."

"Just so, but my 'viewpoint' was negligible as it all occurred from behind me. I was on my own, though quite a few people were about as well as taxis etc. I was reflecting on the Midnight Service which I had just come from, humming some carols, even. I can remember some vocal noise, shouting perhaps, then the sound of running. It was then that I felt I was being shoved, quite forcefully. I don't know whether I remember being struck on the head, or because I know that is what happened next, I think I remember. Other than that, my next definite memory is of waking up in a hospital bed with Mavis Missily and Ken Peterson sitting either side of me. Everything else that I know, I have been told about since waking up. That's it really. Tell me, do you know my close friend, Daniel Harrison, colleague of yours I believe?"

"Yes, I know him well, have done for a few years but Sergeant Jones has never met him, but he knows of him. I should say that Daniel spoke to me this morning and told me what had happened, as relayed to him by Mr Peterson. On the strength of that, we contacted the local police station, left thanks for the quick action of their Constable, but explained that we were under instructions to follow up various aspects of the case as there were possible security issues involved. Being in Central London, they are not unfamiliar with that happening. Sergeant Jones popped in a little while ago and collected their paperwork, which of course didn't amount to much.

You don't surprise me about remembering so little and I doubt if you will remember anything more. Just one or two points I need to raise with you. I assume you were a first-time visitor to the church and that nobody there would have known you. However, were you aware of anyone having followed you into the church, did anyone seem a little, how shall I put it, uncomfortable or out of place with their surroundings?"

"That's difficult, I was among the last few to arrive and there were only a small number left to collect books and find somewhere to sit. It might be worth asking those members of the congregation who were welcoming visitors. I was there in the afternoon as well, so the same questions arise, although the congregation was much smaller."

"Thank you, Mr Warnock, certainly points worth following up. How about Peterborough, anything out of the ordinary going on in your hometown, sorry, City, I should say?"

"If that were the case, I think I would have been more likely to notice. I will have to give that more thought. Should I ask my neighbours, or would it be better to leave them out of it for the time being? I take it that you have asked Mavis or will be doing so?"

"Yes, indeed, we have already spoken to Mavis. She was most clear and quite confident that nothing untoward had been happening while you were both travelling. We'll stop this discussion now, mustn't tire you out and we'll leave you our contact details so that you have a point of reference should anything else occur. Daniel said that he will be flying home before the weekend so he should be able to talk to you about the whole affair. He said I was to tell you to expect him Friday afternoon, that you would understand."

"Message received and totally understood Chief Inspector; there is a malt whisky involved about tea-time on Fridays! There is though, one other matter of which you need to be aware. I have recently had an unexpected and valuable find in my secondhand book business and in the next week or so there may be quite a bit of publicity. I can't avoid this, but I hope it won't make matters more difficult. I had better ask Daniel about it. Do you have any immediate thoughts on the matter, Chief Inspector?"

"Nothing obvious, Mr Warnock. Publicity can be a bit two-edged, might help identify any attacker but it could also increase any risk you may be facing. See what Daniel thinks."

The two police officers stood up, shook hands, repeated their concerns for me over my having been attacked and promised to keep in touch. As they left my bedroom, I heard Muriel call to them so perhaps she had some refreshment all set out.

I must have fallen asleep for a while because when Ken came in it was almost dusk. Like a perfect man servant, he pulled the curtains, turned, and picked up a small drinks tray and brought it to my bedside table. "This is Glenmorangie, which I gather you have a certain fondness for, at least that's Mavis's opinion."

"She's absolutely right. Your very good health, Ken."

"Now, don't miss interpret this Monty. It's Wednesday evening now and I believe you are expecting to talk to Daniel Friday afternoon. I wonder, in view of your recent 'bump', whether it would be a good idea for Tony to drive you up to Peterborough Friday morning? I might say that Mavis thinks it an excellent plan and she would like to stay on over the weekend with Muriel. Tony and you can chat about book illustrating or some other topic of interest which you may have in common."

"Would you think me grabbing if I just say, thank you very much, Ken? That's a splendid idea and just at this moment travelling across London and taking the train north doesn't appeal too much."

"Nothing grabbing at all. Tony will enjoy putting his foot down for a run up the A1, probably won't be busy, Friday after Christmas. I've already dropped a hint, so I'll let him know that the plan is on. Don't forget the malt, now."

17. THE FEAST OF HOLY INNOCENTS

A light tap on my door at 7.30 Friday morning found me just awake and Tony calling in to suggest we left at about 8.15. That was fine by me as I was not one to take long to get up and be ready to go especially if someone else was preparing the porridge, my breakfast of choice. Everybody was up and about to see us off and much to my surprise outside the main entrance was one gleaming 1950s Humber Super Snipe. Tony noticed my amazement and explained that he and Ken had decided that a steady 50mph run up the Great North Road would do the engine some good and provide me with a luxurious ride.

On our way I reflected on the previous evening of which good company, good food and two glasses of excellent wine ensured that I had the best night's sleep since the attack. We had been eight for dinner, we five, Jon Mostang, his solicitor John Prendle, and his wife Joanne Wyndham. Introductions all round and conversation flowed happily. Muriel presented Ken with a wonderful joint of magnificent looking roast beef to carve, while Mavis carried in most of the other dishes. There was no starter, clearly the roast beef was the focus of the table and the first mouthful told me why; Harrods' food hall provisions at their absolute best. We all chatted away while eating enthusiastically and it was then that Joanne happened to mention that she and Ken were cousins.

Apparently on a previous occasion they had been discussing surnames when Joanne told everyone that she had two surnames, one on her birth certificate, Fortnum, and a second, when her stepfather became her official adoptive parent, Wyndham. Her mother was Ken's mother's youngest sister by many years and when she was at Exeter University, second year undergraduate reading history, she discovered that she was pregnant. She could have stayed at University but decided that looking after a child while studying would be just too complicated and given that the prospective dad had all but disappeared from her life, she left.

Two years later she met David Wyndham and happiness became assured thereafter, and Joanne acquired a half-brother some eighteen months later, and he, Andrew a scientist, was working in the United States. It had been the mention of the name, Fortnum, which had alerted Ken to a possible connection and had sent him off to look up some family tree information, something which Joanne had never done. I always love hearing these odd bits of family tree information.

John Prendle explained that their children were staying with his parents for a few days and so he and Joanne were fancy free and visiting friends in London. Somewhat facetiously, I had asked Jon Mostang if he had seen anything of his colleague, Nat Lawton, over the Christmas holiday. His face gave me the answer before he so much as uttered a syllable. The single word 'No' can make an effective and very bleak sentence, two letters conveying so much meaning! Ken joined in at this point, telling me that he and Jon often met over aspects of work which involved them both. Apparently when the three of them were together back in early December, Jon Mostang was telling Ken about several troubles being experienced by some immigrants working in Lincolnshire and who were in Nat Lawton's constituency. It turned out that Nat was of little help with their discussion, no surprise to me. Later, with John Prendle's involvement, it was clear that they were being badly exploited with the threat of deportation hanging over them. John was quickly able to establish that this threat was illegal and that their temporary status in the UK was regularised. This was clearly another aspect of Ken's sense of philanthropy at work.

My attack on Christmas Eve came up in the conversation and much surprise was registered regarding the circumstances. I think they would have liked to know more, but there was little I could add, certainly not until after I had met up with Daniel. The arrival of French Apple Flan and a Chocolate Trifle brought the questioning of me to a speedy halt; better things to do.

I had looked forward to my drive back to Peterborough, wanting to know more about Tony's painting career, I had also wondered whether he had ever heard anything about Mavis having studied art. Without my even noticing, sleep overtook me (a tribute to the old Humber) and when I came to, I noticed road signs pointing off to the east for Huntingdon and Peterborough, only another fifteen miles or so to the north. This was helpful, as I was able to give Tony verbal instructions to my house rather than him having to rely on his portable 'satnav' sitting on the back seat. He saw me in, carrying my various bags and 'Christmas' bits and pieces and then was off. He couldn't be persuaded to stop long enough for a cup of coffee. I wasn't sorry really, although I felt somewhat guilty, as I suddenly felt extremely tired again. I went and lay down and the next thing I knew it was the middle of the afternoon and I had been home for a good four hours.

Getting up, I quickly organised a few things for Daniel's visit as I wasn't sure when he would arrive, but a text message just then alerted me to expect him in about thirty minutes. Tea, coffee, or whisky were all available as were some of Muriel's mince pies in addition to shortbread which I found had been popped in my bags. I also had out Tony's painting, an old Cross fountain pen, a vintage Nuits St George and Muriel's home-made chocolates – these last to taste! Just then I saw him walking up my back-garden pathway, perfect.

It took him about five seconds to opt for a malt though he reserved the right to a coffee before he left. We exchanged a few pleasantries while he told me about his brother and family, his two flights but soon we were onto the major matter of the Christmas Eve attack. Daniel had been very upset on hearing about the attack from Ken, but relieved to have learnt that his security arrangements had succeeded in ensuring that the attacker had been chased off; he knew, though, that it could have been far more seriously.

Daniel wanted to know that I agreed with his decision not to alert me to the risk but just to put in place some effective precautions. I understood him fully, glad not to have been constantly looking over my shoulder for fear of what might be about to happen; the bodyguard arrangement had worked. I would have worried greatly about Mavis had I known. I wanted to know more about him, was he under threat? In fact, he was, although in London things were better organised as far as officer safety was concerned, and of course, he wasn't alone in being under threat. In Peterborough he explained that he organised things for himself. He reminded me of Junaid Anwar, his colleague who was involved with the two lads caught stealing. Daniel explained that Junaid's brother ran a small security firm, activities involving personal courier work, individuals feeling the need for someone to travel with – it seemed there was an increasing demand for quite different aspects of security. Anyway, by arrangement with Junaid and his brother's firm, he managed to ensure a reasonable degree of personal safety.

My main concern was to know who or what group of people might be involved. Daniel was uncertain although his colleagues in London thought it most likely to be Middle Eastern, it all seemed a little vague. I asked him about the two MPs that he had been talking with when we last met, and I wondered if he thought either of them might be involved. He explained that that was difficult to answer as there was still a lot of uncertainty about Mostang's background. As for Nat's background, the field was clearer although any reasons would surely be rather obscure.

His marriage had long since broken up and his former wife, Rosemary, lived quietly on her own in Lincoln, she and Nat were not in contact. There were two children, a daughter, Angela, who had largely been brought up in Spain by an aunt, her mother's older sister. Now grown up, she still lived in Spain, well to the south and she was obviously bi-lingual. Nothing was known regarding her work. The other child, Benjamin, a little younger, had studied French and the Travel Industry at University. He was employed mainly as a courier for groups travelling in various European Cities. He also did free-lance work for various firms who wanted someone to accompany individual senior staff on overseas business trips. Neither of us could think of any reason why Nat or family members might have anything to do with threats again Daniel or family or friends.

I asked Daniel about his family again, were there other relatives beside his brother. He explained that his family was rather limited as both his parents had been only children and had married latish in life. He recalled mention of elderly great aunts and uncles when he and his brother were small boys, but he wasn't in touch with any distant relatives. We batted various thoughts to and fro. Although an attack against me was clearly a warning for him, it couldn't, after thirteen years, be a continuation from when his wife was murdered. Nor could he think of any on-going work which might generate such activity. He and his colleagues were always remembering to be aware of possible threats but only in a general way. The security watch for him in Peterborough hadn't revealed anything sinister.

I mentioned to him that Trumpingtons would be putting out publicity soon regarding the Arthur Conan Doyle book and that this would likely involve me. I wanted to know if he saw this as a source of danger, would my attackers in London pick up on the connection. Daniel did not have a clear answer one way or the other, just that one must exercise some caution. In the event it proved not to be a worry. A couple of the national newspapers picked up on the story of my find and the forthcoming auction, but it only seemed to merit a couple of small paragraphs.

I did make a short local television appearance in which I described the moment of discovery and I was able to show a photograph of the dust jacket prior to restoration and I also displayed the facsimile of the finished article. The interviewer at least had done a little homework and knew all about the story of the Hound of the Baskervilles. He also asked about why it should seem to be so valuable and quoted the Trumpington estimate. I explained the rarity of the book with a unique dust jacket, the unusual nature of the three pieces of Arthur Conan Doyle's writing and signatures in this copy. 'Had I any idea who might buy it?' was another question but, of course, I had no answer beyond some polite waffle.

I was also invited to take part in a radio discussion: this was more interesting as it broadened out to talk about secondhand books in general, what sort of books did I sell, had I ever had great finds before. The interviewer was also interested personally as he collected books in a general way, he had a collection of first editions by John Buchan including a nicely signed copy of 'The Thirty-Nine Steps'. It made for a much better discussion with both of us being interested in old books. The only other result of the publicity was an invitation from a village branch of the Women's Institute, would I consider giving an illustrated talk about old books and the secondhand book market. I certainly didn't see that as posing any sort of threat, so I was happy to agree, might even be good fun. I could easily put together twenty or thirty interesting volumes, some photographs which I could place on a computer and briefly talk about each as well as throw in some amusing anecdotes such as what you do when, as a dealer, you discover you have posted two volumes, but the wrong two, to an individual in New York, and that someone in the west country has received the other two volumes, but who was about to embark on a one month cruise. Over the years I have had my share of such mishaps! I could also take a box or two of books for the WI members to sell or buy inexpensively, they could give the proceeds to charity. I thought I would get Mavis to accompany me, perhaps lend a hand. Afterall, she did have a share in the actual discovery of the dust jacket.

18. THE AND THAT, EVEN AN ENGAGEMENT

In the event, the talk to the branch of the Women's Institute proved great fun. I made it last about an hour with a brief break in the middle. Mavis kindly supervised the computer display for me. I was able to talk without notes because I was familiar with everything I wanted to talk about, illustrations on the screen, individual books which I held up to talk about and passed around. They were impressed with an old C19th Bible which I had because of an inscription linking it to an Irish Aristocratic family. On one of the blank pages at the front I was able to describe how I had successfully removed a modern biro ink inscription which had rather marred the overall appearance of the copy and I showed them a 'before and after' photograph.

One of my anecdotes was about selling an item close to Christmas one year, a booklet which described how Scarborough had been shelled from the sea during the First World War. I was supposed to post this to the buyer who lived in Scarborough, it was to be a Christmas Present for his Grandad because the Grandad's father remembered the actual event. Unfortunately, I popped the item in the post with nothing on the package other than stamps. Obviously, I caused much disappointment, refunded the money but that of course did not solve the problem. Computer to the rescue: a google search alerted me to the fact that all undeliverable mail went to one depot in Belfast; I was able to write to them, describe the envelope and its contents, mention almost to the minute when and where I posted it and what time the collection would have been made and therefore the likely date of their receiving it; I explained why I was so worried, that it had been intended as a Christmas Present; I enclosed a £10 note for their trouble and requested that if a search was successful could they use the enclosed correctly addressed self-adhesive label and post it on to Scarborough. The happy outcome was that on the 23rd of December that year I received an email from the buyer telling me that it has arrived that morning. They were amused when I told them that I had written to the local MP about that success, because it was at a time when privatisation of Royal Mail was under discussion, and did he think a private organisation would be as helpful in the future?

The WI members were also amused to hear that I sold some perfect but old copies of Penguin paperbacks back to Penguin. On that occasion Penguin were planning an exhibition of a series of translations of the 'Classics' – these had appeared from the late 1940s through to the early 1960s. They bought three copies from me because when they went to their stores of old copies, they found that they were missing some and my three helped fill the gap. That's the only occasion on which I have sold back to the publishers. The evening ended with the sale of my spare unsold books and this raised nearly £100 which they donated to a local charity, a jolly evening which led to my being asked to repeat the event with one or two other societies.

Back in Peterborough my daily round of repairing and selling continued with varied success. I called on friends, including Cynthia and her neighbour, Wendy. I also visited Fr Blakeston and continued my weekly visits with Mavis to St Petrie for Compline. Friday visits from Daniel decreased somewhat as he was engaged on more work in London. I gathered from Mavis who had heard from Muriel that he had been to visit Ken on several occasions, sometimes accompanied by one or two of his London colleagues. It wasn't quite clear to me what these meetings would discover but no doubt they had in part something to do with the attack on me. It may also have had connections with some of Ken's work as he was known to have contacts with some quite shady people, from overseas as well, and that this had led him to travel with Peter Prendle to engage in more of his 'righting of wrongs'. He was discovering more semi-illegal immigrants and others from many different parts of the Middle East and Asia who were being badly exploited and enslaved, the sort of things that one read of almost every day in the newspapers.

Coincidently, I had a call from Daniel asking if he could call later, as he had a piece of news, he thought it would amaze me, perhaps delight, perhaps both; he was being most enigmatic. Needless-to-say, my brain went into overdrive but no notion of what this 'delight' might be was forth coming; I would just have to be patient. It may not have been one of his regular Friday evening calls, but it didn't prevent Daniel from accepting the usual glass and with a refill ready when the need arose.

"Monty, we have a romance among our group of acquaintances and as from this weekend it will become an engagement! Daniel seemed thrilled to impart this gem of gossipy news. "I may have told you I was involved with Ken a little more than previously and the other evening I was having dinner with him and a London colleague of mine when Ken suddenly asked, apropos of nothing, whether I had heard about Jon Mostang. He assumed I hadn't and went straight on announcing that this weekend Jon would become engaged to be married to Genevievre Renoir, the newly emerging star of the Paris Opera.

He explained that Ken seemed incredibly pleased to have had this news. Apparently, he had met with Peter Prendle and wife for a meal and also present was an international Lawyer, one Pierre Renoir, who was over to discuss some business with John's firm, and with him was a much younger brother, Jean, who was studying piano in London, both brothers of Genevievre. It was Pierre who revealed the news, asking if anyone there knew of Jon Mostang, and of course they all did. It turned out that our Jon had made all the running after attending a concert just after Christmas with some friends in Paris. He was over-whelmed by her beauty and voice and within two days he had met Genevievre and they had been in touch with each other every day since. "As I said, engagement this weekend."

"That'll make his fellow MPs sit up and take note, be chatting him up for tickets so they can entertain on the grand scale – there is never anything inexpensive about Opera. I wonder whether she is planning to perform in London any time soon?"

"I don't know Monty, although I believe she has been giving a number of concert performances in Paris and elsewhere in France. Ken said that the younger brother thought she may be presenting a similar concert in the UK. I wonder if Jon will want her to perform at their engagement celebration, that would be unusual."

"Is there a date for the wedding because that will be a huge event? Of course, his family is particularly small so it may perhaps be a quieter affair."

"We will have to wait and see as I have no more information. Changing the subject rather, have there been any more incidents that you are aware of? My people in London tell me all has been quiet, no sightings of anything suspicious involving me."

"Mavis and I both keep watch and we have noticed nothing, won't let our guard down though."

"I'll away now, really only came to tell you about friend Mostang. Keep in touch Monty."

As he got to the front door, he pointed to my Christmas present from Tony, the small oil painting of the robin on the pillar box. "I do like that; it has a gentle charm about it." I had placed it just to the left of the main door so anyone leaving would catch a view of it, it seemed to work well in that position. I was pleased and I reminded myself to tell Tony when I next saw him. As Daniel went on his way it occurred to me that I might stroll round to Mavis and bring her up to date on the news about Jon Mostang. No doubt she would ring Muriel to see if there were any extra gossipy titbits. I also had a book that I wanted to show her and to see if it would help me raise the delicate matter of her art studies. The book was a history of knitting, not exactly an everyday topic for one's library shelf. It was signed, and anyway, I had an ulterior motive. I needed to tell her about Anthony Breakspeare's suggestion regarding the holiday in Italy.

It must have been talk of John Mostang and MPs in general, but just before I went out Nat Lawton crossed my mind, reminding me that I had never heard any more about his right-wing activities which were being investigated by the Parliamentary Conservative Whips. A quick search on Google and, just as I thought, a brief announcement that after an investigation no further action was required; it was suggested that there had been some mistaken identity, even the possibility that it was his son who had been seen. Nothing like a prolonged Christmas recess for burying some unwanted 'Parliamentary' news. Thinking no more about one Nat Lawton, I marched round to Mavis to deliver two exciting pieces of news.

19, MAVIS, MURIEL AND MONTY

I found Mavis tending to a little 'spring' gardening, not too arduous, but she didn't mind stopping to put the kettle on.

"This is an unexpected pleasure Monty, any problems?" Mavis queried.

"No, nothing untoward, quite the opposite in fact, somebody's engagement to tell you about." That caused a smile and a raised eyebrow. "And nothing that involves me!" I hastened to add. "Daniel called a little while back and as well as checking on our continued safety, he sprung the surprise of telling me that this weekend would see the announcement of the engagement between Mlle Genevievre Renoir and Mr Jon Mostang, MP. Apparently, something of a world-wind romance which started about Christmas time; Daniel has no knowledge of when or where the wedding will take place. He got the news from Ken, who had been dining with Peter Prendle and the party had included Genevievre's two brothers, one, Pierre, an International Lawyer, and the other, Jean, much younger, who is studying piano here in London.

"I must ring Muriel later, as she is sure to know a few more details."

I smiled at that but said no more, rather, broached a slightly awkward topic which I had been putting off. "Mavis, I have a book which may interest you. I've brought it round because it has only just come my way, but it connects with a conversation I had with Joseph and Charles, from Trumpingtons, from when I first met them." I thought Mavis suddenly looked a little tense, but it might have been my imagination as perhaps I expected some reaction. I pressed on regardless. "It was when I had mentioned to them that you might be calling, they recognised your name, your surname being a little unusual."

"You don't surprise me Monty, as soon as you mentioned the name of Trumpingtons, I thought something of my background would emerge. Carry on, I'm over all the troubles from when I was in my early twenties, just never told anyone from round here. You'll realise now why I didn't call to meet the staff from Trumpingtons. I deliberately didn't tell you, left you to think that perhaps I had forgotten."

"It's been on my mind for a while now but haven't felt able to say anything, didn't want to intrude on your past so to speak. It was just getting this book, I thought it could give me an opportunity to ask. Look, this is the book, 'The Sacred History of Knitting' by Heinz Edgar Kiewe and this is a signed copy from 1967. Actually, the first time I called here after the Trumpington visit, I looked again at your various pieces of art on display and thought then that Joseph and Charles had been correct in what they remembered. It's only now because I have glanced at this book and made one or two internet searches about wool being used in art that I discover that there is far, far more to knitting than 'two purl, two plain and casting off!"

"Gosh, Monty, you have no idea. The possibilities for wool, knitting, visual arts, three dimensional forms are totally endless, and if it hadn't been for a particularly unpleasant and narrow-minded lecturer, I might be working in my own studio even now. Look, I have said too much, so I must tell you the whole story, but not now, leave it a few days. I'm going to talk to Muriel about the 'wedding', so I'll raise it with her first as she was involved in my troubles when I was at college. By the way, I'll do a swap with you, as I have a copy of your book, same edition, but mine isn't signed."

"Thank you, Mavis, for what you have told me. You don't have to tell me what happened, and I don't want to cause upset between us. We'll say no more, and I'll leave the 'ball in your court', no pun intended. We can swap the book though, my pleasure."

Now, I need to tell you what Anthony Breakespeare has found out for me and I think you may find this a much happier topic. When I came back after Christmas, I told him about The King's Tower, Gardone. He hadn't heard of it but made enquiries. He rang me after a few days, pointing out that my original plan could be very exhausting as it would involve three different hotels, while looking after all the luggage required for a couple of weeks or so. He pointed out that if I didn't mind using a taxi or a coach, I could go on trips from Gardone, just taking what was required for a couple of nights and the Verona and Venice visits could be spaced out.

"Anyway, I've had a better idea since then. Do you and your sister ever go on holiday together, because it occurs to me that a very nice way for me to show real appreciation for all her cooking and care over Christmas, would be for the three of us to go to Gardone and sample this hotel which Ken praises so. All with the compliments of Arthur Conan Doyle – why don't you add that to your conversation for this evening? Anthony said a very good time for that part of Italy would be late June, early July for a couple of weeks, temperatures not usually killingly hot and most schools haven't finished their summer term by then; see what she says?"

"That's a lovely idea Monty, but you are talking about a great deal of money, wonderful as such a holiday would be. And to answer your question, yes, Muriel and I are always happy to travel together and have been on many holidays, not so often abroad though. I'll see what she says, thrilled I expect. On the strength of your lovely plan let me make some coffee and you can taste my latest cake, lemon cream sponge."

While Mavis was in her kitchen, I felt I could wander around and look at various pieces of art on display. Catching my eye from the sideboard was the Red Kite sculpture which I had given her at Christmas. She had set it off very well by creating space around it. Closest to it was something I had not seen before, a small model of part of a mountain range, rocks, crags, tiny valleys, a small waterfall. As I looked more closely the 'penny' suddenly dropped – this was all constructed from fabrics, braids, wool, silks, and other pieces which I didn't recognised straight away. There were tiny pieces of knitted items, weaves, incredibly thin pieces of wire of various colours. I stood there fascinated by the complexity of how it all held together although I couldn't work out what gave it bulk, stuffing, for lack of a better expression. That was when Mavis came in with the tray of goodies.

"I only placed that there recently, thought it would look nice near the Red Kite. It dates to my student days, perhaps not typical of what I was experimenting with and not remotely like the works which Trumpingtons sold for me. Now, how about this lemon cream cake? There is some crème fraiche if you fancy it and I'll pour some coffee."

I suspect that Muriel forgets that not everybody starts the day as early as she, because I was woken the following morning by the telephone at just after 7.00am.

"Monty, wonderful idea, yes please and thank you very much!" was Muriel's shout for my start to the day. "Oh dear! I thought it was eight o'clock, but I see it's only seven, sorry about that. You must tell Mavis I rang and that everything is sorted. Tell her that I have spoken to Ken, he'll be away for quite a while at the same time, but it will be okay because Tony can help him. It's all going to work out brilliantly."

"Good morning Muriel. I take it then that you are quite happy with my little plan. We just need to make sure that Trumpingtons get some keen bids for 'The Hound of the Baskervilles'".

"Need to tell you about our security as recent activity here has made a need for some changes. Had you heard about our scare? Ken thought he was being followed the other night and a couple of nights later he was positive. Your friend Daniel has organised something of a watch, and when I look out in the mornings now, I notice someone wandering nearby, our 'guardian angel' as I call him. In recent weeks Daniel has been here more frequently but he still doesn't know whether there is a connection to all these threats. Ken has no idea who might be targeting him but feels a little more comfortable about it all, knowing that there is some security. I expect Daniel will tell you about it. The last time he was here was when Mavis was visiting, he urged her to be alert when out and about. They had sat chatting for some time."

"That must have been worrying for Ken, but I'm reassured to know that you have people watching. Daniel seems to find it relatively easy to organise. On a different note, did Mavis tell you last night that she started to talk to me about her art studies. She didn't touch on what brought it all to a standstill, but she did explain about the kind of techniques she was trying to develop. She has a long way to go but I think she might regain some of her earlier enthusiasm."

"That's very encouraging Monty, perhaps I'll be allowed to display the items I have. Must ring off now, breakfast to prepare, Tony is leaving early on a journey for Ken. And Monty, thank you again for your wonderful idea."

The mention of breakfast and the early awakening seemed to have perked up my appetite, so I determined to cook some scrambled eggs and eat a little more than usual for the beginning of the day; coffee called me first. Later, I needed to contact Anthony Breakspeare and get this Italian venture booked.

I got somewhat side-tracked with book repairs and it wasn't until after lunch that I gave Anthony a ring. He seemed quite amused to think that I was taking two women on holiday but said he would get on to making some bookings. He also wanted to know about any preferences regarding quality of flight, pointing out that if we flew with BA we could opt for 'club class' and enjoy a bit more comfort. The only drawback would be going down to Gatwick. I was all for comfort, asked him to book that and find out about the cost of a taxi to the airport – I certainly didn't want anything arduous about the journey. Knowing that, he said he would also explore easiest way for the transfer from Verona to Gardone. Having set that all in motion I decided to stroll round to Mavis again and let her know the progress made and tell her of Muriel's 'midnight' phone call.

"Monty, you're just the man and the first, come in. Sorry, that sounded a bit ambiguous, but you couldn't have timed your arrival better – look!

Whereupon she threw open the door to her lounge. To say that it was transformed would be an understatement; it was an art gallery. I had only ever known this room with three or four discretely placed works of art, now there were pieces everywhere, different colours, sizes, moods, effects, as well as a small number of models. The effect was breath-taking and revealed a totally different Mavis. Standing there stunned, totally silent, I could see that there was nothing haphazard about this display – the groupings were all as meant to be.

"Mavis, this is magnificent, how on earth have you got this sorted and arranged with such balance so quickly?"

"I'm glad you realise that there is a pattern to it all. Other than taking account of the different arrangement of available wall space, this is, as near as I could manage, a remounting of my final exhibition at the end of my college course. There are just a few pieces missing, the ones sold by Trumpingtons and the few I let Muriel have. She also has the two that I gave our mother." More quietly, she explained that she hadn't felt like taking them back for herself.

"Well, I can tell you now, those that Muriel has will be on display just as soon as she hears about this exhibition. She woke me up at seven o'clock this morning to talk about the holiday and how it would all be superb because Ken and Tony would be away at the same time. You know, sometimes your sister talks like a machine gun, her words come out with such speed. As soon as I mentioned that you had spoken a little about your art, she was off, hoping that it would soon be all right for her to hang up the pieces of your work which she still has hidden away."

"She mentioned last night that she would be ringing you, sorry about her choice of time."

"No matter, and you don't have to apologise for your sister. Anthony Breakspeare has the holiday requirements in hand and will let me know soon what he has booked Of course, he must let me know soon because he'll need some money. Some things he mentioned I have agreed to already: he will book flights with BA, opting for their club class – more luxurious and more space – and he'll sort out using a taxi to Gatwick and also a taxi from Verona to the hotel."

"That's excellent, I had meant to tell you that travelling in a coach makes me ill so to use taxis, wonderful, expensive but an essential luxury. You know Monty, we're not that far into this New Year but with your gift of a holiday and getting all my art unpacked I feel like someone coming out of hibernation. It's better than any medicine."

"And you need to know Mavis, I think you're having something of an epiphany. Now, change of subject, I gather you have heard about Ken's need for some security watch where they live. It is worrying that the source of the threat remains something of a mystery and it's hard to believe that it is all to do with the Middle East. I can't help wondering if it might not be a little nearer home, but I can't imagine what."

"Daniel must believe it a real threat to be able to organise so much security, never mind the cost! He's taken to telephoning me a couple of times a week to check all's well. I enjoy chatting to him, but he never fails to mention these threats. Let's not talk anymore about that. Time's getting on, you sit here with a glass of wine, contemplate my works of art and I'll produce what my mother would have called a 'high tea'; there wouldn't have been wine though."

20. MAINLY MAVIS

Well into spring, and I found myself spending more time on my own. But for the Wednesday night service of Compline at St Petrie's Chapel, I would be having difficulty in keeping up with Mavis – she was a person transformed, lovely really, but it did mean she was out and about so much more. 'Art' had suddenly become 'big' again and she was sketching, taking photographs, gathering materials, and making notes for future ideas. She had also joined a local group of professional artists who met from time to time, shared ideas and arranged exhibitions. If I needed any information, Muriel was the one to put me right.

My last chat with Muriel had been all about the holiday – Anthony Breakspeare had certainly done his stuff: booked return flights with BA, Club Class; two rooms at The King's Tower, Gardone – a twin and a single both overlooking Lake Garda; taxis booked for journeys to and from Gatwick and finally, he had telephoned The King's Tower and discovered that they were happy to arrange a taxi to meet us at Verona. All I had to do was to give an undertaking to have cash to pay the driver. How easy it all seemed, not forgetting, of course, that I had written a rather hefty cheque for Anthony! If there were any drawbacks it was that the journey to Gatwick would start from Peterborough at about three o'clock in the morning. Muriel had decided she would come and stay with Mavis for a couple of nights. She had remained as excited as she was that early morning when she rang to say a very loud. 'thank you'.

I wasn't seeing Daniel quite so frequently either, as his work was keeping him in London more often. I heard from him probably every other week or so and perhaps just a quick telephone call at that. This quiet spell was definitely only a 'lull before the storm' because opening my newspaper one Monday morning in April there was the headline:

'Gunman Disarmed at MP's Wedding in Paris'

'On Saturday morning the wedding between the French Opera Singer, Genevievre Renoir and the British MP, Jon Mostang, took place at a small church in Paris, close to the Bride's family home. It was a quiet occasion, attended only by the Bride's family and some close friends of both Genevievre and Jon. It was just after the service had finished when some photographs were being taken outside the Church. Some pressmen were also there, and able to witness subsequent events. According to some of the guests, a man had run across the road towards the wedding party, waving a gun around and shouting various unclear threats. With lightning speed, another of the guests, Daniel Harrison, a former Commander of Scotland Yard, leapt in front of the gunman, flooring him, and knocking the weapon out of his hand. It seemed, that as Daniel Harrison retrieved the gun, the would-be assassin was able to make a run for it. No shots were fired, and on close inspection the gun was found to be an accurate looking replica, but a dummy never-the-less. French police are still hunting for him, but descriptions are vague. It is thought that an accomplice was close by with car or motorbike. Genevievre and her parents looked visibly very shaken, but relieved on learning that the gun was only a replica. Once the police had finished initial enquiries, everybody was able to be driven away to a nearby hotel where a small reception was being held. Two policemen stayed with them as extra security. There has been no further information and at present it seems the gunman was acting alone other than a possible driver to help with any escape.'

I was shocked to read this. I hadn't seen Daniel for over a week, and he hadn't mentioned the planned wedding on that occasion. I rang Mavis but got her answer service so left a message telling her to look at page two of today's Times. On the other hand, Muriel was full of it – Ken had been one of the guests, and he had telephoned on the Saturday night as he was concerned in case the event made the UK television news. We were both surprised that it hadn't and wondered if someone had been able to suppress the story; the account in 'The Times' had been relatively restrained. She hadn't heard from Mavis over the weekend, and assumed she was out on some 'arty' activity this morning. As far as she knew, both Ken and Daniel were still in Paris. It occurred to me that Daniel could well be liaising with the French Police. As I said to Muriel, no doubt they would return soon and bring us up to date on the 'unpublished' story. We both felt just relieved that nobody had been hurt.

There was another paragraph of news in the same newspaper. It concerned the finding of two bodies, washed up on a Lincolnshire beach. It was thought that they may have been immigrants trying to make an illegal entry into the UK. I don't know why I happened to mention this to Muriel, but we both went on to have the same thought, wondering whether Nat Lawton knew anything.

Muriel suddenly changed the subject. "Monty, isn't it the auction in two or three weeks? If you're thinking of staying in London for a night or two, you'll be more than welcome to stop here. I know Ken is excited about your find and may well attend for the big day. Will Mavis be there, or does she still want to avoid Trumpingtons?"

"I should like Mavis to be there, especially as she helped find the famous dust jacket. Perhaps now she is back to her art with such joy and enthusiasm, she won't be so concerned about Trumpingtons. Do you think, Muriel, you could persuade her?"

"I'll certainly try, I'll send some text messages and see what she thinks. I'm sure she would be incredibly excited to be there, it's almost a historic event, given how unusual is the way that Arthur Conan Doyle signed the book. I should like to be there as well so perhaps that will help convince her. I'll work on her – did a lot of that when we were teenagers. I'll let you know how I get on or tell her to ring you like she told me, when you suggested the holiday. I'm sure you haven't forgotten my early morning call!"

"No, Muriel, no, certainly I can say, not forgotten." If I was being a tiny bit sarcastic, Muriel chose to ignore it. I was warming to her personality greatly as in her bursts of enthusiasm she could be quite over-whelming; subtlety seemed to be a trait of personality with which she did without. "Going back to your invitation, yes, it would be lovely to stay with you, Mavis as well, no doubt; I'm sure she will come."

"I'll let Ken know, he'll be charmed. "I'm going to set about tracking down Mavis now, so you should hear from her soon. Bye for now." And with that, Muriel was gone.

Later that day I received an email from Joseph to let me know about the auction. There had obviously been much interest in this newly discovered copy of 'The Hound of the Baskervilles', from all round the world apparently and quite a number of provisional bookings had been made for telephone lines. He also said that most of the book fraternity that they were in touch with, had approved of the restoration to the unique and unusual dust jacket, especially when they learnt that no surface restoration had been necessary, just a joining of the three sections. There had been many visitors requesting to inspect the book and at the auction house, they had had to arrange for a table to be available, and some degree of supervision. These were all good signs and explained why Joseph was tremendously optimistic as far as achieving an excellent price was concerned.

I sent an immediate reply, thanked him for his continued enthusiasm and confirmed that we would be staying with friends for the two or three nights of the sale. I then had to spend a few hours catching up on my secondhand book business. Cleaning and repairing books and pamphlets and then listing them for sale is quite a time-consuming activity. It didn't do to get behind, especially with packing and posting. If my buyers were anything like me, they really wanted their items to arrive 'yesterday'! I couldn't quite manage that, but I liked to post within 24 hours of payment, and it was always nice to receive compliments about speed of service. I was just finishing up and tidying away various bits and pieces when Mavis telephoned.

"Monty? Glad I've got you, been meaning to ring for a few days but didn't know quite how to explain myself."

"You're being very mysterious, are you at home?"

"No, I'm in Paris. There, that's probably says it all."

"Well, I don't think so or………Oh, yes it does. You've been to a wedding, you're with Daniel! So, did you go to partner Daniel or were you there as a close friend of the couple?"

"First suggestion, I'm with Daniel, actually not at present, as he is still helping the French police and I'm keeping my head down at a Paris hotel. You probably didn't notice that this phone is showing a different number and is for a one use only and then I must bin it. Daniel has given me about half a dozen, each to be used only once. Just so you know, I think we are returning tomorrow but I don't know yet by what route and if I don't hear from him this evening, I'll probably make my own way home. I haven't been in touch with Muriel as I know she will not let me keep any call short and that is important. As well as letting you know where I am, can I ask you to let Muriel know all is well. She knows Daniel and I have been chatting quite a lot, but she doesn't know I've been to the wedding."

"Mavis, I shall be delighted and please let us know just as soon as you are safely back on UK soil. Ring off now and chuck the phone."

"Bye Monty."

I telephoned Muriel straightaway, although I was a little apprehensive as she can be quite bullying in a nice sort of way. As it happened, she was out, so I just left a vague message about both Mavis and me, said I would be in touch in a day or so. I went to bed that night somewhat nervy and stressed. I needed a lengthy read before I felt like sleep.

The following morning, I contacted various acquaintances, told them of the auction being less than a month away. Plenty of well-wishers, plenty of chat but I knew I was getting very fidgety over the wait. It was Tuesday morning and I was struck by a flash of inspiration, threw a few things into a bag, rang the car hire company and within a couple of hours I was driving out across the fens. I couldn't have chosen a better day, clear blue sky, pleasant sunshine but not hot and I didn't stop until I was at the roundabout which divided the traffic in two – continue north towards Sandringham and Hunstanton or turn right, east, also to Sandringham, then on to Fakenham, the Georgian town of Holt and so on, if you went far enough, Cromer and Sheringham. Holt really tempted me, so I popped into the Knights Inn Hotel and was able to book one night, drank some welcome coffee and was in Holt by early afternoon.

21. NORFOLK AGAIN AND FR BLAKESON SOLVES A PROBLEM

The Georgian town of Holt is one of those delightful places which never changes, obviously it does, but I never seem to notice, so never get upset and hence, I always enjoy a visit. Plenty of ancient corners to browse and I never fail to make a find, often quite humble, but satisfying, never-the-less. Slightly better than 'humble', my first find today was a small set of Peter Rabbit bookshelves, probably 1950s vintage and containing about a dozen different Beatrix Potter stories, some with dust jackets. A quick glance enabled me to date them all to the late 1930s and 1940s. This find was in something of a warren, many dealers spread over two floors of what probably had once been a terrace of cottages, changed into single shops and then gradually combined with various doorways knocked through to make a continuous walkway. It all ended up as a charming muddle, the kind of building which no planner would pass for construction today; any proposed alteration to the 'charming muddle' and the same planner will probably raise all sorts of objections. I can nose my way around this kind of warren for hours and I generally unearth something to make the search worthwhile – not so much the search, more the acute backache!

Today's second treasures were some maps, probably 1930s, certainly pre-war. These were town centre street maps and there were always collectors for these so that comparisons with later maps could be made - to study the changes caused by the war damage. Any further hunting was prevented by my stomach beginning to drop hints about some tea and there were plenty of eateries to choose from in Holt. I gravitated towards the double window display of mouth-watering cakes, made a suitable choice of a creamy fruity gateaux plus a crab and salad sandwich. The pot of tea which accompanied this was the sort to keep one at the table for a good hour if one so wished. My next forage was in a converted chapel – sad how so many such buildings had to be given over to commercial uses – but as an antique centre, excellent, as one could walk right round the first floor gallery, where once Sunday school children had probably been a little less than devout! Look down on the table tops below one could spot things unnoticed at ground floor level.

One find was an early C19th hymn book – just words – of Charles Wesley's hymns, an appropriate find for a converted chapel. This was very small, leather bound with a closing clasp, would easily slot into a lady's handbag. I also came away with some children's books including two or three pop-up books, quite old and with the pop-ups in good working order. The best find of the afternoon was a Rupert Bear Annual from the 1960s with its magic painting pages untouched – now that was rare because generally these were rendered a terrible mess. Mind you, it also made me sad as I wanted to know why the child who had opened this, who had unwrapped it one Christmas morning, hadn't had a go with brush and water. Perhaps one can hear the mum even now: 'don't make a mess of that straightaway', 'keep it clean for a few days', 'why don't you play with your other things first', 'you can't use the table now as I'm about to set out tea'. With such 'encouragement' it didn't surprise that the book was put away and just forgotten about.

It was sunset when I drove back to Kings Lynn, made for a most attractive drive with the sunlight flickering through the treetops. It was a slow journey, evening rush-hour traffic across Norfolk didn't go in for record breaking speeds. Before dinner I dozed in a deep bubbly bath and planned the following morning's visit to Hunstanton. The only certainty was that it would include an ice-cream while looking out across The Wash towards the Skegness coastline. If that wasn't visible, then I would gaze at all the wind-driven sporting activities along the Hunstanton shoreline. I was even capable of spending half an hour being mesmerised by the spinning of the wind turbines further out towards the North Sea. However, daydreams over, and down for dinner which turned out to be a baked camembert, roast lamb, and a delicious old-fashioned trifle. All chosen to please the palate, not rest heavy and not prevent sleep.

The following morning commenced with the kind of breakfast which one never cooked at home, the kind of breakfast that caused aromas to waft along the corridors, the kind of breakfast which would defeat all ill-judged good intentions and the kind of breakfast which left one feeling that further food could be missed for the rest of the day; never the case, though!

As planned in my thinking the evening before, Hunstanton lived up to all expectation: I ate a tub of ice-cream as I looked over to the Skegness shoreline, I watched the wind turbines and I also watched the mixed fortunes of the various guys out wind surfing. How easy some of them made it seem whereas others seemed to spend all their time falling in or climbing up out of the sea. Just a little different from the norm was when I witnessed a collision between experience and inexperience – they seemed unhurt and 'Mr Experience' was quite kindly disposed towards his opponent, helped him to get going again and watched him for a short while. It was all lovely to watch as far as I was concerned; I was far too old to consider participating and would, no doubt, suffer the fate of 'Mr Inexperience'.

I was about to drive on to Old Hunstanton when it occurred to me that Mavis would be home. I tried her home landline and she answered at once. "Monty, I'm very pleased to hear from you. Where are you?"

"At this moment, looking out to sea from Hunstanton but I can be home in an hour and half, I have nothing fixed for the rest of the day. Just a minute, where are you?"

"Sorry, you don't know of course. In the end I did as I suggested I might. The hotel booked me first class on the Euro-Star. I rang Muriel and she was able to arrange for Tony to meet me off the train and drive me straight to Peterborough, but I do feel a little nervous now. Would you mind cutting short your trip? Daniel has stayed in Paris and I sent him a brief text to say I was going back on Eurostar and then with Tony back home. I don't know where he is or what he is doing."

"Say no more Mavis. I'll ring again when I'm close to Peterborough and then you can call a taxi and meet me at the car hire office."

"Thank you, Monty, I'm relieved to hear that plan. See you soon."

I didn't exactly put my foot down or try to break any records, but there was little traffic about, and I encountered no slow tractors, so I was back in Peterborough in just over the hour. I contacted Mavis as planned and we both arrived at the office at about the same time. Mavis had held the taxi, so I gave the address for Fr Blakeston. Raised eyebrows was Mavis's only indication that she had noted where we were going. I hoped he was in as I had only just thought of the idea and hadn't had an opportunity to contact him. I asked the taxi to wait until Fr Blakeston had opened his door. If he was surprised to see us both he didn't show it.

After quick greetings I began to tell the tale. He had known what happened to me at Christmas, so I brought him up to date from then. I explained who Ken Peterson was, and Daniel, but didn't say too much about his 'double role' as far as his work was concerned. I mentioned the security incidents, and then what had happened at the wedding in Paris. He knew of Jon Mostang and had read about the engagement. With a nod of her head, Mavis let me carry on with telling of her involvement with Daniel and the need for her to be cautious, especially until Daniel was able to return. Fr Blakeston showed his understanding of where this was all leading and with a clap of his hands, he interrupted me.

"Monty, are you trying to tell me that Mavis here, needs 'sanctuary'?

"Yes please, Father." That was Mavis's first contribution to the conversation.

"Do you know the Dean and his wife? You'll remember them from the funeral of Ernie. She would be ideal for this role. Let me make a quick call and see what can be arranged."

Fr Blakeston was incredibly succinct in his explanation, having got straight through to Mrs Ellerton. With a common sense approach for security, she said she would drive straight round to pick up Mavis and that once she was safely installed at the Deanery she would take a taxi to Queensgate, make it wait, go to M & S and buy all that Mavis was likely to need for the next couple of days or so. Within a quarter of an hour Mavis was off to be installed into the splendid safety of the imposing building that was the Deanery.

"Would you like some coffee, Monty." How unruffled was Fr Blakeston and he was hovering around the age of ninety. Once coffee and biscuits appeared, I was able to explain in greater detail all that had been going on.

"It seems to me, dear boy, that the 'even tenor of your ways' has been most cruelly interrupted. Let us pray that there will be no further incidents; we live in dangerous times it seems."

I noticed that time was pushing on, so I gave Fr Blakeston another surprise by asking if he liked Chinese food. He did, although he admitted to having had only limited experience. I suggested I order a 'take away' to which he agreed, leaving it up to me to choose the dishes. All I had to do was to engage in a delightful conversation with The Yang King Kitchens and then wait thirty minutes. I took the liberty of going into Fr Blakeston's kitchen and putting plates to warm. He was equally thoughtful and poured two large dry sherries. We sipped in quiet contemplation of the food to come; Fr Blakeston confessed that the arrival of a 'take away delivery boy' would be a first for him and probably a first for the Priest's house at St Petri's

22. JUNAID AND ANIK ANWAR

Later that evening I thought back over the changes that the day had brought, from a breakfast just north of Kings Lynn to a Chinese meal with a ninety-year-old cleric. My life had certainly become terribly busy and full of the unexpected. I rang Muriel and brought her up to date with Mavis's activities and explained where she was staying for a few days. I sent Daniel a text asking him to get in touch when he felt able, but as I didn't know what he was using by way of mobile phones I had no idea if he even received the text, let alone reply.

Quite late that evening I received a phone call from Junaid Anwar. He introduced himself very fully, so I didn't have to strain my memory. As he explained, he and his brother's security firm had been keeping a low-key watch on Daniel's house. His brother or one of his staff did little more than drive by at different times, different cars, and different drivers. Junaid could contrive some police business to take him that way without being too obvious. Junaid explained that at first nothing untoward had been spotted but just lately they were concerned because they had seen the odd individual hanging around, different guys but occasionally each would reappear a few days later. They had taken some photographs. Junaid's reason for contacting me was that they had been unable to contact Daniel for a few days now and they thought he ought to know of the development. It was all beginning to get just a bit beyond me and I had no knowledge of anyone, other than Daniel, involved in this security world. I did wonder if any senior colleagues at local level knew of the unofficial watch that Daniel had arranged for himself locally but didn't know how to ask Junaid about this. I felt I hadn't been particularly helpful as far as Junaid's concerns were concerned but I promised to get back to him as soon as I heard anything new.

Although I didn't mention it to Junaid, I did have an idea, because I remembered Daniel telling me that the Chief Constable knew about Daniel's unusual role and it occurred to me that he could make sure the right person was alerted to the situation. I had no idea how to contact the Chief Constable in a suitably confidential manner, but then I thought of Kenneth Peterson.

A call to Muriel told me that Ken would be home in just a few minutes, and she would get him to ring me; I didn't wait long. As soon as he got an indication of why I was making contact he stopped me. He explained how to set up 'chat' as this would be more secure. I had used this system before when getting technical support for my computer. As I was a very speedy typist it didn't take me long to bring Ken up to date with the security concerns about Daniel's house. As I thought, he knew how to make direct contact with the relevant Chief Constable and for the time being I could leave the problem with him. He also gave me an email address to which Junaid could transfer the photographs.

Sooner than expected, I was able to tell Junaid what was happening, and I told him I would text the email address he needed. He contradicted this and said he would call for it later, suggested that would be safer. Then he changed his mind and said he would transfer them to a memory drive and post it to Ken if he could be given the address. I dictated this at once and as a final thought I suggested that he and his brother cut back a little on the checks they were making, didn't want them putting themselves at more risk than necessary.

The following morning it was the telephone which woke me up, Junaid's brother, Anik, was shouting at me as soon as I answered. I had to tell him very firmly to calm down and tell me the problem although I had a nasty feeling I already knew. Junaid was in hospital; he had been beaten up the previous night not far from Daniel's house and at that moment he was undergoing emergency surgery to relieve pressure on his brain. I was horrified and hardly knew what to say. Anik butted in to say that it was all very awkward because Junaid's colleagues didn't know what he had been doing in that part of Peterborough and Anik hadn't known what to say. The police were keeping a watch on Junaid and Anik was staying until he heard about the result of the surgery. I promised that I would join him as soon as possible.

I was fortunate that it was still early, and most people hadn't gone out yet. I telephoned Muriel and was able to speak to Ken immediately. He explained that he had spoken to the Chief Constable as soon as he had finished speaking to me. He would ring him again and get him to explain to whoever was the senior officer at Peterborough the whole business of Daniel's security arrangements. We both understood that it was going to be difficult to maintain the same level of limited knowledge about these matters, impossible really as the whole of the Peterborough Station Force would be talking about Junaid. Ken said he would think about how to let Daniel know and I undertook to tell Mavis.

She was very shocked, bewildered really, and didn't quite know what to say. For the time being she would continue to stay at the Deanery and Lucinda would make sure she had all she needed. Mavis explained that they both had some art interests in common, so they were getting on quite nicely. She told me that she hadn't heard from Daniel. Just before I rang off, she mentioned that she and Lucinda had gone to Compline the previous evening, just remembered in time, but they were pleased because Fr Blakeston mentioned the need for God's protection for several local people and mentioned by name Junaid as well as Mavis and me as we were regular members of his congregation.

There was nothing more that needed my urgent attention so, as promised, I went to see Anik at the hospital. I tracked him down in the restaurant as Junaid was still in theatre and he felt he hadn't got anything to say to the police officer on watch outside Junaid's hospital room. I was pleased to see that he was eating so I joined him, fetching a bowl of porridge and two mugs of coffee, my first drink of the day. We sat quietly for a while and then I explained that the Chief Constable was going to explain to senior staff at Peterborough Police Station exactly what Daniel had been involved in and how Junaid had been brought into the security side of the affair on a non-official basis. I didn't say anything to Anik, but I thought that this one aspect of the whole affair could lead to a great deal of trouble, especially if Junaid was left disabled.

Just then Anik's mobile rang. Other than his name he said nothing, just listened for what seemed ages but was probably well under a minute. He switched off his phone and told me very quietly that Junaid was back from surgery and that he was required to see the doctor. Looking rather desperate, he asked me to accompany him explaining as we went that the security police officer had telephoned him. As I wasn't a member of the family, I suggested he should go into Junaid's room and speak to the doctor; I would wait out-side. I sat next to the policeman, Cliff, he said his name was, but we had little to say to each other. I hadn't worked out quite where we were: we had entered a main ward, spoken to the nurse/receptionist, and been directed to a pair of double doors with a keypad lock. The nurse opened these for us, and we walked along a short corridor off which were doors to four private rooms. We went through one, found ourselves in a tiny vestibule where there were three chairs outside a further door and this was where I currently sat, next to Cliff. The only thing he explained to me was that Junaid's room was the only one with this inner waiting area, it was very private and quite secure because a warning light came on just as soon as anyone entered the corridor.

Just then the row started, someone was shouting Junaid's name saying he was his best friend and that he must be allowed to see him. We could hear the nurse trying to reason with him, but he carried on shouting and pounded on the door. I didn't know what would happen, but Cliff's mobile rang. There was quiet for a while, as Cliff was listening through an earpiece, "OK, yes I know that name, I'll come along the corridor and talk to him through the window. Just give me a moment?" Cliff picked up various pieces of equipment, asked me to wait where I was, and he went through the door to see what he could do. I couldn't hear anything of this conversation, but it was short because Cliff was back within a couple of minutes.

"Mr Warnock, do you know Sanjay Bhatt? He claims to know you."

"Yes, I do, he was one of two lads involved in rescuing an elderly lady who tried to drown herself sometime last year. I think they are now reformed shoplifters and have become leading members of the youth club which Junaid runs. Have you not heard about them, something of a success story?"

"Well, I'm fairly knew on the force, only started last September. I do know about the youth club though."

"All I can say Cliff, is that Junaid speaks very highly of these two boys. He feels they have been under-achieving at school, idle minds finding petty crime outlets. In fact, they seem to have transformed themselves and the school reports on a tremendous improvement in their work and behaviour. Junaid will be quite touched to know that one of them has turned up here to find out what has happened."

"The thing is, Monty, should I let him through to sit here, leave him fidgeting in the ward, or send him on his way?"

"If he is anything, he is tenacious, so don't try and send him off. I've met him and liked both him and his friend. They, together with Junaid, came to the funeral of the rescued lady's husband. Presented themselves very well and attended tea at the Deanery afterwards. I think it's safe to go and fetch him."

"I agree, we'll have him here where at least we can watch him rather than have the nurse getting worried. Not really her responsibility."

As soon as Sanjay sat himself down he was off with his version of the story, about gangs fighting, police being called and unable to cope, reinforcements brought in……..it all bore remarkably little resemblance to what Anik had told me; exaggerated rumours were running rife.

Just then Anik came out; he looked rather grim and said nothing, but the doctor told us that he had explained the situation to Anik who asked if he could give a summary to us. He went on quickly, explained that the operation had been successful in so far as relieving the pressure on Junaid's brain was concerned. At present they had placed him in an induced coma to allow healing. The outcome would only be known when Junaid regained consciousness, when tests would reveal any likely long-term damage. At present, all appeared quite well but they would be monitoring his condition very closely. The doctor promised that he would see the patient again later in the afternoon and with that he went on his way.

"Shall you stay with him?" I asked Anik.

"I will for a while, but he is very deeply asleep. I don't really know what to do." At that moment, his face crumpled up and he began to cry.

It was Sanjay who saved the moment. "Come on Anik, we'll both sit with him. We can tell him what we're doing about Daniel. We can also tell him how we can keep the youth club going while he's not too well. He'll want to know everything is OK. Mr Warnock, do you think you could get Anik a cup of coffee, he looks in need. Would you prefer tea Anik?"

Anik just looked blank, but I remembered that when we were in the hospital restaurant earlier, he was drinking tea, he had been sitting and stirring it quite endlessly. "That's all right Sanjay, I know what to get him. But before I go, what about school? Does anyone there know where you are?"

"Because so many of the boys wanted to know about Junaid, Mr Taylor, he's our form teacher, said it would be all right for one of us to go to the hospital to find out so that's why I'm here. I'm OK for the morning Mr Warnock."

As I went to get Anik a cup of tea, I just hoped that Sanjay hadn't been spinning me a yarn. I decided I didn't want to know so I wouldn't make any more enquiries; I'd just give him the benefit of the doubt and reflect on the fact that there was a lad transformed.

23. JUNAID AND SANJAY'S LOYAL FRINDSHIP

I seemed to spend most of that day making phone calls, ensuring those who needed to know were informed about Junaid. I still hadn't heard from Daniel and nor had Mavis when I managed to speak to her later that morning. Muriel told me that Ken had made several calls and then gone out with Tony and she knew nothing of his plans for the rest of that day, not unusual and she would expect a phone call by late afternoon. She promised to text me if she had any specific information. At about tea-time I decided to take a taxi to the hospital and check on Junaid's condition. When I got there I found different staff so I had to explain myself to the duty nurse, but fortunately someone from the police force had provided her with a list of approved visitors – quite a short list but it included my name, other members of Junaid's family, Sanjay and his friend, Kieran Overton. There were also names of four police officers. When I got through the doors to Junaid's private entrance, I found a different officer on watch. He explained that he had replaced Cliff late morning. His name was Peter and he expected to be there until 10.00pm. He had no news about Junaid, so, very quietly I went in and was surprised to see Sanjay sitting there. He had books and other bits and pieces on his lap but as I walked in, he was in the middle of telling Junaid about all the boys who he thought Junaid would remember and want to know about. He was totally calm, and had I just overheard this rather than seen, it would never have occurred to me that he was talking to someone in a coma. Sanjay continued talking, telling Junaid that I had arrived so he would be talking to me as well. He turned and greeted me with a great smile.

"Goodness, Sanjay, I take it you haven't been here all day?"

"Oh no, Mr Warnock, I left when Cliff left because the driver who brought Peter in was able to give me a lift back to school, Cliff lives not far from the school and he was taking him home. I told all my friends what had been happening, got the original rumours all squashed, then it was just a normal school day, well, perhaps not that normal. I went home and mum said I could come back here after tea, but I was to bring my homework and try and do that during breaks in conversation with Junaid. I wasn't here when the doctor came to check on Junaid, but a nurse who was here a few minutes ago said that the team looking after him were all very pleased with his condition; they seemed quite optimistic about his recovery."

"That all seems good news Sanjay. Did you ever hear about me and what happened at Christmas? I was attacked in London in a similar way, but my head injury amounted to no more than mild concussion. Somehow, having had a similar experience, encourages me about Junaid. I hope that doesn't sound too silly, there is no logic there."

"Have you got any news about Daniel to tell Junaid? I didn't know whether talking to him was a good idea, but the nurse said it was. People who have regained consciousness after being in long comas have often said that they remembered things that people had said while they were unconscious."

"Hello Junaid, this is Monty Warnock. I'm very sorry about what has happened to you, but you may remember a few hours earlier you rang me at my home wanting to know how to contact Daniel. Well, other people have done that, but at this moment I don't know where he is, perhaps still in France. By the way, I hope you are pleased with young Sanjay here – he is being a very loyal friend and he was also especially kind with your brother this morning. If nobody has told you, rest assured that you are safe here and that the police are watching your door 24 hours a day. I hope that Sanjay has explained that when he is not speaking to you, he is probably doing some school homework that his mum insists he does."

"That's given my voice a rest Junaid. Mr Warnock is good at letting people know what is happening."

"Junaid, I expect you are wondering why this has happened to you. At the moment, we still don't know. It may have connections with Daniel and his work, or it may relate to his friend, the MP, Jon Mostang. I expect you heard about the gun attack at his wedding in Paris a week or so ago. Daniel was at the wedding and his quick action led to the gunman being disarmed. The gunman hasn't been caught yet."

"A change of subject, Junaid. Did Daniel ever tell you about my discovering a rare book by Arthur Conan Doyle, one of the Sherlock Holmes stories? I mention it because soon I'm going to be away for a few days. The book, which was signed by the author and which also had an unusual dust jacket, is being auctioned in London in a week or so. All being well, Mavis and I will both be there to see the result. It is an amazingly rare item and may make a lot of money. Mavis is particularly interested because she was partly responsible for finding the dust jacket which had been torn into strips and was being used as bookmarkers in some old gardening volumes. You'll probably be home from hospital while I'm away."

"Now, Sanjay, how long are you staying with Junaid and how will you get home?" I wasn't surprised to see from his face that he hadn't given any thought to such hum-drum matters. In short, his answer to both my questions was that he had no idea. Fortunately, I had some ideas and I gave him £20 and told him I would sit with Junaid while he went to the hospital restaurant and got something to eat and drink and that he could keep the change and use it to call a taxi when it was time for him to go home. I suggested that I didn't think his mum would expect him to be too late. I think he must have been hungry because he didn't take much persuading to act on my suggestion. It made me hope that Junaid did hear all this as I thought he would find it amusing.

I couldn't help being impressed with Sanjay and I told Junaid this while Sanjay was out of the room. There was a wise head on young shoulders and so unexpected, given what I saw him doing when first he crossed my path. I would like to get to know his parents because I felt he was young man who could go a long way with his education and later in subsequent careers. I wasn't going to turn him in to a mission, but I would like to know that help was around over the next few years, if help was ever needed. Sanjay came back after about half an hour and through the door at the same time came the nurse to do the observational checks. She looked a kindly individual and she was happy to tell us that all the readings were as they should be, nothing going on to cause his medical team any concern. She also explained that the two hourly checks would continue for another twenty-four hours and if all were still well, they would reduce the number of checks.

It seemed very encouraging and I decided to pass this on to Mavis and Muriel, also Ken. I turned to Sanjay and Junaid and explained that I would have to be leaving and was there anything more that either needed. I think Sanjay was pleased that I didn't forget to include Junaid in the conversation. Sanjay assured me he had kept enough change for the taxi, and with that I went on my way, remembering to thank Peter who was still on watch outside and also the nurse on the reception desk, just inside the ward.

By the time the taxi dropped me off it was the middle of the evening and I was starving. Unusually for me, but another take-away meal was called for and within thirty minutes an Indian curry was being delivered. I had a bottle of red wine open and both went down a treat. Now, much restored, I set about checking emails, telephone messages and made calls to Mavis and Muriel and I also tried sending an email and a text to Daniel hoping that he would see at least one of them.

Mavis sounded happy and obviously she was getting on very well with Lucinda and her husband. I didn't know his first name and Mavis just called him Dean – sounded straight out of a Barchester novel. She was still somewhat worried about Junaid but encouraged by my reports. She said little and I assumed from that she was still concerned to have heard nothing from Daniel. I expect because of that, she had spoken to Muriel a couple of times, hoping that Ken might have news, sadly, nothing.

I was feeling quite tired, too much rushing around and too many things to think about, people to contact. It was all so totally different from my normal everyday evenly paced existence. One thing that occurred to me, to lesson some of my difficulties and it would be my first task in the morning. I would telephone the car-hire people I used regularly and rent a car for at least the next week, perhaps to the time of departure for the auction. It would help if I weren't telephoning and waiting for taxis and there might be occasions when I needed to give people a lift; without conscious thought, two young teenage lads were crossing my mind.

For the next hour I caught up as far as was possible with my book business. Fortunately, there had been little fresh activity and it wouldn't take me long to catch up with the post in the morning while I waited for a car. I spent a while just contemplating where Daniel might be and what he was doing and whether he was safe. I also remembered that I knew nothing about Jon Mostang and his bride, bride of a few days now. I was startled by something of a clatter and realised that I must have dozed off and sent flying a tray of pens and other bits and pieces; bed called.

24. MUCH NOISE AND SOMEBODY UNEXPECTED

Several loud and frightening bells were ringing, and police were pouring into the bidding room of Trumpington's Auction House. This cacophonic row obliterated the actions of the auctioneer who sat frozen with his mallet poised on the final bid for my 'book'. A telephone bid had just been accepted at £3.75 million, people were stamping and shouting, Joseph and Charles were dancing a jig on their table, a group of the porters picked up instruments which were to be sold later and provided an impromptu accompaniment for this visual display. Another porter was juggling with books one of which was 'The Hound', 'My Hound'! Police still charged in, firemen sliding down poles, their hoses squirting feathers. Nothing but nothing seemed to be able to silence the bells, indeed they got louder and louder. Mavis and Muriel were clashing cymbals, Ken jumping from kettle drum to kettle drum beating them with steel heels. I screamed, reached down, opened my suitcase, and stuffed in my head, pulled the zip until I was choking on a mouthful of smelly socks.

A voice! At last a voice! A quiet, calm, and gentle ordinary voice: "Monty, Ken here, if you can hear this, ring me." A click and blissful silence. I was surrounded by black and trapped in this choking cloth, no not cloth, certainly not smelly socks, just the corner of a pillow which I was chewing while buried under the duvet. At once police and firemen disappeared, nobody was dancing, Mavis and Muriel with cymbals had vanished, not a kettle drum in sight because Ken was awaiting my call. Something of the automaton in me took over, one click, and light showed my bedroom in absolute normality, not one book on the move. My mobile displayed 5.30! Now, that was a horror to generate any nightmare.

I stumbled down to my kitchen and although the phone call had to be of great importance, I felt I could steal a couple of minutes to get a pot of coffee made, nibble a biscuit and then settle down to make the call.

"Ken, I do sincerely hope you have momentous good news which has caused you to ring so early."

"Ah Monty, you're right, good news, sorry about the time. I should say that Muriel told me to wait but I couldn't. We've heard from Daniel, he has spent a very curious few days since the famous wedding, but now he is in police protection, staying in a safe house in the Paris suburbs. Needless to say, we haven't got an address."

"So, how did you receive the news? Stop! Before you answer that, Muriel was right; the ringing of the telephone fired me into the most horrific nightmare and didn't stop until the ringing was replaced by your voice. Never mind, though, over that now and I'm halfway through a pot of coffee so back to Daniel."

"Oh dear, Muriel will crow about that. A Parisian police officer telephoned about four hours ago. He spoke impeccable English, apologised profusely about the time but they had only just got Daniel into safety and he telephoned at the first opportunity. You'll gather we haven't heard his voice yet, but pleasing news just the same.

"Yes, excellent. What of the young dreams? Jon Mostang and Genevievre Renoir, or more correctly, Mr and Mrs Mostang?

"We can certainly tell you about them. Nothing like being an MP of interesting standing as well as being immensely wealthy. As soon as they could decently leave Paris, anxious not to upset her parents, he hired a private helicopter which took them to Dover, where they were met by chauffeur and bullet proof Bentley and driven to a private entrance of one of the more exclusive five-star London hotels. We're told they took a most luxurious suite for a few days. They even managed a box for the opening night of, ah, I've forgotten, at The Royal Opera House. Which of the two of them had the influence for that I wouldn't know. We might not have known but a lucky member of the paparazzi caught a photograph which was only identified when someone on the editing staff of 'The Telegraph' spotted it. Now, any better news of Junaid because it might be good to tell Daniel – we can get messages to him?"

"No change as far as I know Ken. I'll be visiting in a while and let you know if there is anything different to report. I'll also get this news about Daniel to Mavis, she'll be pleased."

"Thank you, Monty, let's hope for good news."

Seeing that it was still not seven o'clock I decided to pop back to bed and wait for the knock which would herald the arrival of my car. I had been able to ring the night before and leave an urgent message about a car. Needless-to-say, I was sound asleep when the bell rang, but without the devastating effect as when the bell last rang. A couple of pieces of paper to sign and I was the possessor of a pleasant little Ford Fiesta for a week. I decided to make the hospital my first visit, calling at their restaurant for some breakfast. The arrangement for seeing Junaid remained the same and I was signed in. It was nice to see Cliff back on duty, but he had nothing to tell me about Junaid's condition. I crept in quietly, just thought I would say hello and bring him up to date on Daniel. I was taken aback to see Kieran Overton sitting by the bed.

"Hello Mr Warnock, nice to see you, I haven't been here long, but I'm hoping to take some news back to school."

"That's most kind of you Kieran. When do you need to leave?"

"There's a bus which will get me to school by 9.40. I'll be all right being only a few minutes late."

"I'll just go and ask the nurse if there has been any change in Junaid's condition."

Unfortunately, she had no information but just then another nurse who I recognised from my last visit came by and mentioned that she was about to go in and take the observations on Junaid. I walked back with her.

"Kieran, the nurse is just going to check on Junaid, you need to move back a little."

"Don't move on my account. I can see all I need quite easily. Just as I expected, no changes from last night so that is excellent news. Shall you be in touch with his brother? We need to tell him about Junaid's progress; it is likely that he'll be brought round from the coma in the next day or so, as the medical team is very impressed with how he is doing."

"I can certainly call on him quite soon, I wasn't intending to stay too long. Junaid, I hope you're hearing all this, sounds as if you might be back with us soon. I hope Kieran has brought you some youth club news."

"Oh yes, Mr Warnock, I've told Junaid all the latest from school and the club."

"It's getting towards 9.20, so Kieran, I can run you round to school if you like and then call on Anik. If he's not in, I'll get a message to him."

Kieran seemed happy to travel with me and I went on to see Anik. Fortunately, he was still at home, so I gave him the message from the hospital. He said he would ring the hospital later in the morning and find out when he should visit. He promised to let me know any news. It occurred to me that perhaps, just perhaps, matters might be settling down a little. That was a thought too soon as I could hear the telephone ringing as I opened my front door.

"Mr Warnock, Mr Monty Warnock? This is Chief Superintendent Tomlinson, Peterborough Police Station."

"Yes, this is Monty Warnock, how can I help?"

"Well, this is a bit tricky really, but I believe you are a good friend of Daniel Harrison. As you may know it is not easy to get in touch with him at present, but we have had a visitor from Egypt, a young man, Husani El Masry, asking after him. He says his visit was unplanned, but that an unexpected opportunity brought him to Cambridge, and he realised that Daniel lived this way so thought he would try and track him down. He claims to be Daniel's brother-in-law. He went on to say that Daniel probably wouldn't remember him, may not even know of him, as he was Noura's youngest brother and was only a small boy when Noura left Egypt with Daniel to travel to England. He is coming back this afternoon and I have promised to see if I am able to help him. I should say that all his credentials seemed to be in order. He is in the UK working at one of the London hospitals."

"That all sounds rather difficult Superintendent. I only know what Daniel has told me about his marriage and the murder of his wife. He gave me to understand that the rest of her family had nothing to do with the wedding, particularly as she had become a Christian. Of course, if this individual, Husani, was just a child at the time of the wedding he may never have been given the details. When Daniel told me of his personal history, I got the impression that he was somewhat upset to have no knowledge or any contact with Noura's past. After her death he felt very cut off. It would certainly be interesting to talk to this Husani, learn more about what he is doing in the UK and whether other members of his family know whether he is attempting to meet Daniel. Would it help if I came and met him as a friend, making the conversation more social than official.?"

"That could indeed be helpful Monty. I am expecting him soon after 2.00pm so if all seems favourable, I'll send a car for you about 2.30."

"Thank you, Superintendent, I'll look forward to that, might be rather interesting. I won't say anything to Daniel's friends until later and only if you approve."

"Thank you, Monty, and the name is Matthew, less of a mouthful than Superintendent."

How much more was I going to have deal with before I could just sit back and contemplate the auction? For ages it had seemed an event well in the future but now, suddenly, just a handful of days remained.

Replacing the receiver, I noticed that there had been a message. Anik had called the hospital and was going in that afternoon to meet the surgeon, he would ring again. I made one more call to the Deanery and told Lucinda about Daniel and she promised to give the good news to Mavis.

For a while I let all these concerns about Daniel and Junaid, Husani as well, take a back seat and instead spent a couple of hours replacing some endpapers in old library books. Sometimes private library stampings, those from universities and clubs for example, can be of historic interest but often books from local authority libraries were best if their endpapers were replaced and the dust jacket, which frequently has been well preserved in what becomes a filthy plastic sleeve, can be made to look extremely fine with just a new non-adhesive protective sleeve. I always found work like this quite restful; didn't have to do it in a hurry and the finished result always pleased.

True to his promise, a phone call from Matthew's secretary told me that a car was on its way and I was soon off to meet Husani. The Superintendent was quite formal in explaining who I was, and he also showed me Husani's passport and other documents. He was a very relaxed individual and my immediate impression was most favourable. He was highly intelligent and had obtained a degree in Physics from Cairo University. Attending some voluntary lectures in aspects of radiation therapy he soon developed an interest in specialising in medical physics and had obtained funding to study at King's College London where he obtained an M.Sc. For the last two years he had been working at St Thomas's Hospital. A colleague, who was intending to be at a conference in Cambridge, had been taken ill at the last moment, and Husani had been asked to take his place. There were gaps in the conference timetable and that was how he came to find himself with the opportunity to make enquiries about Daniel. He went on to explain that his memory of his sister's wedding was very slight, but he came to understand how his family viewed the marriage. It was only after he was away from home with studies and then in England, that he started to view matters differently, hence his wanting to meet Daniel.

I found Husani very plausible and had absolutely no reason to disbelieve anything that he said. Matthew had passed me a short note to say that all the facts given about his time in the UK had been verified and that people spoke extremely well about him. On the face of it, I could see no reason for not helping him with his quest, and in any event, we were not going to be able to put him in touch with Daniel straight away; we couldn't even manage that ourselves.

I told him very briefly of how Daniel and I came to know each other, our shared interest in secondhand books and the chance discovery of a copy of 'The Hound of the Baskervilles'. His eyes lit up with this piece of information, he wanted me to know that he had read the book in both Egyptian Arabic and English and that he had seen most of the films which had been made. This amused me, it all seemed so far removed from the intellectual demands of Medical Physics.

Matthew went on to tell him, slightly more formally, about the shooting incident in Paris, the threats which have surrounded Daniel, the attacks on his friends. He also explained that there seemed to be terrorist connections but not proven, nor was it known whether any of the recent events were connected with the death of Noura. The look on Husani's face clearly indicated his genuine concern. Matthew also explained how the precise whereabouts of Daniel was unknown at this moment and that contact could only be via the Paris Police although it was hoped that Daniel would be able to return to the UK quite soon.

Husani's response and suggested plan was one of plain common sense. He was very pleased to have made contact in the correct place, sad to hear of all the on-going attacks and he sincerely hoped that everything would be resolved as soon as possible. He would like to leave with us and for Daniel, his complete contact details and he would return to Cambridge and then to London and wait on us for news, as and when it became available. He and I also agreed to keep in touch on a less formal basis and Matthew appeared happy with this plan. We shook hands all round and Matthew saw him on his way.

I explained that I needed to leave very soon as I was hoping to hear fresh news about Junaid. Just before Matthew sent for the car, he mentioned that he would let his opposite number in London know about the meeting with Husani. In a few moments, the car arrived, and I was taken home.

25. THREE BROTHER SMILING & PROMISE OF KIPPERS

I hadn't been home long when Anik called round. He explained the team looking after Junaid was incredibly pleased with how he seemed and that as all the observations were as they should be, they were going to let him come out of the coma. They explained that this would take some time so Anik had decided to tell me in person and then go back and wait with Junaid. I was pleased to see that Anik seemed far less panicky about his brother.

I took the opportunity to ask him about his family as really, I knew little about them. He explained that his mother had died several years back and that their father had returned to India a couple of years back. He had wanted to do this for some time but had waited until Junaid, Anik, and the youngest of the brothers, Kabir, were all reasonably settled. Kabir was the cleverest of the three and had gone to university. He was coming towards the end of his second year at Hull where he was reading mathematics. The father had made their house over to them with Junaid and Anik living there all the time and Kabir just there for holidays. It was an unusual arrangement, but they knew their father wanted to be back with his family; they had grown up in the UK and were quite happy to stay. Perhaps more unusual was the fact that all three of them got on so well together.

I hoped he didn't want anyone with him as I didn't feel like going out again; I'd been so busy and was tired, feeling my age. It occurred to me that Kieran or Sanjay may well be there or certainly they would come if asked. After Anik had left I drove round to Sanjay's house only to learn from his mother that he had already gone to the hospital. His mum smiled and I thought she was probably pleased with how her lad was behaving even if she ruled with a rod of iron as far as she was concerned Sanjay had to be kept in order. I was relieved to get back home.

It wasn't until late the following morning that I decided to call at the hospital and see what the news was. Perhaps I had been a bit selfish, but I hadn't wanted to be part of the group sitting and waiting for something to happen and hoping that when it did it represented something good. The same visiting arrangements were still in place but a different policeman on duty. I knocked quietly and the door was opened by a total stranger, but his appearance didn't confuse me for one moment; this was Kabir, the third brother. I introduced myself, Anik rushed over to see me meet Kabir and it was as if we had all known each other for a long time. And in attendance too was Sanjay. Of Junaid nothing was said immediately so I looked in his direction to be greeted at once with a grand smile and that said all I needed to know.

"Junaid, this is incredible, and you look so well and only just a few days since brain surgery. I haven't liked to ask, but does your father know about the attack and your being in hospital?

"No, he doesn't." It was Anik who answered. "I hadn't known what to do and I was on my own so I decided to wait and just pray for good news and then Junaid would be able to tell him all that had happened, it would be more gentle for our father."

"Have you been awake long Junaid?"

"He woke up on hearing my voice of course!" This was Kabir's smiling contribution to the conversation.

Amused, I felt I could warm to this young man. "What of the future, Junaid? When do you think you'll be going home?"

"All being well, the surgeon thinks it will be right for me to be discharged on Tuesday. There will have to be some check-ups and he doesn't want me to consider returning to work for at least two months. We're going to ring our father in a few minutes as it is not often that all three of us are together when we contact him and the family. Anik's mobile has the best speaker so we will place that here on my bed-tray and we'll have a loud chaotic conversation. Perhaps though, it would be better if I speak to father on his own before we all join in."

"Shall we make a trip to the restaurant Monty?" This was Sanjay speaking up for the first time since I had arrived and what a tactful idea that was.

"Good thought, Sanjay, I'll buy us a celebratory lunch."

Sanjay smiled and got up then to join me when Junaid spoke up again.

"You know, Monty, that Sanjay has been a wonderful friend these last few days, and Kieran, I knew when they were here."

Sanjay beamed and the two of us left to find some food. He and I stacked our trays and I knew I wouldn't need to eat again but no doubt for the teenager it was just a snack. "Junaid's seemingly good recovery is a load off my mind, Sanjay. I was terrified that there might have been some permanent damage."

With the confidence and resilience of youth I don't think that thought had even crossed Sanjay's mind.

"Mr Warnock, Anik has said that when Kabir has gone back to university and that he feels he can start work again, he is going to leave the door unlocked so that Kieran and I can pop in after school. Not every day, but we want to make sure he is OK. My mother rang Anik this morning to say that if he wanted, she would be happy to bring some cooked food round for Junaid. I hope he agrees."

"You know, Sanjay, I feel it's time you started to call me Monty. I haven't been a teacher for a long time now and even though I'm old enough to be your grandfather, I think I would prefer it, a bit more friendly. And Kieran as well, shall you tell him? It might feel strange at first, but we'll get used to it."

"Well, that's all right, er, thank you, Monty. Mr Warnock, is your name short for something?"

"Yes, my father was a great admirer of Lord Montgomery, he was an important General in the second world war, so 'Monty' I became. There was another 'Monty' when I was at school, so I don't think it was uncommon. How are you getting on at school these days? I only ask because I have heard that you are doing rather well. What are you best at?

"I was ever so nervous at the time of the last parents' evening, but I needn't have been. It was the first time ever that my mum came back from one of those with nothing to shout about, well, apart from good things that is. I have been getting good results at most subjects but I'm best at History and English as I like writing essays, sort of arguing about things. I'm also quite good at French, enjoy it. Some of my friends think I'm a bit weird but I don't take any notice. I think Kieran does all right as well, we're not often in same classes, but I know he's good at design and art 'cos he's got some wicked stuff on his bedroom walls."

"So, two good friends, but with different talents. Several years away yet, I know, but do you think you might like to do what Kabir is doing, and go to university?"

"I don't know about that. I'm an only child but my mum, well, and me, dad want me to get on, as they put it. It may have to be university."

"It's worth setting your sights on something to achieve. Most of your teachers will have been to university, you ought to ask one of them."

Sanjay had finished eating long before me but eventually we both got up to return to Junaid. "I'll only pop in now to wish him well, I've got things to do at home. I'll leave you Sanjay, to chat with him and his brothers. Kabir seems fun, not quite so serious as his brothers."

"Yes, he is. According to Anik he is supposed to be brilliant at table tennis. It would be great if he could come to the club, some of the lads would put him through his paces."

I looked in on Junaid briefly, wished him a good recovery and promised to let Daniel know how well he was doing. Promised them all that I would keep in touch. Smiled at Sanjay, and I was on my way.

Back home I rang Mavis to bring her up to date and to ask if she had heard any more news on Daniel other than what we knew from the French police. She sounded quite calm about everything, but she still didn't know precisely where Daniel was, and she wondered what kind of investigations he had been following and what might have happened to make the use of a safe house necessary. She was enjoying herself at the Deanery, particularly sharing art activities with Lucinda, and she promised to let Muriel and Ken know about Junaid. Like me, Mavis was relieved that he seemed to be making a total recovery as it might have reflected badly on Daniel as Junaid had been carrying out some unofficial surveillance work on Daniel's behalf.

With my line of work, I could always find something to keep me occupied, books to repair, books to research, sometimes foreign language books to get to grips with. I could be busy for most of the coming week and so put my mind off the auction which was now only ten days away. I sat doing nothing for a while, may have even nodded off, a pleasurable entitlement arising from age. As if knowing the state of my vacant mind, the telephone rang.

"Monty? Lucinda Ellerton here. Do you like kippers?"

There was something, just slightly ultra, cultured about the accent of the Dean's wife, and I could hear her porcelain 'Ks and Ps' echoing round the Deanery.

"Yes, this is Monty, and, yes, I do like kippers."

"Oh good, I gather Mavis enjoys them too and they are a favourite of the Dean's so if you would care to come to supper Tuesday evening, we'll feast on Kippers, poached eggs, tomatoes and asparagus. How does that sound?"

"That, sounds absolutely delightful, so what time shall we be feasting?

"She chortled. Seven o'clock will be fine but it doesn't matter what time you arrive. I believe Mavis has some things to show you. 'Till Tuesday then, Goodbye."

I reverted quite happily to my semi lazy state, did a bit of this and that, read the paper, watched a number of DVDs, enjoyed my way through a thoroughly idle weekend; I did just squeeze in one of the Cathedral Sunday services. Some calming music, very traditional hymns and nothing too thought provoking from a very standard Church of England fifteen-minute sermon. Other than a few jobs about the house now completed, a drive out in the countryside returning via Stamford, on Monday, was little more than a weekend extension.

Late Tuesday afternoon I was just having a spell of book cleaning and pondering what I ought to wear for the Deanery Kippers, when my doorbell rang. To my surprise Sanjay and his mother stood there. I invited them both in with Sanjay looking a shade embarrassed.

"Mr Warnock, I hope it is all right to call like this, but Sanjay has been telling me of some of the things you said to him on Saturday. About school and such, what to do when he leaves."

I didn't answer quite immediately as I was distracted just a little by how splendidly 'Peteroroughish' she sounded and then I worried that perhaps that thought wasn't quite p.c. "Ah, yes, we did talk a little about school. I wondered if Sanjay had thought about University after he finishes at school. Some years away, I know, but the thought crossed my mind. Probably our meeting Junaid's younger brother, Kabir, drew it to mind. He is studying mathematics at Hull University."

"I've met Kabir and Anik of course, nice boys, well behaved. I took them some food yesterday. Sanjay was at school, so he didn't come with me. I asked Kabir if he enjoyed university. He seemed pleased indeed to be there."

I noticed Sanjay fidgeting a bit, and it was not like him at all to be so quiet. But this was the first time I had met him with his mother and in this kind of semi-formal situation. "Does Sanjay's father think university might be the thing to do?"

"He's rather quiet, will go along with what I think, but he would want it to be right for Sanjay. Who is the best person to tell us that?"

"Well, I'm only giving an opinion based on my reaction to him in conversation and social settings. He gives me the strong impression of being very sharp of intellect, good thinker. He must get opinions from those who teach him. I think he is doing GCSEs next summer – Sanjay nodded a yes – how he does in those examinations will be a strong indicator. I know Sanjay hasn't always worked hard at school so he ought to make sure he can catch up on anything which he is still a bit hazy about. His teachers will help if they recognise his determination. I hope that helps Mrs Bhatt, and you too Sanjay?"

"Thank you very much Mr Warnock." They both answered in unison and probably just as well that Sanjay used my surname, another example of his common sense. They both smiled and were on their way.

26. EATING A WORK OF ART

When I got to the Deanery, a bit before 7.00pm, it was Mavis who responded to their splendid bell.

"How lovely to see you Monty and is that your car?"

"Oh no, unlikely I shall ever own one again, too much bother, but I enjoy hiring one; trouble free motoring only as far as I'm concerned. I've got it until Friday as I realised that because of visiting Junaid and other journeys to make, I would be spending too much time waiting for buses and calling taxis."

"Very sensible of you. Well, in you come and straight ahead."

I found the Dean just pouring some sherry. "Monty, welcome, can't really say 'to my humble abode' living here, but welcome to supper. Here, have this and I hope your palate approves.

"Your very good health, Dean. Tell me, I always call you, Dean, but is there an alternative?"

"Some years back, I used to answer to Algy, my father being a 'Biggles' fan. If I were to hunt, I think I could find my father's flying goggles from his Air Flying Corps days."

He must have interpreted my expression as one of mild surprise because he went on immediately to explain that his father was in his mid-sixties when he was born; it was a second marriage for both his parents, and he imagined that his birth was rather unexpected.

"We're both in similar circumstances when it comes to names, both having been named after heroes even if one was fictional. My father was a great admirer of Field Marshal Montgomery. I remember when I was at school, I wasn't the only 'Monty'. Of course, your 'Algy', if my memory is correct, is one Algernon Montgomery Lacey."

"Good memory, Monty." Before he could say any more a bell rang from some distance. "Is that your signal, Mavis?"

"Oh yes, I'm off to assist in the poaching of eggs." Mavis put down her sherry glass and departed for kitchen duties. I realised then, rather guiltily, that I hadn't included her in any of that conversation.

"Lucinda will be pleased to have you lending a hand, Mavis. She always likes to get the poached eggs just right when she is serving them with kippers. Over here Monty, we can sit by the French doors for a while and admire the tulips, almost at their best just now."

"This sherry is a lovely Manzanilla." He just nodded at my comment and I looked out through the doors. "You have a large garden Dean. You won't mind if I choose not to call you Algy. Your grounds couldn't be more different from my patch and for which I have adopted a 'minimum work' approach. Various paths weaving about and a goodly number of planters and pots of all sizes and shapes, and in some, tulips are now on show. One extremely useful feature I have is an old red-brick wall running right round the garden, keeps it very sheltered."

At that moment the unmistakeably dulcet tones of Lucinda interrupted us. "Ready gentlemen?"

As we gathered about the table the Dean said Grace: "Benedictus, Benedicat, per Jesum Christum, Dominum Nostrum, Amen."

"It must be over forty years since I last heard that particular Grace. It preceded every formal dinner for three years when I was at College, in Exeter. Sometimes, just abbreviated to the first two words; rather lazy that, I thought."

The kippers and perfection-poached eggs looked wonderful, and together with some delicately flavoured mashed potatoes, asparagus, and grilled tomatoes, we were caused to be silent for a while, engrossed in the tasting. The Dean had already poured some dry white wine; all was delicious.

He was the one to first break the silence. "I don't know why, but kippers have always been at the top of my culinary favourites. It is fortunate that Lucinda enjoys them as well, as they are inclined to pervade the atmosphere for a day or so."

"You have two favourites today, dear, as Mavis has prepared a very exotic looking trifle, and quite a work of art, as you shall see. Of course, it's hardly surprising given her great artistic skills. Monty, I gather you have seen Mavis's original college art display, I saw it for the first time yesterday, quite breath-taking."

I thought Mavis looked a shade uncomfortable with this effusion of praise, but the moment passed quickly as Lucinda gathered plates and went off to collect the 'sweet' delight. It was a work of art, but more important, it was magnificent to eat!

Polishing his helping off with the enthusiasm of a small boy, the Dean suddenly asked about 'The Hound of the Baskervilles' and the famous dust jacket. This caused me to jump up and with speedy apology, left the room. I returned just as quickly, explaining that I had left a bag by the front door, and I proceeded to give a pot plant to Lucinda, one which featured some very well patterned foliage; a bottle of port for the Dean and then I spread out in front of Mavis the facsimile copy of the dust jacket. "Mavis deserves more than half the praise for this part of the find as she was first to unfold the page markers in the old gardening volumes."

The Dean stood up and came around the table to stand behind Mavis. "I know this is a facsimile, but it looks superb, hard to believe it started off in pieces, folded up and left inside some books for decades."

"This copy does have on the reverse an acknowledgement that it is a facsimile, but really there is hardly any visual difference between this and the original. I think the people at Trumpingtons are delighted with the finished product. You may have heard, I'm hoping to find an old, very tatty first edition, and then I can make real use of this antiquarian gem. "

"I remember seeing the news item involving you and the find of this rare item on television. A few months back was it?" asked the Dean. It all sounded most exciting, and now the auction is just next week."

"Yes, not much more waiting, and just hoping there will not be any more unpleasant incidents."

"Those have been very frightening for all concerned. This last one involving, er Junaid was his name? Lucinda and I were most thankful to hear of his great progress."

"Mavis and I will go to London by taxi next Tuesday. This is our attempt to protect ourselves against the 'roaring lion' that we pray to be guarded from most Wednesday evenings. I must confess though, to some intermittent attendance of late."

"And I ought to include myself in that confession." This was Mavis's quiet contribution to our conversation for some time. "It will be good to see Muriel again, fingers crossed for a good result on Wednesday."

"If you don't think it will affect your driving, Monty, can I pour you just the smallest glass of port? It will make a nice conclusion to our evening," As I watched the Dean pour, I was glad that I had spent enough to class the port as of a good quality. Certainly not what might be laid down, a dozen cases for someone's twenty-first birthday perhaps, (Do people still do that?) but good quality, never-the-less.

Mine was only a small amount but combined with wine and sherry I realised that I was getting rather verbose in my thanks to Lucinda and 'Algy'; I wished Mavis well and was soon negotiating, with considerably extra care, the Cathedral Yard.

There were no messages when I got back but I did ring Junaid and was most pleased that he answered himself, a good sign. Kabir had returned to University as he had examinations quite shortly, so it was just Anik caring for Junaid. All sounded to be fine. Anik got a fair amount of help when one or other of the lads turned up and Sanjay's mother was a very regular caller with a mid-day meal.

I checked on the book business to discover that I had little outstanding work, only a small number of purchases to wrap and post. Better weather and the arrival of the gardening season always put my business on the 'back burner' but come a day or so of torrential rain and sales would rise. I decided I would use Thursday to catch up on domestic activities and some of Saturday to visit Junaid, but Friday would see me out exploring some book hunting spots.

I had in mind a drive over to Olney, a fascinating place with great historic connections. It also had the widest main road I had ever encountered where vehicles could park at right angles to the pavements. With several cafes and charity shops, including a specialist Oxfam book shop, a small antique centre, yes - Olney would be a good way to spend Friday. I had the car until first thing Monday morning, and this was useful as I was booked to play the organ at Fotheringhay on Sunday morning. With its octagonal lantern this church is one of the ecclesiastical jewels in the whole region. The great historic connections with Richard III and the execution of Mary nearby, the church and village had become well established on the tourist map.

I was keeping busy, which helped pass the time to auction day the following week, and so I could begin to look forward to what I hoped would be a memorable event. I was as a child, waiting for his birthday.

27. NOT A NIGHTMARE!

Finally, there we were: Mavis, Muriel, Ken, and me, all pleasantly seated about two thirds of the rows back in Trumpingtons main room and our lot was next. So far, the auction had been quite tame with most items running close to estimate, no shocks, or surprises for anyone.

"Ladies and gentlemen, we come now to lot 141, the first edition, Newnes, from 1902, of 'The Hound of the Baskervilles' containing three pieces of verified handwriting by Sir Arthur Conan Doyle and of which two have been signed. Despite research, we have been unable to identify the lad, Albert, nor his father, knowing no more than what the author has told us: Albert, a son of Arthur, who was employed by the publishers, George Newnes. In addition to finding this copy in a job lot of books purchased at a provincial auction, the vendor also found a dust jacket, torn into three pieces, each folded up and being used as book markers in some old gardening volumes. No dustjacket was issued by the publisher, this one has been 'homemade' using materials contemporary with the book. The design makes use of the motifs used on the boards and makes further use of some of the illustrations – all who have seen it agree that as a dustjacket it works well and is worth keeping with the book. As you know, after much discussion between experts and our highly experienced paper restorer, it was decided to reassemble the three pieces of the dust jacket. You'll be pleased to know that all who have seen the finished work, including some quite eminent people in this field of paper conservation, are united in saying that an extraordinarily successful and most satisfying piece of restoration has been achieved. One facsimile only, and marked as such, has been made and given to the vendor. Another facsimile has been used during the viewing period, but this will be destroyed as soon as the item is sold. Lot 141 may not be the most valuable item in today's sale, but many would argue its being the most interesting. There has been a great deal of presale interest: several bids left with me, five telephone lines have been booked and the internet is singing with activity. I can therefore open the bidding at…. did I detect the merest hint of a dramatic pause? £45000, looking for £50000. £50000 bid, thank you sir, looking for £55000."

With speed the price rose to £75000. Here it held momentarily, the auctioneer looking at those holding the telephones, glancing at his on-line monitor.

"At £75000, £75000, I can take £2500 if it helps. £77500, £80000, £82500, £82500 on line two. £82500 then, are there any more bids? fair warning then, at £82500 once, £82500 twice, sold for £82500, telephone line two, number? 1944, Thank you."

A resounding knock from the gavel, set off a good round of applause and brought to a close, in a breath-holding spell of only a few seconds, a delightful piece of bidding; I was thrilled. My fellow enthusiasts and supporters, (can I use that expression?) were all, like me, smiling. Without the auctioneer's introduction, the actual bidding was probably over in less than a minute, but how memorable that minute. It was the culmination of action and thought which all started with my choosing those scruffy boxes, scrabbling round the bottom of one and unwrapping a most tatty looking brown paper parcel, one wet autumnal Saturday.

We were at the end of the row, so were able to slip out quietly, to meet Joseph and Charles in one of the nearby adjoining rooms. They too smiled as we came in, handshakes all round and it was Muriel who asked the obvious. "Do you know who bought the book?"

"In this case, yes, but frequently we don't. Today the actual winner is not here but his nominated agent is, and he'll be through in a moment. The book has been bought by someone in Italy, and his agent, ah, here he is, Andreas. Come and meet the vendor of your Conan Doyle item."

"A pleasure, Joseph."

Just the merest hint of an accent revealed that Andreas was not from the UK originally, but clearly, he had lived here for many years. "I take it that you were at this end of telephone two?"

"And you must be Monty Warnock. I hope you were pleased with the outcome? It might have been higher because my instructions were very precise: bid until you win! The final price was a bit above top estimate, but the buyer will be well pleased. I don't often have the pleasure of bidding at auctions, and this is the first time I have been able to do so using someone else's money and with no upper limit.

"Have you told the buyer the good news?"

"Oh, no need to do that, the call was being relayed automatically so he could hear both me and the auctioneer. He said nothing, the buyer, that is, nothing, from start to finish. Just breathed a sigh of relief and thanked me. But then, he couldn't lose."

"Am I right in thinking you are from Italy?"

"Yes, but I have lived nearly half my life over here. I finished my schooling in this country, went to London University and have been here ever since. I go back to my parents frequently, they live near Venice, but over here I live with my grandparents, my mother's parents; she is English but married to an Italian. I have a brother and sister, but they never wanted to leave Italy. They both speak good English though, because our mother brought us all up bilingually. Being outnumbered four to one, our father has been forced to learn English too, he's pretty good now. My brother and sister both speak German, mother is fluent in French and I'm not far behind, it was one of my GCE A levels.

"It's Italy where we intend to celebrate this auction result. Mavis and Muriel will be joining me in about six weeks when we're off to Lake Garda for some glorious sunshine, Italian cuisine and some local wines."

"I know that area very well, lots of beautiful lakeside resorts."

"Well, we've chosen Gardone, staying at The King's Tower."

Joseph and Charles suddenly interrupted us at this point. "Look, sorry, we need to return to the auction now, But, Monty, we'll be in touch very soon. And, just so you know, our accountants will have dispatched a cheque by the end of month. Good luck with your hunt for another first edition so you can make pleasant use of that facsimile dust jacket." More handshakes and they disappeared.

"We need to celebrate. Well, I want to, even though it's two or three weeks to cheque receiving day, but let's go to the Wellington Hotel and celebrate with a couple of bottles – perhaps Andreas, you can choose something good from Italy?

"My very great pleasure, indeed. My father is in the wine business, so he has imparted some good knowledge."

It was little or no time before we were comfortably seated and awaiting the fruits of Andreas's discussions at the bar. He sat down after a few moments, explaining that the staff would arrive with a selection of three bottles, together with some Italian nibbles – olives, cheese, bread, and some variously sourced nuts. True to his word, there arrived several plates of tasty morsels to eat, including, I noticed, with some pleasure, a plate of different sliced salami. There was a selection of glasses, a bottle of Monsanto Chianti, a Pinot Grigio and a bottle of La Marca Prosecco – these last two in their own buckets of ice.

"How wonderful," Muriel showed her enthusiasm. Ken read the labels and nodded some clear approval. With the help of one of the waiters Andreas took our orders and passed round the glasses as they were filled.

"Provided you remember to eat plenty of bread there is not a limit to the number of bottles. In fact, I think it would be a good idea to put another Prosecco on ice in readiness. It may look a little unseemly, but we can always take the bottles away if they still contain a goodly level! After all, it is not every day that I sell a book for just over £80000!"

"Now, Andreas, what is the Italian for 'cheers'?"

"Saluti quando si beve!"

28. THE RETURNING COPPER

We stayed at the Wellington for some time, gradually getting pleasantly, how shall I put it, reddish of complexion. It didn't look as if we would need to carry away any bottles and it was Mavis who suggested a change of brew. "I don't know about the rest of you, but I'm in need of a large pot of tea, lest I start snoozing the afternoon away."

Andreas caught the eye of one of the guys who had helped bring over the first order; the second was to comprise tea, a selection of different coffees and one of those tiered cake-plates, now very much back in fashion, laden with a nice range of their kitchen's finest and most delicate sweet offerings, prepared earlier and now ready for the afternoon tea trade. By the time I had sampled them and swallowed a few cups of coffee I was beginning to feel quite full in the stomach department; sleep would call me before the afternoon was out. Andreas was the first to leave, explaining that he had to get back to his grandparents. While I was settling the bill, Ken gave Tony a call and he brought the Humber round, so we all returned to Leopold Mansions in some style.

It was Ken, who having checked some telephone messages and then his emails, came into the kitchen with the news of Daniel. He was flying into Heathrow that afternoon and would get a taxi to bring him to the Mansions. Any hint of sleep left Mavis's face at once.

"Did he have any more information about where he has been or what he has found out?"

"No, sorry Mavis, that is all there was apart from an apology for missing the auction, but he hoped it would been successful. We will just have to wait on his arrival to learn anything more."

"If you'll excuse me, I'll do that waiting horizontally. I'm sure the noise of his arrival will wake me but just make sure it does. There is much to learn from all his activities I'm sure, and I want to tell him all about poor old Junaid." I toddled off and left them to moulder the afternoon away, remembering yet again, that mid-day alcohol always left me very lethargic, truly disastrous if one wanted to complete any work.

I slept quite peacefully, no 'auction house nightmares' and, in fact, I came to quite gently, becoming aware of lots of voices all trying to vie for attention. I toddled into the kitchen and there was Daniel, looking none the worse for his strange time spent in Europe. He was sitting next to Mavis and she was looking quite radiant; no questions needed to be asked about their possible intentions.

"Monty, I am so sorry about the auction although I gather if you blinked it could all have been missed most easily. Anyway, I'm extremely glad it was a great success. I take it that that was the best and most successful find you've ever experienced?"

"Without doubt! A 'once in a lifetime' event."

"What have you found out?" Muriel brought us back to a more sombre moment which automatically raised memories of attacks, failed attacks and a pseudo shooting."

"I've travelled hundreds of miles, held a number of telephone conferences with colleagues here in London, spoken to officers in France who carry out similar work and the only thing we're all probably agreed on, is that it has nothing to do with the events in Egypt immediately following my marriage. I may even have been chasing 'red herrings' for the last few days."

I didn't say anything just then, but I was suddenly reminded that I had to tell Daniel about the unexpected arrival of Husani El Masry, Noura's youngest brother. He must have been reading my mind as Daniel started to tell us about Husani. Apparently, he had been contacted by Chief Superintendent Tomlinson's senior contact in London. Daniel knew of a very much younger brother but beyond that had no knowledge of him at all. He was most impressed with his current career achievement and had decided he would endeavour to meet him where he worked, and soon.

I think he must have been burning up his mobile because he had contacted several people while in his taxi and gained information he wanted to share. Firstly, he mentioned a concert, which was scheduled to take place at The Palace of Westminster at the end of May. The concert was to be part of a larger event to promote greater international awareness and help for orphaned refugees. Music would be interspersed with two or three high profile speakers and amongst the performers would be Genevievre Renoir, accompanied by her brother Jean. Daniel had been speaking to Jon Mostang who promised to send him some complimentary tickets. He wasn't sure which room would be used but perhaps the Members Dining room. Speakers were not mentioned by name, but they were likely to be well known, perhaps former politicians working for the United Nations. Obviously, Jon was going because of Genevievre and because of his foreign affairs Parliamentary work. It sounded to me a rather prestigious event, so I hoped a ticket might come my way.

Daniel had also heard from Peter Prendle, because of there being more work involving immigrants whose legal status was under question. This was again in the Lincolnshire area and a Mr Lawton's name had been mentioned as being vaguely involved. It sounded like a case of 'muddied waters' or perhaps, 'muddled waters'. He wondered if Pierre, Genevievre's brother, had been involved.

The last call Daniel had made was to Junaid. It was obvious to all that he was very relieved that Junaid had made such a good recovery from an injury which could very well have had disastrous consequences. Daniel promised that he would get to see Junaid as soon as possible.

At Ken's invitation everyone was to stay the night at the Leopold Residences and how grand that made them sound. He also invited us all to dinner, and, looking at Muriel, said that it might be at a nearby restaurant. He needn't have hinted that Muriel might not have been able to cater at such short notice, because within two hours she had produced one of her excellent fish pies, a roast chicken and the promise of an omelette should anyone want something a little lighter. There were vegetables to feed an army, a quite grandiose mixed fruit crumble, a selection of cheeses and had the said army been in the vicinity, Ken opened enough bottles to render the entire force legless. While this banquet was in preparation, a phone call had found Jon and Genevievre unexpectedly free to join the party. It seemed to be a stunning way to round off the 'auction day' and by the time everyone was replete there was that sense of worry-free bonhomie.

I had slept well that afternoon but that was as nothing to my next eight hours of trouble-free slumber. On the Thursday I returned to Peterborough, but Mavis was staying on in London, perhaps until Daniel decided to visit Junaid and they were both staying with Muriel. Getting a first-class seat on a mid-morning train from Kings Cross to Peterborough was not difficult and for the entire journey I had the compartment to myself. I dozed intermittently all the way and I must have been worried about the possibility of sleeping through Peterborough because I gave the ticket inspector a suitable tip if he would ensure I left the train at Peterborough; he didn't forget me and we both left the train together.

I was able to think over the previous forty-eight hours, especially meeting Genevievre, she was quite charming, and I heard a little more about her programme for the House of Commons Reception and Concert. She was intending to sing some French songs.

She also knew that a trombone player, from Iran she thought, and a recent graduate of the Paris Conservatoire, was intending to play some unaccompanied traditional Middle Eastern melodies. Of the rest of the programme she was unsure, but she thought that a student from the London Royal Academy was intending to perform some Vaughan Williams. It would seem that there was an intention to feature young musicians, perhaps pointing up the frightening consequences of what might be missed when the potential of tens of thousands of youngsters caught in the international refugee nightmare is totally neglected, even rejected, given the current tendency of many countries to increase their border restrictions. It wouldn't escape notice that the music would reflect each musician's nationality.

All this made me think about my own good fortune and the cheque which would soon be coming my way and it occurred to me that I must speak to my accountant very soon to see what could be given away using any permissible tax benefit; I'm all for enhancing the value of any gift, especially when the Exchequer foots the bill! I had in mind Sanjay and Kieran's futures, also Cynthia, as I suspected she may be getting a little hard up depending on how Ernie's pension arrangements affected her. I also reflected, somewhat guiltily, on the fact that whilst I had eaten incredibly well over the last forty-eight hours, those who were to be helped by The Palace of Westminster Reception, most certainly hadn't.

29. NORMALITY RETURNS AND WESTMINSTER BECKONS

For a few days, normality returned! A restful experience, but it also made me realise how easy it was to get mixed up in all the excitement of what could readily be described as 'the unusual'. It reminded me of a documentary programme I had watched about the immediate aftermath of the second world war, of how disorientated many returning servicemen found themselves. This experience was decades before we started talking about the terrible effects of post-traumatic stress disorder, the term hadn't even been invented, certainly not in everyday conversational usage.

I determined that my first .normal. act would be a round of visiting. So, I set off one morning soon after getting home to visit Fr Blakeston. He was, as ever, 'in the pink' and seemed pleased to see me. The lady who helped him in the mornings was there, so he was able to produce coffee and cake very quickly. My news pleased, all good news and for once no dark shadows shedding a worrying gloom. He was excited about the auction result and encouraging about some of my charitable plans. Fr Blakeston doesn't go in for wishing people luck, but he could understand my desire to find a suitable first edition copy and make use of my souvenir of the whole auction process, the facsimile dust jacket. Like the Dean, he cautioned for continued care as far as the unexplained attacks were concerned.

I got the impression that had he felt up to the journey, he would have enjoyed a visit to Westminster Palace for the music and speakers, hoping to raise support and awareness for the many thousands of youngsters caught in the misery of being a refugee in the Middle East. If I got there I promised, silently and only to myself, to report back on the evening's proceedings.

Next on my calling list was Cynthia, and as it happened my visit coincided with a morning call by Wendy, she would have been my third visit. Pleasingly, I found them both in great spirits, and it didn't take much conversation before I discovered that they had both been quite active; helping in two charity shops where they found they enjoyed the work. Cynthia surprised herself by learning how to use a modern till and they both enjoyed chatting with all the different people who popped into the shops, getting to know some of the regulars very well. Cynthia was keen for me to know that she had started attending the Sunday Morning Cathedral Service again and with just a confirming phone call the evening before, somebody from the congregation would pick her up so that she didn't have to walk. She thought that most kind and was thrilled when Wendy had asked if she could join her. Years seemed to have fallen from Cynthia's shoulders.

By the time I had consumed more coffee and biscuits it was late morning before I returned home, so I rang Junaid and arranged to see him the following morning. Mrs Bhatt must have called with his lunch just then, because very soon she was ringing me.

"This is Mrs Bhatt," said the voice when I answered the phone. I struggled with my memory momentarily but was rescued! "You remember, Sanjay's mother?"

"Hello Mrs Bhatt, you only caught me out for a moment. How are you, and your family.?"

"We're all very well and Sanjay is continuing to do well. I am ringing to ask when you visit Junaid tomorrow you time it so that you can have lunch with him. I will bring enough for both of you. I know that Anik can't be there. The food will be curry but I will make it very mild. You will like it I think."

"Mrs Bhatt, that is a lovely idea, most generous of you, and I will enjoy having lunch with Junaid. Do you have lunch there as well?"

"O no, no, I must get back to Mr Bhatt. I will see you tomorrow Mr Warnock. Goodbye."

I suspect she was slightly embarrassed by the thought of eating with us and I hoped I hadn't caused any discomfort. I enjoyed the multi-racial aspects of modern Peterborough, but I was conscious of my ignorance when it came to my needing more understanding of unfamiliar ways and customs.

With welcome respite from telephone calls for a while, I set about getting some lunch, something akin to a 'ploughman's and I was just finishing this when Daniel rang to ask if it would be all right to visit later that afternoon.

"I will be delighted; glasses and malt as usual?"

"Absolutely, but we'll need an extra glass."

"I understand perfectly," was my 'knowing' reply. He may have sensed my smile, but he couldn't see it.

There were several recorded messages to go through but the only one of any concern was from Anthony, to say that he now had all the travel documents for the Italian excursion, as he put it. He is something of an early bird, so I called him at once and arranged for him to come to breakfast the following morning. Jet-setting politicians and businessmen go in for these working breakfasts (I imagine they think it sounds impressive and makes them appear 'busy, busy') so why not more humble mortals. Anthony's only additional comment was his fondness for bacon and mustard toasties, a fondness for which I was more than happy to share; he rang off feeling well pleased with himself.

Internet and email checking prompted me to wrap a small number of books and get them ready for immediate posting. I would obtain breakfast goodies at the same time. Dictionaries were obviously the flavour of the week as among the six books I set about packing, three were dictionaries, all earlyish copies of German, Russian and Hebrew, each to English. I was always pleasantly surprised by the number of different sorts of dictionaries which would pop up in job lots of books and they sold very well to an international market, and especially when near the beginning of any academic year. This done, books posted, and breakfast purchased, I was back just in time to get ready for my lovebirds.

"Come in you two, and don't sit holding hands and looking coy; I'm thrilled for you both but don't wish to feel like an elderly out of touch has been. If you sit just here you can reach out and choose one of three malts, plus ice, water or fizz as you wish."

As Mavis did this the light reflected from a cut-glass beaker caused a wondrous coloured sparkle to fire from an appropriate finger and catch my eye; no further explanation as to their visit was required!

"Hand quite still please, Mavis. I need to inspect some baubles, I think. No, that would be rude, let me just say, 'Heavenly Blessings to you both', and as I like being rather corny occasionally, 'It couldn't have happened to a nicer couple'. There was a raising and chinking of glasses all round, and for a while we basked in a little silent bliss. Pretending to sound a little peeved, failing, of course, I went on: "If I had be given some hint, I would now be handing over a well-chosen and suitable engagement present, but at present it is a case of 'watch this space'. They both chorused their thanks and retained slightly bashful smiles.

"And what does Muriel have to say? Let me think: 'I've been waiting weeks for you to say something and I bought a very costly bottle of champagne on the expectation.'"

"Along those lines." Mavis smiled through everything she said. "The champagne was rather good, Harrods served her well."

"I say, Daniel, my taking your lady away, quite soon now, not causing any worry, I hope. It's a jolly good job Muriel is coming, or I would be booking some professional chaperone, if such people exist these days."

"Worry not, Monty. London colleagues have me well booked up for a lot of the summer. Emails, texts and skype will keep us together very well indeed." They gave each other a blissful smile and took the opportunity to hold hands again. It did so remind me of my teenage years, but I was never sure if my parents ever approved of my romantic choices. I snapped out of this tiny moment of nostalgia and pushed the tray of bottles towards them, waving my hand in the direction of their glasses.

Daniel reached into his pocket. "Before I forget." Passing an envelope in my direction he added: "Courtesy of Jon Mostang."

There was no mistaking the portcullis envelope. "I hope this is what I think it might be." I took out a personalised invitation for the Westminster Palace evening. "Well, I am pleased, my thanks to the Member of Parliament. Who else will I know?"

"Mavis, of course, I'm there in a semi-official capacity so don't need one of his tickets, Muriel, Ken and we hope the Dean and Lucinda will like to come –

they've been so helpful and kind just lately – so with you, Jon has used all his six tickets in our direction."

"That is amazingly generous, and I feel quite privileged to be going. Not long to wait I see, first Wednesday in June. Some questions, mustn't do the wrong thing: Is it a black-tie event, do I need to acknowledge this ticket in any official way, and shall I be required to have a suitable cheque at the ready?"

"You are very practical, Monty. Daniel smiled. "Yes, yes, and probably yes, answers you, I think. A dinner suit is a must on these occasions; on the reverse of the invitation are instructions regarding acknowledgement and security matters and as far as a donation is concerned I'll make some discrete enquiries – there will be, hopefully, some sizable corporate donations- but with private individuals there will be wide variations. In days long since passed, five guineas would have more than sufficed, now perhaps fifty pounds. After all, you are retired."

"You've made that all perfectly clear. I shall air the dinner suit; I'll check all security matters and I will have a cheque for £100 available. Shall I get my accountant to set it against profit from the auction proceeds, or am I being a little facetious?"

Mavis was just finishing her drink when she looked up. "I enjoy your common-sense approach to such matters, always tinged with a touch of humour. By the way, we visited Junaid this morning and found him seemingly very well. Getting a bit restless about not being allowed to resume work yet. Daniel told him quite firmly to wait, he has known too many injured colleagues in the past who have tried returning to work far too soon, never a good idea. It would have caused my mother to utter one of her well used phrases: 'It will all end in tears.'

30. MRS BHATT'S CURRY AND OTHER MATTERS

I was with Junaid by late morning but well before he expected Mrs Bhatt. I didn't take any drink as I had no idea whether he ever consumed alcohol. He was up and about and appeared quite active but was obviously restless and soon mentioned the need to get back to work. I could only repeat what Daniel and Mavis had told him and add some memories of mine from teaching days when some colleagues were always trying to return after perhaps a bout of flu – back for a couple of days and then away for another week or even longer; he wasn't convinced.

Mrs Bhatt appeared soon after this somewhat fruitless conversation; she was laden! She refused to let me help in any way whatsoever, and I noticed Junaid was quite used to this 'take over'. She laid the table put out cutlery and water and got out plates which unnoticed by me Junaid had already placed in the oven to warm. She then served the food and only when she thought everything was satisfactory, did she allow us to sit and start. She left the remaining food in the oven in case we wanted more and off she went. Clearly this was not a time for any social conversation; she had smiled at me when she arrived, so I think she was very pleased that I had turned up and in time.

She was true to her word: this was a mild curry with all manner of vegetables, many of which I did not recognise. There was rice, cooked to perfection and two dishes containing different kinds of chutney.

Junaid explained that these were her own preserves. There wasn't a pudding in any sense of the English use of that term, but there were some crisp pastry-coated sweet confections – quite delicious- several varieties and which I had never eaten before. I felt just a little humbled because there I was, having lived in Peterborough for years, and yet I knew nothing of this cuisine which was being prepared in countless houses and restaurants. It was a shortcoming which I must determine to rectify. I thoroughly enjoyed this lunch and given my enthusiasm to eat some more I think I convinced Junaid of my pleasure. He was pleased I ate some more because he told me that Mrs Bhatt took offence if too much was left uneaten although it didn't matter, as she always came back later in the afternoon to collect dishes and placed all the leftovers in the refrigerator for Anik to eat when he got home. These brothers were being well cared for and I wondered how long it would go on for. It occurred to me that the situation had all the ingredients for some embarrassing awkwardness.

Junaid made us both tea; he was so fidgety when he carried it through, that I wondered what else was causing his nervousness.

"Monty, I need to ask you something, but it is a little difficult."

Here was the explanation, I thought to myself.

"It's about Kabir. He has always telephoned or sent texts quite often and these have mainly been about the university and what he was doing, nothing specific, more about groups of friends, sport, all the usual things."

My next thought was that there was a romance brewing.

"I think Anik is much more bothered that I am, but lately he has been talking about someone called Stephen who studies mathematics with him and lately they have been doing some project work together, set by one of the tutors. It's just we suddenly hear so much about this Stephen and this is first in his calls to us. They have been out to cafes, cinema and the other night he mentioned a club called 'The Christian Union'."

"I don't like to interrupt you Junaid, but I think I begin to see where your worries are leading. Tell me, I have never enquired before, but do you as a family belong to, not sure how to phrase this so please don't be offended, belong to the Muslim Faith?"

"Yes, we are, the whole family is, but in all honesty we three brothers are far less practising of the faith than the rest of the family back home, where our father is. What is a Christian Union?"

"I can answer that Junaid, quite easily. At nearly all colleges and universities, especially where there is a large resident body of students, there is usually a colossal large number of clubs, sport, cultural, drama, politics. Mention any activity and there is probably a club for it. The Christian Union is a club and is for those students who come from

Christian backgrounds and want to meet other students from similar backgrounds. They might meet for services, prayers but they would also meet for lots of quite general social activities. In the situation you have mentioned I expect Stephen is from a Christian family and he has joined the group to help him maintain his faith, or just to meet some like-minded friends. I imagine Kabir has gone along with him, perhaps just out of interest."

"It's difficult for us Monty. Kabir and Stephen seem such good friends; what if Kabir were to become a Christian?"

"Well, what indeed? I imagine from your worried manner and despite the fact that you have mentioned that all three of you maintain only 'token' links with your background faith, it would be very difficult, perhaps impossible, if Kabir became a Christian, is that what is really worrying you both?"

"Yes, and we think our father would be particularly angry indeed, and he would accuse us of not having watched Kabir with enough care. I know Anik is livid about it. He mixes with more traditional Muslim people than I do. I'm a policeman so I meet a very wide range of members of the general public, the whole community, I must, it's my job. With Anik, deliberately or not, he can keep closer to his own background and I think this is what he has done. He is already taking a dislike to Stephen and he hasn't even met him, it's not fair. I'm frightened about what might happen when Kabir comes home for the summer."

"I'm sorry you have this worry although it may turn out to be no more than friendly curiosity on Kabir's part. I must be careful how I put this, don't in any way want to cause offence but Christianity and Islam do have roots in common, along with Judaism. They're sometimes referred to collectively as Abrahamic religions. There is a lot I don't know about your personal lives. Do girlfriends exist for any of you or is this something your family would be planning?"

"Our father hasn't said anything. We don't think he has arranged marriages in mind. He probably hopes that we will marry within our culture. I've had girlfriends, friends who are girls, nothing long-term, but I think Anik has had girlfriends about whom he has been a bit serious, he hasn't said much. Kabir has never talked about girlfriends. Think he's hung around more with just a group of blokes. I suppose while he is at university he will always be with a wider range of people, from every kind of background. It's only just recently, he's talked a lot about this Stephen guy. He mentioned playing badminton, doubles, well more people get to play that way."

"I don't know what more to say. You and Anik must talk it all through and it won't help if either of you bottle up anger about Kabir. You need to choose your moment and try and keep Anik calm. If Kabir is coming home for the long summer vacation it will be bad if you all start arguing. I can't remember, does Kabir work when he's home, does he keep up with local friends?

"He's worked in shops with people who knew our father. He has usually managed to get something so at least he has kept himself in pocket money. When he's at University he is existing on maximum loan. It's a colossal amount of money but he says it will be all right because being a mathematician he should find it easier than many students to find work. As far as work goes, he could stay in Newcastle if he wanted to, because the house he shares has been rented for the whole year. I don't know how easy it is to get work up there.

"Well, Junaid, I have to be on my way soon. You have a lot to worry about but whatever happens, remember that you three have always got on so very well in the past and that must count for a lot. Don't let go of family love; it can be a rare commodity. Do tell Anik he can come and chat with me if he thinks I can help."

31. A COUPLE AT COMPLINE

Sitting on the bus on my way back from having lunch with Junaid I couldn't help but wonder if the connection between Kabir and Stephen was something more than just friendship. Different kinds of love and relationships will occur quite regardless of race, religion, or family background, never mind the personal opinions of one's relatives and friends. I could see the whole situation getting incredibly difficult indeed for Junaid and Anik. I didn't mind talking to them about such matters, but I would have to step very carefully. Once home I quickly wrote a thank you card for Mrs Bhatt, telling how much I had enjoyed the lunch. I told her that I needed to get a bit more adventurous about food and that I would come to her for lessons! I also asked after Mr Bhatt and Sanjay.

I needed now to think about the Palace of Westminster Concert – I knew it wasn't just a concert but that was the easiest way for me to understand it. I had already got my dinner suit out and sent it away for cleaning, sorted out appropriate shirt, bow-tie, cufflinks, and anything else I thought I might need for my evening attire. As with most of our previous 'trips' to London, Mavis and I were planning on going by train on the day of the concert, along with the Dean and Lucinda and then meeting up with Daniel at Leopold Mansions for a meal before the concert. We would stay there afterwards; the Dean and Lucinda were invited but they had relatives with whom they often stayed when in London. Mavis and I would meet up with them at Kings Cross for the train journey back the next day. I had replied to the invitation and awaited email instructions regarding entry to the Palace of Westminster.

Working from home always keeps me well grounded; needless-to-say there were a few orders to process and books to parcel and post and that kept me busy for the rest of the day. That evening I began to give more thought to the holiday; not long to go. I didn't want to be weighed down with luggage but I didn't want to be without the essentials of the kind of everyday living that I had got so used to; old-age, older age, a better description, was beginning to make me just a little more inflexible and a detailed list of what to take and plans to make was definitely called for, so I opened a fresh 'page' on word. Among the essential planning was the need to work out how to close down my web-site so that I didn't get endless queries which I couldn't answer while I was on holiday and nor did I want to return to a long list of orders to dispatch. I'm quite good at organising myself and I could see that I needed to start; 'a typing I must go'
.
I was just beginning to think about some food for an evening meal when Mavis telephoned to ask if I had remembered that it was Compline that evening, and would I be calling round in the usual way. She surprised me then by inviting me to supper, joining her and Daniel as he was going to Compline and travelling up to London afterwards. I had never thought of Daniel as one who would be attending Compline; there was always something to take one by surprise. I was pleased to be meeting up with them

both as I wanted to sound out their opinions about Junaid and his brothers. Mavis had prepared a lovely supper meal, having cooked a magnificent cheese souffle served with a medley of vegetables. She had heated some deliciously crusty rolls. Mavis followed this with some locally grown strawberries with which came a large dollop of Cornish cream – a favourite of mine and, as it turned out, Daniel's as well. Over some coffee I broached the matter of Junaid and his brothers. It was all news to them, so I didn't go into too much detail. They could immediately appreciate the potential for some inter-cultural conflicts and Daniel was aware that Anik could be quite prickly as far as his personality was concerned; he was not as broad minded as Junaid. I didn't hint at my other thoughts about Kabir's possible relationship with Stephen, leaving that to wait on time.

It was soon time to stroll down to St Petrie's for Compline, a beautiful evening for early summer. If any of the regular Compline attendees were surprised to see Daniel, they were far too polite to raise so much as an eyebrow. The restful atmosphere of this ancient service soon enveloped us all and yet again I was caused to ponder the activities of the 'roaring lion'. It caused me to realise that this magnificent but potentially ferocious beast had been taking a frighteningly long rest; vigilance was still necessary. As we came out, Fr Blakeston greeted us, exchanged few pleasantries with Daniel. They seemed to know each other, of how or when I had no knowledge. Also attending, but we didn't see them until they came out, were the Dean and his wife, and I could see at once she was very intrigued by Daniel's presence, especially as it was clearly obvious for all to see that he had accompanied Mavis. As soon as she heard that he was heading back to London I could sense her planning; Mavis would be invited to morning coffee very soon.

I was right because I had only been home about an hour when Mavis rang up. "Monty, guess what?"

"Lucinda has invited you to coffee tomorrow morning."

"Almost right; afternoon tea in the Cathedral Tea Rooms."

"Mavis, I could see Lucinda's mind planning the event just as soon as she heard Daniel was going back to London and I take it that he is on his way as we speak."

"Yes, indeed. I'll ring about this time tomorrow evening and tell you how I got on." At that she rang off.

And, true to her word and almost to the second, Mavis was speaking to me the next day having been 'grilled' by Lucinda. I imagine that Mavis didn't say more than she wanted to, but no doubt Lucinda felt she had had a good gossip. I didn't think the Dean was one for idle gossipy chit-chat so Lucinda would have to enjoy this romance with her imagination only, doing her own private 'pumping' for juicy titbits. Perhaps she would try to get Mavis to drop the odd planning hint on the train to London, but with the Dean present, not so easy. Still, lots for us all to think about, a bank holiday weekend, a special concert in London, a holiday in Italy and the possibility of a wedding come Autumn.

I was still thinking about the joys and delights to come while I was checking recent emails and found the potential for another delight, certainly for me, anyway. An email from Joseph Mallings alerted me to the possibility of their having another vintage copy of 'The Hound of the Baskervilles'. I wondered how often that could happen, two copies of a rare book within weeks of each other. Apparently, they were unsure of the actual date because the copy was missing its main title page and so the publication details couldn't be immediately checked. As well as missing this important page it was also in rather a battered state, loose pages, some torn, binding a bit weak and some colouring to a couple of the illustrations. Even if they were able to prove that it was a first edition, they still expected it to have a low valuation. He would let me have further details as and when he could. This was without doubt another piece of exciting news.

But then, another phone call brought Junaid, sounding very disturbed; the 'lion' was waking up! Slowing him down a bit, I gathered that Kabir had telephoned and spoken to Anik while Junaid was out. By all accounts they had argued very badly, and the call had been cut short. All Anik would say when Junaid got back was that Kabir would not be home for the summer vacation because he was staying in Newcastle. Junaid thought that there must have been more to the conversation to cause such anger, so he sent a text to Kabir while Anik was getting ready to go out and received back a quite different version of events. Kabir would be staying with Stephen whose family were not far away from Newcastle. Apparently, Stephen usually worked for his father's firm during university holidays and that a friend of the father would be able to employ Kabir. Because they were not too far from Newcastle they could go back at weekends, meeting up with friends who were staying near the University rather than going home. It took some time for Junaid to relay all this. He was very worried about telling their father.

When he finally paused, I asked him if it was important for him to tell his father yet, and Junaid explained that they had always kept their father informed about what they were doing as a family, it was a duty. I found it difficult to know what more to say but again I repeated previous advice about keeping in touch with Kabir. After he had finished the call and I thought more about these three brothers, I realised how difficult it was for me to help them; I was just too far outside their culture. It all cast something of a shadow over the good bits of news that I had been privately celebrating and I went to bed feeling rather discouraged.

The following morning Junaid telephoned again but this time with awful news. One of his cousins had called during the night from India to tell him that their father had suffered a heart attack and died. This was a terrible shock for Junaid but not apparently to his cousin's family because the father had been ill for some time. Obviously, the dutiful boys in the UK had not been kept informed about their father. I offered him my sympathy as well as I could and asked about

Anik. Junaid went silent for quite a while and then said Anik had gone quiet on receiving the news, then he went back to bed and now he was out, and he didn't know where.

"Junaid, can I ask about your father's funeral?"

"That's the problem for Anik I think. Father died yesterday, I believe, and the funeral is tomorrow. It is our duty that we should be there, but it is simply not possible. We haven't the money and even if we did, we could never get there in time. I think our cousins deliberately delayed telling us and so prevented us from going."

"And Kabir, have you told him yet?"

"No, I'll ring him a little later this morning."

"Well, Junaid, I'm so sorry to hear about your Father's death as well as all the difficulties you're having. I don't suppose there is anything I can do to help but I'm always around if you want to talk.

"Monty, you are truly kind, thank you. I will ring again."

32. TRAGIC NEWS

It was late afternoon when Junaid rang again, and if anything, he sounded even more upset.

"Monty, it's about Anik, I don't know what to do, he hasn't come home since early this morning. I think I told you that when he heard about our father's death, he went quite silent and then went straight out. I know he went off in his car, but I've no idea where and I don't know any of his friends well enough to have phone numbers or anything. I don't know what he took, wallet or…. hang on, there's banging at the door."

I could just make out fragments of talking, then a shout, then a voice telling Junaid to sit down. There was some unidentifiable noise and then a strange and rather formal voice.

"Good evening, this is Sergeant Armstrong, Peterborough Police. May I ask who I am speaking to please?"

"Yes Sir, my name is Monty Warnock and I am a friend of Junaid and he was telling me about his concerns for his brother, Anik. I take it something has happened?"

"Yes, you're right, and if you know Junaid well it might be helpful if you could come here. Just a minute, Junaid is shouting about a car."

"He is probably telling you that I don't have a car. I'll call a taxi."

"No, don't do that, I'll stay with Junaid and my colleague here will come and fetch you.

Despite the delay of giving him my address there was a police car outside my front door far quicker than I would have managed to get a taxi and very soon I was sitting looking at a tearful Junaid; the news was truly awful. There had been a call to the police about the middle of the afternoon from a car driver at Guyhirn, saying that he had just seen the car in front of him accelerate towards a barrier at the bridge crossing the River Nene just a few miles north west of the City. He hit it so fast that the car somersaulted over and into the river. By the time he got to the bridge, the car was out of sight.

An angler further along the bank had jumped in but had been unable to see the car either. People soon gathered and two others tried to make a rescue but to no avail. When the emergency services were on the scene it was too late; a police diver eventually brought the driver's body to the surface about forty minutes after the first phone call and it was only then that a tentative identification was made, confirmed soon afterwards by a trace of the vehicle's number plate. Anik Anwar was confirmed dead at the scene of the accident and his body was taken to the Peterborough Mortuary.

What a terrible, terrible day for Junaid and his family. Sergeant Armstrong clearly knew Junaid well enough to be able sit quietly with his arm over his shoulder. Junaid continued to sob, sometimes trembling with the shock of it all. I moved to sit the other side, but I said nothing other than to let him know that I was there. We all sat quietly for a while, letting Junaid reach some sense of calm.

It was the Sergeant who spoke first. "Junaid, I'm sure you understand how important it is for us to get the main facts clear just as soon as possible." A barely perceptible movement from Junaid and Sergeant went on, "I gather that when you received the bad news this morning about your father's death, Anik went very quiet and then went out?" – another nod from Junaid – "You're not really familiar with his friends in any details, no phone numbers etc?" -another nod- "Now I don't want to cause any offence but does Anik drink, alcoholic, I mean?"

Junaid spoke at this. "I never drink and as far as I know nor does, nor did Anik. It would have been against his whole upbringing."

Sergeant Armstrong continued. "At this moment we have no reason to suppose he changed his habits of a lifetime. There will be some blood analysis to check for any substances, you know that of course."

"Will there have to be an autopsy?"

"Junaid, I know your background and fully appreciate your worries about any kind of autopsy. The decision isn't mine, but the coroner will be as sensitive as possible when coming to a decision. He will want our analysis of the eye-witness statements very soon. We hope to find somebody who may have spoken to him earlier in the day."

I was very reluctant to interrupt these questions, but it seemed important to me. "Junaid, so sorry to interfere, but does Sergeant Armstrong know about the row yesterday between Anik and your other brother, Kabir?"

"No, I haven't mentioned it.

"I think you had better just give a short account."

"I was out, so didn't witness the actual phone call. Kabir telephoned and spoke to Anik. All Anik said to me was that they argued and that Kabir told him that he wouldn't be home this summer. Later I sent a text to Kabir and his answer was more detailed. He would be staying at the home of his friend's family. Stephen always worked for his father during holidays and a family friend was offering work to Kabir. They would be able to go back to Newcastle at weekends and meet up with other friends not going home. I think Stephen is Christian and I know this upset Anik and along with news that he would not be home caused a big argument."

"Thank you, Junaid, that was quite clear. Let me summarize – Anik is unhappy about Kabir's friend, angry and resentful that he was not coming back here all summer, shocked about his father's unexpected death and very distressed that he wouldn't be able to get to the funeral that he knew from his upbringing he ought to attend. Is that a fair understanding Junaid?"

"Very clear."

"Junaid, as I said earlier, decisions rest with the coroner but he will be guided considerably by our report, which will also include a preliminary examination of the vehicle Anik was driving. At present, much of the evidence is beginning to point to suicide. How do you feel about that possibility Junaid?"

"Obviously, it will have been a tragedy, but the policeman in me sees the logic behind your thinking."

I found it curious, as a sympathetic bystander to all of this, how Junaid seemed to be able to appear, an obviously and understandably distressed relative on the one hand, while at the same time, managing to be a reasonably thoughtful policeman.

The Sergeant spoke up again. "I think we can leave you now Junaid if you're all right with that. Do you want us to give you a lift Mr Warnock or shall you stay awhile?"

"I'll be happy to stay for a bit unless you want to be alone Junaid. I can get a taxi very easily, so you don't have to worry about providing me with a lift Sergeant but thank you anyway."

The police left having promised to contact Junaid just as soon as they had anything of importance to tell him, especially the views of the Coroner. Junaid sat quietly as I did, a pause before anymore conversation seemed very desirable. It was Junaid who broke the silence first.

"I ought to ring Kabir, but I don't know how to break the news. Can't imagine how he is going to react."

"What about yesterday when you told him about your father's death?"

"Actually, fairly restrained. I suppose he was less close to our father than Anik and me. He was a bit lost for words and that is unusual for Kabir. I expect he will react very badly about Anik's death, if only because their last conversation was obviously unpleasant, won't be easy for him to forget that. I had better telephone now, do you mind staying while I do that?"

"No, you go ahead."

"I was pleased that Junaid went into another room, I didn't want to hear the details of this call too closely."

I began to hear voices, so I gathered Junaid had got through. I took my mobile out and checked emails and texts. Junaid didn't have to raise his voice, so I assumed the call was going a little better than anticipated. Quite shortly he came back through.

"I think Kabir was just stunned and he certainly didn't know what to say. He made no mention about his argument with Anik. He asked me to let him know about the funeral."

"Junaid, now you have told Kabir there are two people I would like to speak to about the bad news you have received in the last two days, Daniel Harrison and Mrs Bhatt and she will let Sanjay know who will certainly be upset on your behalf. I wouldn't be surprised if Mrs Bhatt doesn't want to help you, she won't take over, but she will provide you with some helpful organisational skills."

"Yes please , Monty. Give them both a call."

Daniel wasn't in so all I could do was to leave a message, rather difficult, given the nature of Junaid's tragic news. Mrs Bhatt was easier as she was most straightforward. She sent a message offering her sympathy and said she would be round at the usual time with lunch. Having only managed to leave just a message for Daniel I suggested to Junaid that I would ring Mavis as she might know where Daniel was and be able to speak to him. I went through to the kitchen for this call.

Now Mavis was most upset, I think she shed a few tears. She knew that Daniel would want to know and want to offer help in any way possible. She expected him to contact her late that evening so she would find out if he had picked up on my message. Meanwhile she was going to ring her sister. I was pleased to hear that, because my impression was that they harmonised with each other so well. Muriel would know exactly what to say. Before Mavis rang off, I broached another matter, Anik's funeral. I really felt that I ought to attend but didn't know when it was to be, nor did I know whether it was something I should do. The additional problem was that it could clash with the Westminster concert. Mavis agreed with me that it would be kind if I attended and she was sure people would understand my missing the Westminster event. She would mention it to Daniel.

I was beginning to think that it was probably time for me to go and perhaps Junaid needed some quiet time alone, but such time would have to wait as someone was at the front door. One look from Junaid and I got up to answer and to my astonishment I found Sanjay standing there.

"Goodness Sanjay, how did you get here?"

"On my bike, managed without lights. Just had to come over, Junaid was so good to me and Kieran." He slipped past me and through to where Junaid was sitting.

"Oh, Junaid I'm so sorry, can't believe how horrible it all is."

Junaid put an arm round his shoulder. It was as if Sanjay had received the bad news and Junaid was offering the sympathy. There was clearly a warmth of understanding and I thought it would do Junaid good if Sanjay stayed for a while. "You're a good lad to come round like this Sanjay. As you said it is horrible but one thing my father used to say, and I heard others say the same: bad things just happen. Don't try blaming. I look to Allah for guidance and I'm sure Monty seeks that from the Lord Jesus."

I looked at them both and knew they would be all right for a while. They would mutually support each other. I went into the other room and called a taxi. With a quiet goodbye and a promise to be in touch I went out front and waited for my taxi.

33. A COMMUNITY COMES TOGETHER

Saturday morning found me feeling very disorientated, it's the effect of knowing that friends are having to cope with bad news. It always makes me feel guilty, uncomfortable that I am not doing anything to help, even though I really know that there is probably nothing I can do. I remembered then that Mrs Bhatt would be calling on Junaid and I was sure she would bring real practical help to the situation and if she got involved with the funeral arrangements, she would understand what was required. Sanjay would be old enough to lend some help and young enough not to worry if he were occasionally in the way, that adolescent exuberance that so many teen-agers have for a while. He would also be a great friend, along with Kieran, for Kabir when he came down from Newcastle. I was thinking about all of this when the front doorbell rang, and I found Mavis standing there. She seemed enthusiastic with my offer of coffee and I wondered if she had had any breakfast. I didn't wait for an answer, just put some toast on and got the butter out and two different pots of WI jam which I had bought from a market stall a while back. Clearly, she hadn't eaten anything and very soon refills of coffee were being placed before her.

"This is kind of you Monty, most welcome; you've read my mind, I think. I haven't heard from Daniel yet, but I have my mobile with me and ready. I had a long chat with Muriel last night who was obviously most upset to hear about Junaid's family situation. If you need to decide about the funeral or going to London, then I think it must be the funeral."

"I'm glad you've said that because that's the conclusion I came to. Another peal from the front doorbell and there stood Mrs Bhatt. She was happy to come in but didn't need any refreshment. I introduced her to Mavis as they had not met before.

"I've been round to Junaid, a bit early I know, because Sanjay didn't come home last night so I took him some clothes. I wasn't surprised, I knew he hadn't any lights on his bike and he can curl up anywhere and sleep. They were both eating some breakfast when I arrived. Junaid was perhaps a little embarrassed, but I put his mind at rest. The Sergeant had telephoned Junaid to say suicide is certain to be the outcome. He can arrange the funeral for Tuesday, and I've told him to leave catering to me and friends, and we can get hold of small community hall to use."

"Mrs Bhatt, can I call you a treasure? I'm sure Junaid will be very relieved when he hears about what you can organise. Your friends are also to be called treasures."

Just then Muriel's mobile came to life, so she took it to the other end of my large downstairs room and as she looked up, she mouthed the name Daniel to me.

"Now, Mrs Bhatt, what about costs? Can his friends help in anyway? I know that Junaid hasn't a lot of ready money because that was one of the troubles for both him and Anik, that they wouldn't be able to go to their father's funeral."

"You don't have to worry about money Mr Warnock. We a strong community and the boys well known, and their father."

"Thank you for that, kindly and very reassuring. I shall come to the funeral, and I expect some of Junaid's colleagues, those who knew both the brothers, will come. Daniel, who is talking to Mavis at this moment, may well want to be there."

"You will all be very welcome, and I expect it won't be too strongly traditional, things have moved on. There will be a burial though. It may last into the afternoon."

"I understand. Here's Mavis now, she probably knows what Daniel will want to do."

"I think I heard the last sentence or two of what you have been saying. As you know, Daniel's contacts with the local police are still strong so he has already spoken with Sergeant Armstrong, Daniel rang very early this morning. He has also spoken to Ken and I suspect they are both very relieved to hear that the verdict as to the cause of Anik's death is to be suicide, incredibly sad though it was. Daniel expects to be here Monday evening so that he can attend the funeral."

"Mrs Bhatt, you may not know about Ken, he is someone Daniel knows well in London, we know him as well because he is the employer of Mavis's sister, Muriel. I doubt he'll be at the funeral. I don't know anyone else who would wish to go to the funeral. In any case, we'll keep in close touch Mrs Bhatt. By the way, please thank Sanjay for staying with Junaid, that was amazingly thoughtful of him. And thank you Mrs Bhatt for what you are doing and please ask if any help is required from - how can I put it – outside your resources."

"I'll be away Mr Warnock; everything will be good.

"I'll make you some fresh toast Mavis and we both need more coffee." As she didn't refuse, I knew she must be hungry. "Did Daniel have any more news?"

"No, nothing. He and Ken are more than relieved that this hadn't any connection with other troubles and it certainly seems as if Sergeant Armstrong is confident about all his enquiries."

I put the fresh toast down, gave Mavis another plate and poured out coffee for both of us. "I've never been to a Muslim funeral, so I had better make some discreet enquiries, correct clothes, what to do etc. It can be so easy to offend, and I should hate to do that. The only thing that I do know is that family funerals can last a long time. I'll ring the undertakers who arranged for Ernie Brownley's funeral as I expect they'll know. Perhaps better if I call round there."

"I know you wouldn't have minded, but I am glad that you haven't got to miss the Palace of Westminster event on Wednesday, if only because it is the first opportunity we've had to hear Genevievre sing. I'll be going now, things to do and I must let Muriel know that I have heard from Daniel. You know that she is being quite 'Mother Hen' about Daniel and me. I think she would like the next twenty, perhaps thirty years to run past her at high speed; wants to see the highlights before they have even occurred! By the way, Daniel & I want to hold a small engagement party but don't know when or where. Muriel will want to have a lot to do with arrangements."

"Perhaps you need to think of two parties, one in London and perhaps a smaller one here for your local friends. Of course, I shall attend both! Just joking. Might it have to be after the Italian holiday?"

"You've quickly summarized all the little difficulties that we've envisaged. Most likely after the visit to Italy. It doesn't have to be a huge, lavish affair as we're thinking of getting married in the Autumn. One solution is for an engagement party in London and a wedding here in Peterborough, perhaps at St Petrie's. I wonder when Fr Blakeston last conducted a marriage?"

"Doesn't matter; he will conduct your service with love, holiness and friendship."

And on that trinity of thought, Mavis beamed, and went on her way.

The weekend before Anik's funeral was a busy time for many people. Junaid had to pull himself together somewhat and check with the undertakers regarding the funeral arrangements, that they would be able to organise a Muslim burial. Junaid had already followed their advice about registering the death and ensuring that the funeral could go ahead as hoped on the Tuesday. He was in touch with Mrs Bhatt several times until in the end she assured him that everything would be organised exactly as it should be, and that many of those involved had remembered his father well, had known the boys as they grew up and saw it as their duty to them as a family and to the wider community to ensure everything was as it should be. I suspect Mrs Bhatt had to shoo him away as one might a small child who couldn't get out of the way. Mrs Bhatt was a lady of stern love.

Sanjay and Kieran both went to the station on Sunday to meet Kabir off the Newcastle train, in fact it was the London train, as he had changed at Kings Cross. Kabir had been quite a hit with both lads and despite the sadness of the circumstances they were still delighted to be able to welcome Kabir back to Peterborough; they considered him a friend. With Mrs Bhatt's permission, I had given Sanjay some money for taxis and minor refreshments as I thought this would enable them to help in a more grown up way.

I was at Junaid's when the three arrived back from the station and the welcome Junaid gave his younger brother was most moving. It wasn't tearful but you could sense that they both understood how each felt about this family tragedy, their father and brother both taken within a couple of days of each other. They were, I thought, totally sensitive to their mutual anguish and understood the need to support each other. Conversation didn't start until Kabir expressed his sadness for Junaid, that he had had to receive the final and tragic news from the police on his own. Junaid continued to embrace him but explained that I had arrived at the request of the police very soon after they had arrived.

Whatever the circumstances, teenage thinking is often never far from the state of their stomachs and Sanjay started to regale them with details of the food that his mum and friends were preparing for Tuesday. I think Kabir and Junaid both saw the funny side of this, and Junaid went on to tell Sanjay how appreciative they both were for all that she and her friends were doing; they simply would not have known where to start. It suddenly made me realise just how strong this community was, that they could all come together to arrange such a complicated family event in such a short time. It was highly likely that several people had had to change, postpone, even cancel, various planned activities, it reflected a beautiful community warmth. It caused me to remember the rather lonely event, which was my mother's funeral, and to feel quietly pleased that Ernie's funeral had received some genuine community love.

34. ANIK ANWAR LAID TO REST

The funeral for Anik Anwar started at ten o'clock on Tuesday but for Junaid and Kabir it had started on the Monday afternoon as they together with another friend of Anik, had gone to the undertakers to perform what I later discovered is known as Ghusl, a ritualistic washing of the body, quite a lengthy ceremony. After this was completed Anik was, I believe, dressed, and then wrapped in three white sheets, the Kafan; ropes were used to secure the Kafan to the body. These ceremonies complete, Anik could be left with the undertakers to be brought to the Mosque the following morning.

Tuesday was warm, not over sunny and this was ideal as the funeral, led by the Imam, was to take place outside in what could be described as a small courtyard. I had asked about what to wear and was assured that black mourning clothes were not necessary, just neat tidy clothes and nothing in bright colours. For me that meant a grey suit, a white shirt, and a plain blue tie. Those already there were standing in rows, men and women separately. I could see Daniel near the back, so I joined him. I couldn't see Mavis so I assumed that she had chosen to stay away, perhaps she knew that men and women would be separate, and she wouldn't know anyone to stand with. Quite close was Kieran, who was with his father, although I couldn't be sure. Sanjay, being Muslim, was nearer the front. We stood quietly waiting for the service to commence. I didn't know what to expect but as proceedings got underway it was clear that the format was a selection of prayers and readings from the Quran and it was carried out in restrained voices and I was not aware of any loud crying. When it was obvious that the service had ended, I was surprised to discover that it was already after eleven o'clock. There was a silence then and at some given signal Junaid, Kabir and four others stepped forward, lifted Anik's body to their shoulders and walked towards the hearse which had been parked a little distance away and out of immediate sight. Later it was explained to me that had the grave been within reasonable walking distance they would have carried Anik all the way.

When everyone who was attending the burial had gathered, Anik's body was lifted from the hearse. Different people did the lifting, certainly more people involved, but Junaid, Kabir and the four others took over at the graveside and it was those six who lowered Anik's body into the grave. Beside the grave small piles of wood and stone and these were placed on top of the body before any earth was to be added. Junaid threw several handfuls of soil into the grave as did Kabir followed by the other pall bearers. After they had finished, they stood back and others from the crowd of mourners also threw in handfuls of soil. Junaid nodded slightly in our direction to indicate that we could join in this simple ceremony. It seemed that the funeral was now ended, and it was at this point that I noticed that there were far fewer women in attendance. Maybe this was customary, but I also thought that Mrs Bhatt and her group of helpers would be wanting to return early to the community centre to help organise the food.

I walked with Daniel to his car to drive to the hall. He noticed one of Junaid's colleagues looking a little lost so gave him a lift. It took some time for everyone to depart the cemetery and it was near to one o'clock by the time all had got to the hall. The crowd had reduced somewhat so presumably some people opted out at this point; probably had to return to work. I remained mostly quiet throughout this time, ate a few pieces of the food that Mrs Bhatt and friends had prepared, there was iced tea to drink. I was able to say something appropriate to Mrs Bhatt regarding all her work, and she seemed to be pleased with this acknowledgement.

Sanjay and Kieran stayed close together and this helped Kieran. I spoke briefly to his father as he looked a little lost. Time passed and I saw Daniel heading my way to offer me a lift. When we got back to my place, he didn't come in and was off to meet up with Mavis as she would want to know that the funeral had gone according to plan – been successful doesn't seem the right expression.

The morning post was waiting for me and I noticed an envelope marked 'Trumpingtons'. I thought I knew what that would be, and I wasn't wrong. A formal account sheet with calculation enclosing a cheque for the net amount of £62700. There was just time for me to call a taxi and get to the bank for what one may refer to as a 'finale' – pay in the cheque.

35. THE MEMBERS' DINING ROOM

Wednesday morning found five of us on a mid-morning train bound for Kings Cross. At the end of the day we would be meeting for the evening event at the Palace of Westminster but before then we were going in different directions. I wasn't sure how the Dean and Lucinda were spending the day, perhaps something rather ecclesiastical, Daniel and Mavis were spending most of the day with Muriel and I was off to Trumpingtons to inspect another 'Hound'! Daniel and I described some of the funeral ceremony to the others. The Dean and his wife seemed most interested; Mavis explained that she had thought to attend but then decided that as she almost certainly wouldn't know any of the other women attending, it would perhaps be easier not to attend; I understood her difficulty.

It is never easy to think of funerals in good terms but Daniel & I both felt that Junaid and Kabir had achieved a dignified and moving ceremony for their brother's funeral. We also felt that the community had really come together and shown great support for the two brothers who were the only members of the immediate family able to attend.

Quiet, newspapers and magazines took over our group as we travelled on to London and it didn't seem long before we were rattling into Kings Cross. Two taxis completed our journey arrangements: The Dean and Lucinda, to wherever, and Daniel, Mavis, and me, off to Trumpingtons via Leopold Mansions. I was meeting with Henry at the auction house to see the old and tatty copy of the Hound of the Baskervilles'. I found Henry ready and waiting, together with some coffee.

"Well this is the copy." Henry passed over a wonderfully scruffy copy but knowing what Henry and his team of restorers would be able to achieve I had no hesitation in giving this purchase my approval. I had brought with me the facsimile copy of the 'fake' dustjacket, so I was keen to marry the two.

"This is going to be wonderful, I'm so pleased to have a replacement copy, no matter the condition. What are you going to have to do and is it a complicated piece of work?"

"No, not especially. Tightening the stitching of the binding is relatively straightforward, the boards will be transformed with little more than a good clean and a limited amount of restoration to parts of the gilt design. We have some identical paper and some good images of the two sides to the main title page. We won't attempt to set up a period printing block for the lettering of the missing page, but rather transfer a digital image to the period paper. You're off to Italy soon I believe, and we'll have this looking beautifully finished by the time of your return.

"I'm delighted and most impressed, Henry. I think the finished book is going to look rather smart. It won't be worth £70000 but it will make an impressive reminder, particularly with this dust jacket. We're looking forward to going to Italy, but I'll also be looking forward to returning to this piece of history.

Can I leave the dustjacket with you now, so it can stay with its 'new friend'? Do I need to settle up with the accounts department yet?"

"No, no, plenty of time for that. Are you spending the day here?

"Not this time. Sounds impressive to say, but with others, I have a ticket for an event in The Members' Dining Room, at the House of Commons. There's a presentation about youngsters caught up as refugees in the Middle East and as part of the event there are some musical interludes. One is being given by the French Opera Singer, Genevievre Renoir, she married the MP Jon Mostang recently and as we're all loosely acquainted, Jon sent a group of us tickets for the event."

"I heard something about that wedding, got held up at gun point in Paris."

"You heard correctly, but it all turned out to be something of a false alarm."

We sat for a while, finishing the pot of coffee; Henry reminisced about some of his restoration work and I could have listened for hours. Mischievously, I should like to ask him if he had had any disasters. I didn't want to drag myself away from Henry's memories, but I really had to be on my way. I thanked him for what he was doing, expressing pleasure in seeing the book and looking forward to the finished product. I was able to obtain a taxi with ease and was soon at Leopold Mansions, meeting up with Mavis and

Muriel. Glass of wine in hand, I told them about the latest book restoration on my behalf which would enable me to make use of the facsimile dust-jacket and end up with a permanent reminder of the day I found the signed copy of 'The Hound of the Baskervilles'. Mavis and Muriel both thought it was a nice bit of timing that I would be able to collect the finished book on returning from Italy; a rounding off to a very notable chapter in my life.

The afternoon passed quietly, one or perhaps two more glasses of wine and something cold to eat latish afternoon. Muriel was promising something hot by way of supper when we returned from the Westminster event. Ken was organising our getting there by way of the Humber with Tony at the wheel. Daniel was meeting us there as he was 'loosely' attached to the security organisation. The plan was for Tony to go and pick up the Dean and Lucinda, then back to Leopold Mansions for a sherry or coffee. I was rather pleased we were going as a group; I wouldn't have to worry about finding the correct entrance and being organised for what I suspected might be a considerable amount of red tape. I was sure Ken would be up for all that and I could follow in everybody's wake.

It was pleasantly quiet so I would take advantage of that, have a bath, don the dinner suit, including a very long fiddle with cuff-links and bow-tie, then find a copy of The Times and exercise the brain with a few of the day's puzzles. I had completed the sudoku grids, the easier of the cryptic crossword puzzles and was just pondering the harder one when

Ken arrived. Malts also arrived and we relaxed immediately. "Monty, if you don't mind my asking, how long did you spend weaving your bowtie?"

"Too long and until I couldn't hold my arms up any longer."

"Yes, it shows. Stroll across here for a moment and I'll do a little 'unpicking'"

True to his word and at the most, five minutes later, Ken had my bowtie in perfect order. Even better, neither Mavis nor Muriel were present to witness this moment of re-dressing!

"Thank you, Ken." We clinked our topped-up glasses.

The evening was a truly splendid and memorable occasion; I did as I had already decided, just followed everybody else until I arrived at a seat, a wonderfully comfortable one, I might add. There was no waiting around because there was so much to look at in this architectural gem of a room: wall coverings, doorways, panelling, furnishings – all simply perfect, a feast for any eyes.

A hush was brought about by the arrival on the platform of Jon Mostang. He was suitably brief, alluding to his Iranian background, his British upbringing, and his recent marriage to the very lovely Parisian Soprano, Genevievre Renoir. He felt that this trio of circumstances qualified him to bring together interested parties to raise awareness of what he described as a terrible blight on the modern world – young people as refugees. He didn't for one moment suggest that young people in Iran were in a unique situation in comparison with other countries, but it was where he hoped to make his start, to spread out worldwide from the geographic origins of his own birth, and if he was honest, fortuitous circumstances which would enable him grow a cause. It wasn't until he had started, did I realise how personal he was making this evening. It was while I was reflecting on the individual nature of this cause that he introduced the evening's first piece of music: the particularly English composition, Ralph Vaughan Williams'. 'The Lark Ascending' performed by two recent graduates of the Royal Academy of Music, Suzanna Ravenscroft, Violin and Edward McLeish, Piano.

Never easy expressing music in the written word and perhaps this piece required a more natural environment. I was more familiar with the orchestral version but for Piano and Violin was how it was first composed and performed. It was a delight to listen to this performance and not difficult I would have thought for anyone to visualise the gentle agility of the lark as expressed by the violin. The audience showed genuine appreciation and while the applause lasted, I gazed around once more. Just as Jon Mostang appeared to introduce his first speaker, I was somewhat surprised to see the Lincolnshire MP, Nat Lawton, standing by one of the doorways. Perhaps my surprise was because I didn't associate him with this kind of event. It was while I was thinking about this, I realized that not only had our speaker started but that he was one of the UK's former Prime Ministers; at least he was at home in these surroundings. A man of wide experience, he was certainly well qualified to speak on this international issue, an issue which had to be seen both in the appalling statistics involved, the devastating numbers of young people being deprived of their futures, and also in terms of each individual, each set of talents deprived of any chance to be developed. He was an absorbing speaker and it seemed no time at all before he was taking on the task of introducing the next young performers: the recently celebrated Parisian Soprano, Genevievre Renoir, who, accompanied by her younger brother, Jean, were to perform Debussy's Clair de Lune. In contrast with the first solo of the evening, this was a much shorter work, but no less beautiful.

Without doubt, a talented pair and it was lovely to hear how sensitively Jean accompanied his older sister. They rightly deserved their applause and Jon appeared in time to give his wife a suitable bouquet of flowers. They didn't leave the stage, stood perhaps more to one side and Genevievre indicated with the slightest of hand gesture that her brother would perform an encore. The bravura of youth nearly upstaged his older sister not to mention the composer, Debussy, because young Jean swept into a short but highly original set of variations on the song his sister had just performed. However, she applauded just as enthusiastically as anybody, greeted her brother with a kiss and they both departed the stage, leaving Jon to introduce the next speaker.

Like Jon Mostang, the next speaker had an obviously international background but spoke impeccable English with only the merest hint of an accent that would never be easy to place. He was able to draw on wide experience from working 'on the ground' with refugees, sharing their misery and daily deprivations to the public face of international agitation for action. His speaking from the daily experience of young refugees, certainly harrowing to listen to but also riveting in terms of disturbing the consciences of those for whom such experiences were totally remote. He was a stirring speaker and one's attention didn't stray so it was only after he had finished that I looked round and noticed that Nat Lawton was still propping up the 'gothic' doorframe but had been joined by a young lookalike, his son, Ben, I presumed.

The final musical performance of the evening was in total contrast with the previous performances. A young man, slightly hesitant in manner, walked onto the platform. He was to play the trombone, unaccompanied. He explained that he was from Tehran but was now studying in Paris. He was a classical trombonist by study and training but in recent months he had begun to take an interest in traditional folk music of Iran. He had been transcribing some of the folk songs for solo performance on the trombone. With a touch of humour, he explained his solo playing required one accompaniment, a rhythm player using a 'daf', a framed skin drum, about half a metre in diameter, this could provide very complex rhythms as background accompaniment to his more angular Trombone solos. He said no more and his 'daf' player arrived. The trombonist just played, strange bass register melodies, not particularly agile, agility was left to the daf performer. There was a satisfying eeriness to each piece or movement and from the concluding applause I think they were very well received. That they were unusual pieces of music went without saying.

What was not unusual was what followed, a monetary appeal! I must confess to not paying the closest attention to this. I knew that there were some corporate representatives in the audience who could no doubt reach deeply into company coffers. I was not in that position, but I placed my envelope containing a cheque and a note explaining that they could contact me if they wished it to be enhanced by gift aid. We left as we arrived, a slow precession with me bringing up the rear. Tony didn't keep us waiting and we were soon back at Leopold Mansions for Muriel's serving of a late hot supper. Ken opened two very acceptable bottles and the evening concluded with warmth surrounding us all. Mavis set a ball rolling by asking what everyone thought of the evening.

"Well, I'm making the most of it as I don't expect another such evening to come my way."

"You never know," said Jon.

The Dean struck a sombre note, never-the-less, absolutely correct. "Mankind hasn't travelled very far when you consider how basic is the notion of looking after one's neighbour."

"I'm afraid you're right, Dean," said Ken "Much of my work involves trying to uplift the downtrodden and, sad to say, the need never lessens. Ignoring the neighbour is another form of bullying, whether it be one against one or nation against nation."

"Expressed in those terms it makes the United Nations ever more important when it comes to solving some of the problems we heard about earlier, all credit to you Jon." Muriel was being very effusive, how lovely; she could be relied upon for the truthfulness of her emotions.

"Hitting a different note, pardon the pun, did others enjoy the trombone playing as much as me. I found it a very haunting experience which I won't forget in a hurry, just so different."

"I don't know him, but know of him, if you follow me. I've heard that his teachers speak very highly of him." That was all Genevievre could tell us.

"Talking of speaking highly," said Lucinda. "Your brother, Jean, is very courageous to suddenly play a set of variations based on Debussy; very bold."

"Where is he, by the way, not able to join us?"

No, sorry, Monty, he needed to get back to his accommodation, didn't want to be late, but I'll send a text of your comment Lucinda, he'll be very 'chuffed' - is that the right word?"

I gave Genevievre a little round of applause.

"Lucinda, talking of accommodation, we should be heading towards ours I think."

A feeling of 'end of evening' came upon us, and being the oldest, I was looking forward to my bed and, I suspect if they were honest, so were most of them.

Muriel had a lovely and unhurried breakfast ready for us the following morning. We were meeting at Kings Cross just before lunch, having booked a non-stop connection to Peterborough. Over the next week or so I needed to get all my book business in a position so I could leave it unattended, so to speak, while we were in Italy; didn't want to try and answer any queries at distance. I was also anxious to make some visits to good neighbours and friends and I wanted to make sure that Junaid was feeling much better now. I hoped he would be seeing Kabir for some of the long summer vacation but that was outside my influence. I also wanted to have a good chat with Fr Blakeston, wondering whether I could squeeze a few of his thoughts about the forthcoming Autumn wedding at which I knew he would be officiating. Unusually for me, my way of suggesting something of a gossip, but no doubt the foxy Fr Blakeston would out-fox me as far as that was concerned and without my even noticing.

36. MONTY'S EXTRA SLEEP AND PLENTY OF PROSECCO!

As I don't much care for air travel, especially when having been up since 3.00am for the two hour taxi run down to Gatwick, I'll say little about the airport except that the architects and planners must have assumed a very high level of fitness given the distances one was expected to be able to walk. Fortunately, Sir Arthur Conan Doyle's signed masterpiece had enabled us to book club-class with British Airways, so that gave us access to a very elegant 'designer-chrome-glass' lounge for drinks, food, newspapers, magazines, not forgetting the wide selection of wines which were of little appeal to us at 6.00am, but plenty of people were sitting in front of well-filled large glasses. I just sat quietly with coffee and an early edition of the Times.

Handing over luggage and getting through (pure luck that I wasn't laden with contraband) had taken all my spare energy. To my surprise Muriel seemed well at home in all the airport hustle and bustle but Mavis reminded me that Muriel accompanied her boss on some overseas trips, obviously more than a housekeeper at his London flat. She had also advised Mavis on which lotions and potions that could be in hand luggage. Time passed quickly and soon we were trekking to some distant gate. Fortunately, there being no delays, and helped no doubt by a couple of small bottles of wine and some welcome sleep, our descent for Verona Airport had started.

Unlike Gatwick, Verona Airport was very modest in size and it didn't take long for us to collect luggage and get outside to meet a taxi driver, a fortunate consequence of Mavis having a very strong aversion to coach travel, so I had booked a taxi via an arrangement with the reception staff at The King's Tower, Gardone. For a little icing on the cake of this last leg of the journey, the taxi turned out to be a brand-new Mercedes, air-conditioned to a perfect degree. I snoozed all the way, opening an eye for the occasional glimpse of a lake, until Mavis gave me something of a shove as we drew up at the smart entrance way to The King's Tower.

We were soon to be found relaxing in a magnificent period lounge sipping chilled Prosecco while waiting to check in. Our arrival had coincided with a couple of larger parties and all the reception staff were occupied. We gazed about at the painted ceilings, wall paintings, rich décor, and a glorious view across the lake, until we were unexpectedly joined by a very elegant member of staff.

"Mr Warnock and party? I'm Angelini and here to welcome you and show you to your rooms. First, I explain slight confusion of accommodation as we have not two rooms close as requested. We like to offer upgrade to one of hotel suites, this has two large bedrooms with connecting door, two bathrooms, small room for belongings and long furnished balcony and patio. Of course, no difference in cost, we go there yes, and finish checking in then."

"That sounds absolutely lovely." That was Mavis's enthusiastic comment with Muriel's smiling agreement.

One floor up in the lift and we were soon there. By my reckoning we had ended up just above where we had been sitting in the lounge. While we looked around the suite and patio, two porters arrived with all our luggage and another brought in the glasses and ice bucket with the bottle which had been with us in the lounge. I was just quick enough to say thanks and give one of the porter guys a ten euro note. I don't travel much these days but as I dislike carrying heavy cases, I always have a small supply of bank notes to hand; too embarrassing to be scrambling to find some small change and often failing.

All Angelini needed to do was to see that we were happy with this change of rooms, our faces made that obvious, gather up our passports and leave us with the prosecco and with the promise of another bottle to follow, which it did, accompanied by some nibbles. We sat out on the patio for a while until Muriel yawned and announced her intention to have a sleep before any other activity, not surprising given how early we had been up that morning.

"While you do that, Monty and I will go for a little look round, sit in the shade for a while, perhaps drink some tea and watch the Lake 'go by'. Monty more or less slept for the entire journey, so he won't be tired, and I fancy stretching my legs for a bit."

We did all of those and wandered round the gardens, watched various ferries come and go - some were surprisingly large. We found a group of trees which had been pruned over many decades to act as giant umbrellas. Here we indulged in some Italian ice-cream. We walked towards the low lake-side wall and peered down into the water. There were several surprisingly large fish swimming about. Two or three families of ducks paddled by and I wondered how many ducklings had been 'mislaid' by inefficient mothers! Some hardy swimmers were out a fair distance, very hardy as far as I was concerned, as I imagined the lake water was considerably colder than the pool. There was quite a crowd of holiday makers around the pool but not so many as to make one feel the hotel to be over busy.

There was an air of quiet peacefulness, much as I expected, and we were happy to sit in silence for a while. When we went back up to our rooms, we found Muriel just stirring. Another glass of prosecco, a bit more unpacking and then we got ready for our first meal. It was no doubt superb, and certainly most elegantly served. However, the rigours of the journey, not forgetting the early start, caught up with me, so after a couple of courses and the 'nursing' of some more wine, I had the ladies excuse me and went off to my bed. They gave me something of a pitying look, 'the poor old boy's not up to it' kind of look, said they didn't mind and immediately poured themselves more wine. They looked well settled and I never heard more of them that night.

Not unexpectedly, I was wide awake by 6.00am. I got up and thought I would see if anywhere could provide coffee. I slipped a scribbled note under our adjoining door telling of my coffee hunt and promising to be back in time for breakfast. A brisk run down the stairs and I wandered off through the village and saw some preparation going on in the main square for the 'Opera Festival' which I had seen advertised for some time soon. Tickets for that would be good, must ask when I get back, so made a mental note. Sitting at some nearby café tables I didn't wait long before I was being offered coffee. Managing to successfully order a large Americano with hot milk and water I sat back and enjoyed the view.

I booted up my phone, thinking I would catch up with the news. Nothing surprising happening, just much of the usual, but an additional item from a security spokesman for the Government indicating a slightly raised security level to do with Middle Eastern terrorism – nothing new really. I wasn't the only early bird in need of coffee, two suited guys sitting nearby, looked like businessmen, unusually early to be about, I thought, and wondered what business they represented.

I strolled back slowly. The King's Tower was waking up for sure and a member of the reception staff called me over.

"Oh, Mr Warnock, letter here left for you."

"A letter, who knows about me? By hand I see, I expect the tour operator is leaving some information."

As I stood in the lift, I tore it open to find, to my astonishment, three tickets for the Opera Festival which I has seen advertised. Nothing with them to say who had sent them and no other details. Entering my room, I found Mavis and Muriel holding court, having obviously unlocked the connecting door, controlled from their side; how very correct! Were they displaying a little impatience?

"Before you speak, I'm on time and have collected our post, look!" They were as amazed as I was.

"We have an unknown benefactor, how very Charles Dickens," was Mavis's romantic explanation.

Muriel was again more down to earth. "That'll be a great night then, and have you noticed that these tickets are marked VIP?"

Mavis grabbed them back. "She's right, VIP!"

I hadn't noticed the exclusive nature of the tickets and it made the circumstances seem even more odd that we didn't know who had sent them. There was no price on them, so these were perhaps being given out free, just to the great and the good, we included! It made me feel suddenly very up-beat about this holiday and then rather down-beat, realising that I hadn't packed a dinner suit.

"Breakfast then?" Muriel jumped up with this more basic need in mind and off she went. Mavis and I followed.

"Mr Warnock and party?" asked a very superior waiter, absolutely, 'head-waiter' in his superior suit of Italian tailoring. He saw me nod acknowledgement, whereupon he led us out to a lakeside table with two sunshades to provide shelter from what was fast becoming a very warm morning. He took orders for coffee and tea which he passed to a young junior waiter, wished us well, hoped we would enjoy our breakfast and to call him personally if anything were not to our satisfaction. I was most impressed, indeed quite flabbergasted.

This must have shown on my face because Muriel spoke quite firmly. "What on earth is the matter, you look stunned Monty? Come on, let's get some breakfast started, sure to be some lovely choices here."

"I am stunned, how did he know us, I haven't seen him before? He must have been told to look out for us. I realise he is in charge but we're no different from any of the other two hundred or so guests milling about. Very odd, I feel."

"Well, perhaps just a bit odd, but my sister is right, let's get started."

About an hour later and feeling we wouldn't need to eat again until that night, we made our way back to our rooms to get ready for whatever we felt like doing. I noticed that the super-efficient service which seemed to be following us all round this hotel had included the coming and going of chambermaids. I pointed this out to my companions and that in our absence orchid plants and bowls of fruit had arrived. In view of this generosity I told them that I would be most' disappointed if when we returned in the afternoon, we didn't find chilled prosecco to keep us going until evening meal. They scoffed at me but although I pretended that I was joking I felt quite certain about my prophecy.

We spent a while sitting under trees near the pool and occasionally enjoying the sun but not for too long as it was late June and becoming rather hot. A little before lunch, found us in the centre of the village with two beers and a glass of chianti between us accompanied with olives and pieces of cheese pastry together with a large bowl of crisps. It was lovely to sit and just watch: obvious regulars coming and going, ferries arriving and departing, very much to a tight schedule because occasionally one waited a while before docking so that another could land some passengers who needed to change to the waiting ferry.

I'm always happy to study the changing scene but the two sisters went off to look at the local shops, very successfully too, given the number of smart designer bags they held between them on their return. Given the effect of the previous day's travel it was not surprising that the afternoon floated along in a giant bubble of snoozing, tea drinking with the occasional supplement of something a little stronger. As I predicted, on our return upstairs, we found bottles cooling and glasses to the ready in both rooms and a sense of contentment washed over us all.

37. DEFINITELY UPSTAGED

Going down to dinner on our second night we were met by a charming young lady. "Oh, Mr Warnock, our manager Giovanni Baptista, wonders if you and your party would join him for dinner? He will be so pleased and be assured all will be very informal and friendly. Look just follow me please and I can show you. You can have items off the menu you already thought about, or Giovanni make other suggestions.

We found ourselves being led through the main dining room, round a small partition and into a little alcove with a table set for five, and as we arrived Giovanni came through the glass doors from the lake. He left them open and a pleasant cooling breeze wafted in. I vaguely recognised him but couldn't place where I had seen him. He radiated a smile which put us at ease immediately; he was just charming. As we sat, he told us how thrilled he was to meet us, but he was cut short by another voice.

"Ah, Giovanni, am I late?"

"Andreas! Where have you come from?" I was so surprised and turned to Mavis. "Do you remember? He was at the auction and we met him afterwards when he explained that he had been bidding from another room on behalf of the 'winner', but he wouldn't tell us who."

"And that was me," said a quiet voice.

We all looked at Giovanni who stood there smiling away, positively beaming. I remembered then, I had seen his photograph on local television as they had covered the story of my finding the copy of 'The Hound of the Baskervilles', the dustjacket in pieces and all at the bottom of a box of various cheap secondhand books.

"So, when did you connect us with…...?"

"Later, later and I will explain everything, but first, some Prosecco which I believe is a favourite of yours," he said, smiling at Muriel. "We need to order some food, or will you just let me ask the staff to bring a selection of various courses and we help ourselves."

"Excellent, that will be just wonderful. " Muriel's first contribution to the evening and how very sensible.

In the best traditions, Giovanni just clapped his hands and trolleys laden with food were wheeled in. Somebody, very expert, poured some Prosecco and the rest of us chose from the trolleys with a smart guy standing at each to lend a skilled 'waiting' hand. It took little time before we were stuffing ourselves with a veritable feast and there wasn't a pause until Giovanni cleared his throat and started to speak.

"I have been a 'Sherlock Holmes' enthusiast for many years. As young man I spend year working in London, as waiter at Grantchester Hotel, close of Park Lane. I have read much, and Conan Doyle's stories came me when I was young, but I was reading them in Italian then. When in London I was working to better my English, I tried to read English Newspapers, very dull. It was then I tried Sherlock Holmes stories in English. Not easy, but I struggled on. Anyway, how do you say, to make a long story quick?"

"No, short," said Andreas.

"Ah, thank you Andreas. His English is wonderful because his Mother is English, and he spent long holidays there with his grandparents who live in London. Now they are very ancient though and he doesn't see them much but stayed there for the auction.

Back to my skill in English, soon as I could read short stories well, I started collecting early date copies, old bound collections of Strand Magazines, film material, old pictures, maps, information about Conan Doyle – anything that came my way. My first autographed book wasn't a Holmes item, but a Gerard story – a very broken old copy and the signature had been missed because it was at the back, after the last word. That got me begun and as I got money, I could buy more items, now I have hundreds, I show you later. Andreas was thrilled to go to the auction in London and I was pleased to ask him bid. He was unknown and money was not a problem. Keep bidding until you win, I told him."

"That was super fun," interrupted Andreas, "to bid and bid and know it was not my money! What could be more exciting?

"I feel a little awkward knowing you spent all that money, more this evening and now I think about it I suspect that the story about it being necessary to move us to better rooms when we arrived, well, that was just more of you."

"Well, I won't complain. Indeed, thank you so much, the rooms are beautiful." Another pertinent comment from Muriel and spoken with genuine feeling. I was really warming to her very straight forward style.

"Well, never mind all that, there is much still to eat, and you upset my chef if it is sent back. There are chilled and opened bottles as well.

"Don't worry, I'm sure Muriel would love one for later," I added, a bit facetiously, and was rewarded with a thump on the shoulder from Mavis.

"If you are worried about money side of it, don't, because I have a little work suggestion to put to you. More of that later, now, sweet trolleys, coffee and something a little special in a while."

I realised then that I was getting used to Giovanni's English. He had a very wide vocabulary but didn't bother with little words, prepositions, and conjunctives. The effect was charming.

We attacked the sweets and listened as Giovanni told us more of his 'Sherlock' obsession.

"Andreas, you take Mavis and Muriel, start looking at collection and I talk Monty for a moment." Turning to me as they began to leave, "Monty, I run a small group of people, a club, all interested in anything English. In a few days, my turn to host, provide entertainment and……"

"This is the work you mentioned?" So, what do you want me to do?"

"You agree good, good. I want you to talk them about anything, your story, hobby, finding book, collecting books. Talk is short, 45 minutes maybe? What you say?"

"Yes, OK." Giovanni didn't know but my answer was easy to give because I had given a similar talk to that which he wanted earlier in the year. "I can do that, I think. I might want to borrow a laptop." As it happened, I knew that one of my memory drives which I had with me, had on it all the material I needed.

"No problem, no problem, anything you want, yours, you ask just, OK?"

The prosecco was beginning to make our Giovanni rather genial.

"The women, we join the women."

"Yes indeed, and Andreas as well, do you think?"

Giovanni just smiled and we made our way to his apartment rooms; lovely rooms too and exquisitely furnished, expected really, given how well the hotel was furnished with so many period pieces. Giovanni's study doubled as library as well, with his Arthur Conan Doyle items in one cabinet with a glass-topped display table brought into service as well. The whole study exuded an Edwardian tone and feel; with several pieces of 'correct' furniture much of Giovanni's Sherlock Holmes collection should have felt well at home. I could have spent hours just looking at the books, following up inscriptions and little snippets of information which might yield results given some research. At a glance, I supposed most of the items were well under £50 in value, though not so their interest level. Obviously, any signed items were of much greater value. The item which had led to our being here was beautifully arranged in the glass topped table cabinet, most impressive. Time was getting on, we all had full stomachs and I could see my companions getting somewhat worn out. Any immediate thought of going to bed was dashed away with the arrival of a member of staff bearing a tray of exquisite liquor glasses, each containing a small quantity of a liquid of an attractive shade of yellow.

"Ah……"

But before Giovanni could get beyond so much as a preliminary 'noise', Muriel was already exclaiming with clear delight, "Oh, wonderful, Limoncello, Mavis, this is truly delicious!"

The upstaged Giovanni looked highly amused. "I see at least one of you is familiar with our traditional Italian liqueur."

I must admit that Muriel's joy was most certainly not misplaced. It was ice-cold yet gave off an amazing lemon fragrance and flavour, the moment it engaged with one's mouth. Mavis too looked pleasantly surprised – I knew that in normal circumstances she drank quite modestly. Giovanni let the beauty of the drink speak for itself and soon we were all offering thanks, wishing Giovanni and Andreas goodnight, a little premature as far as Andreas was concerned because he escorted us back to our rooms.

Just as I heard a loud exclamation from Muriel next door, I noticed an ice-bucket on my bedside table with an open bottle of prosecco and glasses at the ready. There was a little card and brief note: 'Must never waste opened bottles.' I couldn't disagree with that sentiment, when a little later, glass in hand, I was sitting up in bed thinking over the events of the evening. Giovanni may have been just slightly upstaged by Muriel's knowing about Limoncello, but that was nothing in comparison with how successfully and completely he had upstaged the three of us. Decadent perhaps but sipping this divine wine while sitting in bed was delightful, and how wonderful it was to have seen once again that amazing book.

38. MONTY DOING HIS THING

It was as if we acted in unison, all arriving individually at breakfast the following morning, but about one hour later than might have been expected. We were probably paying a price for late night prosecco. I was first and when the girls (as I sometimes thought of them) had both got started on their purifying grapefruit and herbal teas, I mentioned that there was an internationally famous museum nearby where there was a renowned collection of small statues of the Infant Christ.

"Good gracious, how do you know that?" exclaimed Muriel.

"No amazing piece of general knowledge, but in the card room I came across a superb book, 'I'll Piccolo re la Collezione', written by the collector and owner of the museum, Hiky Mayr. It is quite a modern publication, but I suspect it is already quite valuable. The photography is absolutely stunning."

"Why am I not surprised that you have already tracked down a rare book on the premises, so shall you ask Giovanni if you may buy it?"

I knew that Mavis was being facetious, but I played along with it. "What a good idea."

"Of course, you can't, he would want to give it to you and that would be so embarrassing."

"I'm only joking. As it happens there is a dealer in the next town with a copy for sale and there is only a few on the market world-wide. Perhaps I'll visit him and see what I can negotiate. At present his copy is priced at about £100. Changing the subject, have you noticed those two men sitting over there, looking rather over dressed for breakfast, don't you think?"

"Perhaps lounge suits are a bit over the top."

Yes, you're right with that assessment, Muriel. I've seen them once or twice about the hotel."

"Well, they were in the town when I was about early yesterday morning. A little strange I thought, still, no matter. Anyway, I'm going to visit this museum in a while as the collection is world famous. Nearby are some attractive botanic gardens, might you prefer those?"

More my scene, I think, I'll just look at the book later. What about you Muriel?"

Later that morning we were all strolling along the road, having got some directions from the staff at the reception desk. Shortly the girls went one way and I carried on to the museum. I was just ambling along as it was already getting hot and it was then I heard my name being called.

"Monty, Monty, I was hoping I might bump into you on your own."
"Daniel? Why the secrecy? You know that we're all here and we're enjoying some of the

proceeds of the 'Sherlock Homes' volume. You can join us."

"Yes, I realise that. In fact, Mavis knows I am here, I sent her a text yesterday and I may well call at the hotel this evening. I'm here primarily on work and need to keep a rather lower profile along with a couple of colleagues."

"Two guys in smart lounge suits?"

"Perhaps not a low enough profile then."

"Definitely not."

"Look, can you join me for some coffee, and I'll explain. I'm using a couple of rooms above a restaurant at the other end of the town, 'Sans Souci'."

"Oh, very Agatha Christie."

"Pardon?"

"Never mind, look it up when you have a moment."

"Well, leaving the Queen of Crime aside, my car's just over there, so hop in and I'll explain all."

We drove to the other end of Gardone and then walked down to Daniel's place. We sat and Daniel started to explain, while brewing some coffee. "I don't think I necessarily know what all the attacks and threats have been about but I'm coming to the conclusion that it is all very UK based, and as nearly everyone who has been involved so far is here in Gardone, it seemed sensible for us to be here as well. At present, my colleagues and I are just watching the situation, watching closely, I should say. Did you know Jon and Genevievre will be here soon? She is arriving later today, and Jon will be here as well, but travelling separately. I take it, given your obvious surprise, you didn't know. Genevievre is singing at a private event at one of the larger villas in the hills near here. Some Italian friends of Jon's are hosting a rather prestigious gathering. Jon is only able to be here because he has been in Rome for a few days, some Foreign Office business for which his skills were necessary. He will be on his way home when he arrives here and meets up with Genevievre. Ken will be here in a couple days, after his business, also in Rome, is settled. Clearly you didn't know that either, nor I expect, does Muriel and Mavis."

Is everybody I know travelling to Gardone?"

"Well, perhaps not everybody. More certain, I think, is that most questions will be answered here, but I don't quite know how or when."

"What do I say to Mavis and Muriel about this?"

Nothing but the truth. As I said, I'll be up at your hotel later and explain all that I know. Here, pass me your mobile phone and I'll add my number to it, it's different from the one I have been using in the UK. What are you doing now?"

"When you met me, I was on my way to the Hiki Mayr Museum to look at her collection of statues of the Infant Christ. Perhaps I'll do that another day instead. I shall walk into Salo now, where I have tracked down a book dealer who has a copy of her book about the statues; I may even buy it. The walk will do me good as I am eating far too much. Shall you be going to this large Opera Festival taking place in Gardone centre?"

"Yes and no, certainly at it, but whether as a relaxed member of the audience is quite another matter. I will see you this evening then."

I marched off at quite a pace but slowed down quite soon though. It was a hot but pleasant walk and mainly downhill. With the help of a street map and a copy of the dealer's name and address it didn't take me long to find his place. Frederico, as he was called, seemed quite thrilled that his book advertisement had brought someone all the way from England. He fetched out the Hiki Mayr volume for me to inspect. I shouldn't think it had ever been looked at, its condition was magnificent. Whilst I was leisurely turning the pages and pondering how to negotiate a price, Frederico had disappeared only to return after a short while balancing in one hand a large cardboard box and on the other, in good waiter style, a tray with two small black coffees and two glasses of liqueur, that delicious Limoncello. This man really knew how to look after his customers. I moved the valuable volume well out of the way while I sipped the coffee, and watching him emptying the box, more books, needless to say.

"My British bits," Frederico said, and pushed them over in my direction.

These were not what I was expecting, not obvious volumes such that holiday makers may have abandoned, nothing like that at all. These were mainly slim volumes, old minor textbooks, pamphlets, and papers published by universities. Quite a number were signed by the author, they were all quite old, certainly pre-war. I tried to get him to explain where he had found them, but this seemed a bit beyond him. "You like to buy?" was his main response.

"Yes, I do like to buy." but only thought it. Dealers are dealers, the same the world over. Frederico had paper and pen to hand and wrote down 75 euros while indicating that that was for the whole box load. That was quite good given that there were probably thirty to forty items in the box and all very saleable. I brought the Hiki Mayr volume back to 'centre stage' and indicated with my hand that I was interested in buying everything, even wrote on the piece of paper '?euros'.

He wrote down 160 euros, so he had reduced the large book to 85 euros. I smiled and shook his hand and he responded in like vigorous manner. I suppose he thought he might end up keeping the textbook bits and pieces for years before anyone else showed interest. I could see them all selling quite easily for £5 to £20 per item, a nice profit even allowing for the cost of the Hiki Mayr, as well as a taxi back to Gardone. I handed over a few bank notes reflecting how useful it was that they went in for high value denomination notes for the euro currency. I pointed to my watch and indicated that I would return in an hour or so and with a taxi. With another smile from Frederico and another handshake and a wave from me, I strolled off into the centre of Salo.

I carried on downhill and soon found myself at the waterfront. I walked along, incredibly valuable looking yachts to my left and the most expensive shops to my right – the sort of shops which displayed perhaps just one dress per window with a price ticket in the thousands. With all my walking and the excitement of my book buying I began to feel quite hungry. There were plenty of outdoor bars and eateries to choose from and I soon had a coffee and a pizza in front of me. I would also indulge my taste buds in a delicious looking cake – there looked to be a wonderful selection in the glass-fronted chilled cabinet. I sat and contemplated the joys of my day so far.

I was beginning to feel a little sleepy and would have probably nodded off but for the noise of some squawking gulls, having a 'row' I supposed, over some bits of ice-cream cone that had just been thrown down for them. They all seemed to get something so flew off. I was left looking at a young man tying up a small speed boat. He seemed vaguely familiar, but I couldn't place him, just my imagination I thought. I remembered the chilled cabinet then, so called the waiter over and had him serve a magnificent confection of chocolate, meringue, strawberries, and cream. I also accepted his offer of more coffee. The young man returned soon after carrying three large jerry cans and given how casually he dropped these down into the speed boat, clearly, they were empty. He jumped down then, threw off the rope mooring, started up the engine and with a very loud roar he headed out towards the deeper waters of the lake.

Calling the waiter over again, I gave him what seemed a suitable amount of money and, following his instructions, went in search of a taxi. With a stop at Frederico's, and then, after much handshaking, I was soon on my way back to the hotel at Gardone, clutching my pile of treasure.

39. IDENTIFICATION

Taking my treasures to my room I reflected on the fact that books were heavy so must be careful in any purchases here in Italy, or I would be caught for excess baggage charges. Unusual for me, but I suddenly felt like a swim, something I rarely did at home but the setting of a heated outdoor pool just close to the lake and under radiant sunshine, created a very inviting effect such that didn't come my way in Peterborough. I had taken the precaution of purchasing something up to date in the swimming shorts line so I wouldn't be looking as if I were still wearing swimming trunks from school days. I hadn't seen Mavis and Muriel since breakfast so thought I might find them 'poolside' – they would certainly be surprised to see how I was attired.

As it happens, they were to be found under one of the 'umbrella' trees and as I thought, they were surprised to see me in shorts, shades, flip-flops, and a towel round my neck. "Good gracious, Monty." It was Muriel who spoke up, no surprises there. "You look twenty years younger!"

"It won't last into colder climes, so you won't see me thus attired when back in Peterborough; sorry to disappoint. Anybody swimming?" Now that did amaze them. "Another surprise for you: I've been in Salo today, negotiating with a book dealer for a few volumes which I'll show you later." So, I spun on my heels, and went off to the pool which I was pleased to find had very few people swimming. Like riding a bicycle, I hadn't forgotten how to swim even though it was several years since I had last been in a swimming pool. I found it quite invigorating to indulge in a few lengths of front crawl even if I still couldn't get the breathing quite right.

Returning to the girls I sprayed water in their direction and then sat down. "By the way, I bumped into Daniel this morning, he said he would be up this evening."

"Mavis, did you know this?" Muriel was obviously surprised; Mavis certainly had kept a secret.

"Does he want to join us for dinner or is that likely to be a little too public for him. I'm sure Giovanni would let us have the use of a private room. Are you able to give him a ring or send a text?"

"Monty, did he say anything more specific?

"No, only that he would come up this evening. Send him a text, I think that's the best thing to do. There's plenty of time to organise something different about dinner. Thinking about plenty of time, shall we stroll over to the outdoor bar and have something cooling to drink, we haven't used that facility yet."

"Good idea, come on." Muriel was on her way, so I expected a bottle of Prosecco was about to be ordered.

Mavis was looking at her mobile as she sat. "Daniel's replied quickly, he'll be here about seven pm, private room not necessary."

"That's good, I'll be able to tell him of my successes in Salo."

Daniel joined us in the bar just before seven o'clock and we enjoyed a couple of rounds of drinks before strolling down to the dining room. We had already explained to the reception staff that we had a visitor joining us for dinner and they seemed quite happy about it. He and Mavis seemed more than happy to be with each other again and I think Mavis was also pleased that we all knew about Daniel being in Gardone. Daniel told us that he had spoken to his colleagues but explained that they wouldn't be joining us for dinner. We were amused to be informed by Daniel that the lounge suits would be seen no more.

Dinner was fun as it turned out that this was the night that the hotel offered what they called their 'Italian' night, the menu was all very Italian in style. Daniel insisted on ordering the wine, a red and a white and both Italian. The Head Waiter, who had attended to us the first morning that we were here, suddenly appeared and was most anxious to know that we had all that we needed. I think he would have preferred us to be in their 'Giardino dei Limoni' Restaurant, a more sophisticated venue offering a specialist a la carte menu. We were settled now and didn't want to move so we assured him that we would avail ourselves of the alternative another evening; with this promise he seemed content.

Daniel didn't have anything more to tell us other than what he had mentioned to me that morning. I told him of my little jaunt down into Salo and of my time with the book dealer. Had it been a little smaller, I would have brought the Hiki Mayr volume down to dinner for him to see. Perhaps just as well I didn't, sure to have got splashed with some sauce or red wine. We were eating our way through a particularly delicious Lasagne when my memory clicked into place. "Daniel, I saw somebody in Salo who I feel I have seen before, in London maybe, youngish man, perhaps thirty. I wasn't close and only noticed him because he was handling a rather stylish speed boat and into which he had loaded some empty jerry cans."

Daniel flicked open his mobile and two or three taps later passed a photograph over for me to see. "Is that the guy?"

"Yes, I think it is, but hard to be sure because this photograph is of him in a very formal situation whereas today, he was in tee-shirt and shorts and wearing sunglasses. I certainly know this man; didn't I see him at the Palace of Westminster the other week?

"You did, Ben Lawton, Nat Lawton's son. We know that they have both travelled to Italy very recently but you, Monty, have made the first sighting of one of them. Well done. Just give me a moment, I need to let a few people know." A few taps later and this task was complete.

Daniel didn't say any more about this sighting, so we let the topic be. I told him about my other book purchases and my expectations of enough profit to pay for the one large volume.

"I'm pleased to hear that you're not neglecting your business interests Monty. By the way, are you all going to the Opera Gala Night, tomorrow is it?"

"Certainly," was the united response.

An idea crossed my just then: "I think the staff here would be pleased if we were to avail ourselves of the Limoni Restaurant, so it occurs to me that if we were to eat a lighter breakfast than usual, I could invite you all to lunch, 1.00pm or so. We haven't got that many days left to fit such a visit in. Any takers?"

If I had any thoughts that this would be no more than a gesture, the loud chorus of 'yes, thank you', turned the invitation into a certainty. Before we came away from dinner, I made a reservation for the planned lunch, a reservation which I think met with staff approval.

We spent some of the evening together in the lounge, so I took the opportunity of bringing down my copy of the Hiki Mayr volume for all to see, as it could be placed on a suitable table. Really heavy books such as this are at great risk if resting on someone's lap. I think Mavis admired it most, brought out some of her long hidden artistic instincts, which could do nothing but good. Unusual for me but I drank a beer during the evening, in fact by the end of the evening quite a range of drinks had been consumed including a round of limoncello which rounded the night off nicely.

I suppose because we all knew that a large lunch might be consumed later, we didn't really meet for a group breakfast. In fact, and much to everyone's amazement I went swimming first thing. It rather perked my appetite up, but I managed to exercise some restraint and confined myself to coffee and toast. Muriel roared with laughter when she heard about my swimming, Daniel wondered if I was having some late life crisis regarding fitness. I told him off about the 'late life' bit. Mavis was just politely restrained and hoped that I would feel better for it as the day went on. Mavis and Muriel were planning another walk around the botanical gardens and Daniel said he needed to meet up with his colleagues.

As I had had my fitness burst for the day I went back to my room and spent some time looking up book dealers, seeing if there were any bargains to snap up. I also 'surfed' through the various ebay listings, ones which I kept a watch on. I didn't find any 'must have' bargains, a pity as I usually found something to send for. One book dealer friend (a friendship made entirely on- line) I knew would list hundreds of items over a wide range of subjects and always on a free post basis. He was very amenable to offers, such as my choosing four books and offering £30, and if he agreed, I would just pop the bank notes in the post - a happy arrangement for us both. I passed the rest of the morning leafing through the Hiki Mayr volume.

We met in the bar before lunch. Daniel was in the chair and bought two malts and 'the girls' both opted for gin. While Muriel and Mavis were talking about someone they had met earlier, Daniel was able to let me know the progress on the search for the Lawtons. They had had sightings of the speed boat further along the lake shore but of Lawton senior, no sign. With a little influence from senior officers in Scotland Yard and opposite numbers in this region of Italy, Daniel had been able to enlist the help of local police in keeping a watch on the speed boat in the hope that they would be able to spot both the Lawtons. Daniel was convinced that they had to be here for a distinct purpose, but what he didn't know.

No more time for conversation, drinks finished, and it was time to make our way the Limoni Restaurant. On the way Daniel mentioned that he had received an invitation for all of us to join Jon and Genevievre on board the yacht that they would be using for the rest of the day. Middle of the afternoon was suggested as an approximate time. When we arrived at the Limoni we found a round table ready for us, placed so that we could be looking out to the lake or look at each other for which a round table is perfect.

"Monty, don't be offended but I have already 'nobbled' the wine waiter, so ordering and paying for that half of the meal is with me, too late to argue." Daniel smiled as he delivered this piece of charming interference.

Menus were handed round and while we studied these the wine appeared with waiters seemingly knowing what to pour and for whom. With no surprise, bubbles went to the girls. As if my choice of first course was already known my glass receive some dry white. As it happened. I had already chosen braised scallops. As a pair again, Mavis and Muriel opted for rolled aubergines stuffed with raisins, capers, and walnuts while Daniel went with Prosciutto. The menu was set out in traditional style with Antipasto, Primo, Secondo and a Dolci but nobody minded if we opted for a more UK arrangement. I had already noticed that the hotel offered its own Pizza so thought that would be nice for this meal's main course. Its key ingredients were different cheeses and spinach. Mavis was going to have a lamb burger with quite a selection of 'this and that', Muriel was opting for thinly sliced and incredibly rare beef with a salad. Daniel was going with a pasta dish which included a lot of prawns.

I had even got as far ahead as spotting the sweet trolley but had decided to ignore that in favour of local ice-cream of which the hotel made quite a boast. While dishes came and went, another waiter hovered, always knowing what wine to pour for each of us. It was a lovely lunch and we chatted away most happily.

By the time we had finished, settled bills, and smiled our thanks to all concerned it was soon time to get ready to visit the yacht. Mavis and Muriel needed to change, what was worn for lunch was not suitable for mid-afternoon tea, perish the thought. It wasn't possible for the yacht to moor immediately next to the walkway running along the hotel front, so a small dinghy came across from the yacht and collected us. This was rather nice as it gave us an excellent view of the yacht, indeed we went right round and boarded from the far side.

The Vele Gardone was a splendid looking craft, obviously quite new, absolutely top of the range when it came to décor, fittings, and furnishings; if it was not gold-plated then one assumed there had been an error. Genevievre and Jon were waiting at the top of the gangway to welcome us. They were looking quite resplendent so it had been wise of the 'girls' to dress for the occasion; Daniel and I would just have to get by. There was a crew, about five of them, impeccably uniformed. That seemed quite a large crew given that we were going nowhere and there was a separate galley crew of two.

The Mostangs showed us round and it was really a craft to show. There seemed to be quite an area of deck space for guests to lounge about and below seemed even more spacious. There was a large forward cabin which provided a most elegant double bedroom, another spacious cabin which acted as a lounge during the day but converted into another bedroom with accommodation for up to four. Depending on requirement, a double bed arrangement could be created, two twin beds or two pairs of bunk beds. The lounge furnishings had been very cleverly designed so that the necessary conversions could all be created. Between the two main cabins were two bathrooms. Further towards the stern, the gangway leading down from the deck was to one side so on the other was a sizable galley. Further towards the stern of the yacht were facilities for the crew, two small cabins each with two bunk beds and there was also a tiny shower-room and toilet, the shower cubicle containing a fold-away wash-hand basin. Wherever one looked, if space permitted, there were cupboards. The furnishings and fittings were all finished to amazing standards, wood so well polished it could act as mirror glass; gold leaf or brass, handles, knobs, hinges and hooks all shone jewel-like.

Jon and Genevievre explained that the yacht belonged to the people with whom they were staying, they had a villa in the hills to the back of Gardone. Up on deck a steward was setting an afternoon tea table with the chairs, table, napery, china, and cutlery all oozing Italian design. There was champagne or coffee as alternatives to tea. Two or three plates were set with the most exquisite cakes, fortunately quite tiny, given the amount of lunch we had consumed not long before. Genevievre 'poured' – how very period I thought. Daniel had been the last to sit and I noticed that he had made a brief detour to the stern of the yacht where he had had a brief conversation with two of the crew. I said nothing but did wonder what that was all about.

It was beautiful just to sit, there still being plenty of warmth and sunshine but with the lightest of breezes. No-one could complain of being too anything as far as weather conditions were concerned. Nothing too serious came up in conversation, mention was made of the holiday ending rather soon now, the wonderful hospitality we had enjoyed at The King's Tower. Genevievre was curious as to how an impromptu opera concert would work out in the evening, Jon was looking forward to the fireworks, especially as they would be out on the lake and almost amongst the fireworks. Just then the noise of the dinghy caught our attention and when we looked across the deck, we saw Ken popping up above the gangway. There was some immediate renewal of tea and cakes and another bottle of champagne was opened. It was Muriel who apologised and explained that she had known that Ken was in Rome and that he was flying up to Verona that afternoon. The hotel reception staff had alerted him to our whereabouts and a couple of quick phone calls later and Ken was being picked up by the yacht dinghy.

Ken's arrival gave a boost to our afternoon conversation. He had been in Rome for about a week, but we didn't learn why. I had known from things Muriel had said in the past, that he could be a little on the secretive side as far as some of his journeys were concerned. I think his aeroplane lunch must have been rather light because he almost cleared a plate of cakes. He was also pleased to hear that his arrival coincided with the concert and firework display. As well as hunger, his thirst necessitated the opening of a third bottle of champagne, but I noticed nobody declined when offered more. We didn't stay on the yacht much longer, a few yawns providing a hint of the need to get into the dinghy. We wished Jon and Genevievre well for the concert and firework display later and made out way back to hotel.

40. CHORUSES, ARIAS, FIREWORKS AND MORE

I suppose because of my musical interests I have, from time to time, joined in an impromptu performance of Handel's 'The Messiah'. This has been a popular amateur activity for many years and such performances pop up just about anywhere. There has to be a few enthusiastic folk to form the musical nucleus so to speak, somebody willing to conduct and sufficient local knowledge to be sure that there will be instrumentalists to form a suitable orchestra and enough keen 'wanabe' soloists to cover the many solo items. It is not often that the performance is of the whole composition, but the organising 'nucleus' generally gets all those details clear and usually arranges hire of the orchestral parts and score. The venue needs to be large – parish church, school hall for example. A small fee from each performer covers all the costs. The usual pattern is a rehearsal in the afternoon followed by a performance in the evening to which paying members of the public are invited. It goes without saying, that you only offer your services in any capacity provided you have the required ability and knowledge. The rehearsal is more about organisation than learning of parts.

I'm thinking about all this while waiting for the Opera Festival Performance to start; it is in the same form as a 'come together Messiah' performance, only here in Gardone the local keen singers are joining forces to perform a large selection of famous Italian Opera Choruses. There were to be a few differences:

four keyboardists instead of an orchestra; all performers were to be costumed in something approaching C19th Italian fashions of ordinary people – performers providing their own costumes. There were to be some soloists, mainly to provide moments of contrast between choruses. Like the chorus members, these soloists were to be amateurs from the local area but chosen in advance. The one final and crucial difference from the Messiah performances was that all the singers had to be word and note perfect, to be able to perform from memory! It promised to be a most memorable event and the opening item was to be The Grand March from Aida with performers processing in from all round Gardone – the music from the keyboards was to be relayed about the town and using several keyboards enabled important individual instrumental moments to be highlighted, picked out like orchestral solos. This was to be followed by a solo and then the Anvil Chorus from Il Trovatore.

I think I'm probably much like many thousands of individuals who enjoy the sound of opera, choruses, and solos. It seems easy to sense the drama, the poignancy, the majesty but know nothing of the words, the titles of the arias. I soon discovered that this evening's concert was not going to improve my education in these matters because there was no programme to read. There seemed to be a presumption that everything would be well known. The only help was the conductor in announcing the solo items and as this was done in Italian, I was no further forward. However, it was all immensely enjoyable, some items were more familiar than others; I was aware of a Puccini solo. I suppose, like many, listening to episodes of Morse had made the 'sounds' quite familiar.

At the end of the concert, night was drawing in, and starting so quietly it was difficult to know that anyone was singing, we listened to the unison melody of the Hebrew Song of the Slaves from Nabucco. It has all the feel of a hymn or anthem and is an incredibly beautiful item to sing. It is said that the crowds lining the streets, sang this melody as the Funeral Cortege for Verdi passed. As this evening's performance of the final item faded out, the lights dimmed, and darkness and silence took over and it was a short while before applause broke out.

Looking about, as the echoes of the music and applause faded away into the night, one realised how dark it had become, even though there was a clear sky and moon. The effect of darkness was also due, no doubt, to the contrast caused once the stage and spotlights had been switched off. For a short while there was a great quiet and only gradually did the whispered conversations start up. According to the programme a firework display was set to follow the music. This was to be well out into the lake so that it would be visible over a very wide area. For most of the early evening small boats had been moving about the lake positioning the fireworks. At any time of the day various small privately-operated craft were to be seen about the lake but presumably all craft owners had received instructions about keeping a marked area of the lake clear after a certain time. During the concert there had been several craft - yachts, launches, small cruisers not far from the shore. No doubt they provided a more informal setting for those on board to listen to the music. These craft would all have to move well away before the fireworks started. The Mostangs and friends were the only people we knew who were out on the water.

We were all looking forward to this firework display, the setting could make for a quite spectacular show and with this thought in my mind, it actually started with the simultaneous firing of five rockets which as they rose arched to a converging peak and then outwards where they burst into a myriad of sparkling colours and glitter making for a grand opening moment. Thereafter items were fired from all over this area of the lake, providing a continuous but ever-changing kaleidoscope of colour. The height of the display changed constantly as did the range of volume and nature of the sound – individual explosions, continuous crackles and some which in a sporadic way created a series of changing surprises. Without doubt the crowning glory of any firework display would be the incredible range of colour which can be created: clouds of coloured smoke effects interspersed with sparkling lights and noise, noise which can be changed in intensity, almost orchestrated to accompany the increasing intensity of the range of colour.

Just as the display was reaching its zenith, I became aware of a distant hum, the throbbing of an engine. I nudged Mavis and cupped my ear to signal sound and she nodded agreement and as we realised, so did others, a distant powered boat was approaching from some way out in the lake, headlights bouncing on the rippling surface and far behind, two further powered craft, appeared to be in pursuit. The first boat was increasing in speed and heading off to our left, towards some of the larger leisure craft from which people had been listening to the music and now watching the fireworks. What on earth was intended and how a major collision was to be avoided it was hard to imagine? At that moment, the lights of the fireworks began to fade as did the explosions and we could all see this potential disaster unfolding before us. Chaos seemed to break out: people stood up, were shouting, some leapt down from their raised seating to go to the lakeside wall, but everybody was powerless, nobody could act.

Mavis cried out, "Jon! Genevievre! It's their yacht, their yacht is under attack."

As we looked in its direction another engine roared into life and the yacht seemed to leap forward and accelerate away from its target position as did two other craft, fore and aft. Through this sudden gap the first powered speed boat leapt, careering on towards the wall. The following craft suddenly slowed but their headlights picked out a man making a desperate leap from the rocketing speed boat. With a certainty now beyond question we all watched in unison, awaiting what turned out to be a phenomenal explosive blast of flame and noise which completely dwarfed all that the firework display had left in our memories. Flame and light obliterated everything else from sight, but which must have included a powered boat being blasted into thousands of pieces to land over a wide area of shore and lake.

Almost as an anti-climax and when our eyes adjusted, we looked back to one of the following craft as a man was hauled from the water. Was he the only occupant or the only one able to save himself? Perhaps we had just witnessed the equivalent of a water-borne suicide bomber. Fire boats arrived quite quickly and doused the still burning shrubs along the shoreline at the point of collision; Lake Garda's waters extinguished the rest and pitch darkness returned. This was soon replaced by street lighting and when safety lights came on members of a very shocked audience could climb down from their seats, to wander about, white faced, to huddle in whispering groups, to make for the bars and large brandies, return to hotels, carparks and hillside villas. For many the onset of sleep would be much delayed.

Places can recover at speed and within thirty minutes or so, Gardone returned to its late-night holiday atmosphere and no doubt by daybreak, the staging and seats would be stacked to await the lorries and the walkways swept to impeccable cleanliness. Along the shore the lapping waters would have dispersed much of the debris, and a team of gardeners would have raked smooth the blackened shrubs and flowers.

Before all that though, the ever-urbane Giovanni was supervising the serving of coffee and spirits to all who required such medicinal restoratives in the lounge of the King's Tower. He had witnessed much of the drama from one of the tower rooms and when he realised that there would be a need for late evening service, he issued a few instructions and sent messages out to various guests. Mavis and Muriel were holding large crystal balloons containing equally large measures. Daniel and I nursed malts of choice. Jon and Genevievre were perhaps looking the most shaken, but brandies in hand they were visibly beginning to relax. One or two colleagues of Daniel's were also in attendance, as was Ken who had flown up from Rome to Verona only that afternoon.

"Dare one ask, Daniel, do you have an explanation for everything that has happened?"

"As it happens, Monty, I do, and you may be surprised to know that you observed one of the final keys to this mystery. Serious as many of the individual attacks of the last few months were, tonight's finale, which was intended to be devastatingly explosive, was vaguely known about but not preventable. Your spotting Ben Lawton in Salo was most helpful, remember you only recognised him because you saw him the other evening at the Palace of Westminster. From your reporting of that sighting we were able to discover that a large quantity of petrol had been purchased. Our problem was that we couldn't locate the powered boat, nor did we know what was planned. I only realised the possibility of a detailed plan when Jon happened to mention that he would be on the yacht for the concert and firework display. With the co-operation of the local police we had armed launches fore and aft. I alerted Jon to the need to have a mobile phone at hand the whole evening, as did the crew members and the two police officers we had on board. The police launch crew and officers were all in radio contact. We waited to the south-west of the Isle, just a mile out from the shoreline.

To be sure all would be safe, we kept watch from late afternoon and into the evening, but particularly so once the firework display started. We were alerted from shore about the power boat on the move and we started to follow once it had passed and only then switched on the spotlights. As soon as it was clear where it was heading, we alerted Jon to get the yacht moving. As the power boat passed, we observed two people on board. In silhouette we could make out something of an argument. We witnessed Ben, getting ready to jump and were able to pick him up quite quickly. The eventual explosive collision was completely out of our control and it would have been frighteningly dangerous to attempt any interception.

"But why?" called Muriel, "Why?"

"Plain old-fashioned jealousy."

"Jealousy! What of?"

"Jon Mostang was the sole focus of Nat Lawton's Jealousy."

Jon sat up at that point. "You mean this all about my wealth."

"Far more general than that Jon. Nat Lawton was jealous of your wealth, your immediate status in the House of Commons when you appeared to take over his position on the Foreign Affairs Committee, your intellect, and international contacts. He hated your racial background – don't forget his Jewish background (Nathaniel, Benjamin, Angela and the surname, Lawton – very Jewish names) He came to see all immigrants as people on a different side from him, hence the troubles in his Lincolnshire Constituency. I don't know why we didn't spot all this much earlier, perhaps because it was the opposite of everything we expected. Perhaps we simply didn't allow for the possibility of a Member of Parliament becoming so completely deranged and dangerous. Wickedly, he was able to take advantage of what was an unsolved murder in the death of my first wife, Noura, and this distorted much of my thinking."

"Don't blame yourself, Daniel." One of his colleagues spoke up. "You were not alone in that thinking."

"Where is Ben now?" asked Mavis.

"At this moment in an Italian police station prison cell but not, I suspect, for much longer. Noises are already coming from the Foreign Office to the effect that the precise details of this longstanding vendetta are not to be allowed to get into print. The Government will clamp down on all information with security prohibitions. There will have to be another version which covers all the facts ending with the accidental death of the MP, Nathaniel Lawton."

Giovanni spoke. "I totally confident, British diplomatic speak, more equal to that little job."

Jon Mostang was the only one I think who saw the humour of that. "Giovanni, you should be the Diplomat!"

41. SETTLING THE DUST, PERHAPS NOT MEMORIES

By the time the 'dust' had settled over the previous night's most unexpected finale, we were all extremely late to bed. Jon and Genevievre had returned to their friends' villa; they were flying back to the UK the next afternoon. Before he took himself back to the Sans Souci, Daniel and Mavis had managed some quiet romantic conversation after his colleagues had taken themselves off and Muriel had tactfully retreated to bed on the pretext of being excessively tired; my impression of Muriel was that she never got tired. Ken had been talking to Giovanni for some time; I knew he had a room somewhere in the hotel for a few nights. I just slipped away during a conversational lull, being attracted to a quiet glass of whatever I would find had been left by my bed; I would quiet my mind by leafing Hiki Mayr's masterpiece.

Inevitably, our breakfast party gathered rather late, but we were shepherded by that most dignified of waiters, who had welcomed us on our first morning, to an elegantly arranged table by the Lakeside wall. Several sunshades were strategically placed to provide maximum comfort. I was pleased to see Daniel striding in, he being the last to complete the morning's breakfast party. Our rather aimless chatter came to a stop on his arrival, rather as if we expected him to make some announcement; we were not disappointed.

"It is just as I expected, the Italian authorities want to be as little involved as possible and have released Ben to British authorities which means me, and my two colleagues. They're collecting him about now and I expect they will return to the UK just as soon as they can arrange a flight, hopefully later today. Before that though, they will bring back for me a copy of the 'official' police statement of what happened last night. It has already been given an authorised translation and I shall have to send off a few copies by secure email. I'll stay on just long enough to 'dot the 'i's and cross the 't's of anything official. That should leave some time for us," and so saying he turned to Mavis and gave her a most affectionate kiss; we all applauded.

"Well, I have to prepare my talk today because I'm the official guest for Giovanni's 'English' group who are meeting here tomorrow evening. You may remember he got me to promise to do this when I was telling him at that first dinner that I felt a bit guilty about all the extra expenditure the hotel had gone to on our behalf. If I'm honest it will only take me about hour to get ready because I happen to have brought with me the USB driver which has all the illustrations I used when I gave a talk to the Women's Institute back in the winter. I don't use a script, so the illustrations just remind me of everything I have to say. I must remember to ask reception to let me have a lap-top and arrange for a screen to be up in whatever room is being used. Perhaps I better give thought to our last few days. What about you Ken, much on, or are you able to do nothing for a few days?"

"For once, I have few calls on my time. That being the case I thought I would sleep in this morning, but habits just don't change to order; I was wide awake by six o'clock. I went out for a walk around the town, brought back a few memories of my visit here some years back. I was surprised by how much tidying had been achieved after last night. I walked along to where the explosion had occurred and found that area much restored. I'll come and listen to your talk if that's all right Monty?"

"Certainly, my pleasure, Ken."

"Bearing in mind what you were saying just now Monty, I have been wondering if it wouldn't be a good idea to buy something for Giovanni. I'm sure others will have some different ideas." Muriel looked around expectantly.

"I had been thinking along similar lines because when I was in Salo a couple of days ago I was so impressed with some splendid looking restaurants. Perhaps a bit 'coals from Newcastle' but we could take him out for a celebratory meal and present him with something."

"That's a nice idea Monty," good to take him away from Gardone. Perhaps we can get somebody to recommend a suitable venue."

Pulling his eyes away from Mavis for a moment, Daniel offered to ask at the Sans Souci.

"Well, when you do, ask about a place called Fabrizio's. It caught my eye when I was strolling along the promenade and looking at the yachts."

"When it comes to a gift, I might be able to help." Ken took a fountain pen out of his pocket which he held so we could see it. "For a long time now, I have often found the need for a gift or two when on some of my travels, especially overseas. I have generally found a quality fountain pen in a small presentation case goes down well with most men, an item of jewellery for the ladies. At present I'm in the £50-£75 range. I have to keep up with inflation!" He added this last sentiment with a bit of a smile.

I suppose the ultra-smart waiter thought we might sit all morning and never ever start breakfast because at that moment two younger but equally impeccably dressed waiters wheeled a pair of trolleys to our table, both laden with a wide selection of croissants, butter, conserves, rolls, fruit, cakes and other pastries. There were also pots of coffee, teapots with hot water and an elegant caddy containing a selection of teas. We smiled our thanks, took the hint, and got started.

Just then there was a light tap on my shoulder and Giovanni sat down. I don't know where the chair came from, perhaps attached to one of the trolleys. It then occurred to me that the breakfast order may have come from a higher authority. "Would I permit to join Monty for coffee? Do I find you all recovered last night unpleasantness?

"I think we are all fully recovered now, Giovanni, thank you."

"I come to ask about tomorrow, your talk. OK?"

"You need have no worries; everything is organised. All I'll need will be a laptop loaded with 'powerpoint' and a white screen or suitable wall space."

"No problem, Monty. I tell reception and check later. I stay with you, have more breakfast. OK."

"Giovanni, we would like to take you out to dinner one evening before we go home. Need to check that you would be available. Do you have any nights coming up when you can't leave the hotel?"

"That's a lovely idea Monty, but do you mean not here, at The King's Tower? I have nothing booked after tomorrow evening's talk that you are giving."

"You're right, Giovanni. It will be somewhere else, our surprise."

"How wonderful, just leave a message at reception for me. I shall look forward to it."

I think we all chose to spend a quietish day but every so often my memory would take me back to the previous night. A gigantic explosion at night made for a very visual memory and very frightening given the clear knowledge of just how much worse it could have been had the yacht with Jon and Genevievre on board not managed to move to safety in time. I knew then that this would be a memory which wouldn't go away for a long, long time so not surprising that soldiers returning from several years violent experience are left so traumatised. Jon and Genevievre may well have to give each other much understanding and loving support.

Later I checked with the reception staff that equipment would be ready for the following night. I was able to borrow the laptop for a while and remind myself how to use the powerpoint program, run through my various images and remind myself of the various things I would say. Giovanni promised to bring down his copy of the now famous copy of 'The Hound of the Baskervilles' and he also promised to bring down a few other items to show his friends. I had every expectation of a successful and jolly evening

The following day Daniel was with us at breakfast again and mentioned that he had received many great recommendations for Fabrizio's. In the event we were incredibly lucky because for the very next night, Fabrizio's had had a party of ten cancel as the main guest had been taken seriously ill. We simply took over the whole booking. I should imagine they were relieved to reinstate a large Saturday night booking so quickly. We knew we would be certain for six, hoped that Andreas might join us, possibly his parents and we weren't certain that there wasn't a Mrs Giovanni Baptista or close partner who might like to join us. It goes without saying that Fabrizio's was delighted to get such a replacement booking. They seemed particularly thrilled when we explained who we were, and the name of our Guest of Honour. We stressed that the destination was a secret as far as Giovanni was concerned. I sent a message to Giovanni via the reception staff, apologising for short notice, but hoped Saturday would be all right. I also asked if he wanted to bring anybody, wasn't quite sure how to put that. I also asked him to find out if Andreas could join us, perhaps his parents as well.

The booking was made in my name and later that day a member of the reception staff team sought me out, asking me to ring the restaurant and ask for Fabrizio. She also had a message from Giovanni to say that he, Andreas, and Andreas's mother would all be able to join us. Worried that there was going to be problem with the booking I made the call immediately.

Fabrizio turned out to be a very flamboyant sounding guy, very Italian but he spoke impeccable and lively English. He told me that he knew Giovanni well and had a good idea of the dishes he would most enjoy. He also knew Andreas. Fabrizio suggested, with our agreement of course, that he could put together a typical menu of three or four items to choose from each of several courses. Would we allow him to make some wine recommendations? This all sounded incredibly helpful so without asking the others I put the whole evening's arrangements in his hands. I confirmed that we would be a party of eight. He was quite easy about that and if one or two more came there would be no problem. I also remembered to book a minibus taxi in view of what might be consumed by way of liquids! Later in the day I suddenly remembered to tell the rest of our party about the booking; now that would have been an embarrassing oversight!

42. FABRIZIO'S

The day of our surprise dinner for Giovanni arrived, magnificent looking weather, but, as we had all come to realise after our week or so stay, the weather in this area can change in an instant: glorious sunshine can become a violent thunder storm in a matter of minutes! Being English, I continued to think about the weather, as if it were a calm warm evening and that it would be lovely to eat 'al fresco'. I happen to know, though, that originally this expression meant 'in prison' as far as Italians were concerned. Be that as it may, dinner tonight was something to look forward to especially as I formed the impression that Fabrizio wanted to be proud of menus and choices of wine; the bill might be something else altogether.

Most of us, I think, just pottered our way through the day and I even went swimming again. Normally, I wasn't a very sporty person, I would never dream of jogging or visiting a gym, but I could take up swimming again, future food for thought. Later in the morning I met up with Mavis and Daniel who invited me to join them and Muriel for coffee in the town square. I must admit to thinking of Mavis and Daniel as an 'item' now, taken some time because I've only ever known either them as being single. A tray of drinks soon arrived together with some tasty pastry and because Daniel was having a beer and Muriel was having a glass of wine with her coffee a selection of crisps and olives were also served.

"I'm glad you both could join us." Mavis sounded just a little hesitant as she started this conversation going. "I know we all travelled here as a trio; can I use that expression but…..."

"Say no more!" Muriel jumped in and I knew exactly what she was going to say, I could have put a sizable bet on it, so certain as I was. "You don't want to travel home as a trio and that's hardly a surprise, is it Monty?"

"No, of course it isn't. Rather obvious thinking, really, and so romantic if I may say so? Does anyone know how Ken is travelling and when, because with a little persuasive phoning by someone like Andreas, it might be possible for Ken to take over Mavis's flight ticket?"

"All he has said to me is that he was only intending to be here for a few days. I'll speak to him now. As far as getting the flight ticket transferred, I think I can ring a contact in London and get that sorted." Daniel was very efficient with his mobile contacts listings and he soon got hold of Ken and explained the situation. Silence then ensued for some time. "Well, that's excellent. No, we're in Gardone Town Square. Definitely. We'll sit for as long as necessary, just like the Italians. Fine. Yes, quarter of an hour or so." Daniel ended the call and looked up. "Ken thinks it an excellent idea and he's joining us for coffee."

Ken came marching up to our table looking very sprightly and full of the joys of life. "I'm delighted with this suggestion of yours, because although I was well organised for my outward journey, I hadn't booked anything for the return, left it all somewhat open-ended. How can we arrange it?

Daniel caught the eye of the waitress at that point. "Mavis, shall you get everyone what they need by way of refills and whatever Ken wants and I'll make a couple of calls."

"You might need this, Daniel." From my wallet I was able to pass over the flight details.

"You are efficient, Monty, thanks. Ken, do you happen to have your passport with you?"

"Er, no, but I do keep in my wallet a photocopy of the key pages which should cover all you need."

Daniel made his first call, getting up from the table and walking off, finding a quieter spot. We couldn't hear him, and he wouldn't get disturbed by us; we got on with the important task of ordering more drinks and eats – quite a large order.

Absorbed in our drinks and food we temporarily forgot all about Daniel until he came sauntering back looking mightily pleased with himself. "All arranged, and necessary documents are being emailed as we speak, care of The King's Tower. Additional advice is that you check in earlier than usual."

Even sitting in an attractive town square, looking out over Lake Garda didn't remain the quiet relaxing interlude I had expected, not exactly 'pottering'. In view of the exciting evening to look forward to, I decided then that some sleep would come my way this afternoon.

Our dinner at Fabrizio's was timed for 7.00pm so we planned to be leaving in the minibus about half an hour earlier. As we gathered in the foyer I was somewhat taken aback when a brand-new Mercedes people-carrier arrived. Andreas and his mother were meeting us at the restaurant, an arrangement that would suit their journey better and then after the meal they were coming back to the hotel for the night. Giovanni was looking quite resplendent, seemingly full of joviality and as we went out, he greeted the driver like an old friend. Remembering what happened when we first arrived at this hotel, I placed two sums of money in my pockets, sixty euros in one and twenty in the other. The reception staff had told me to expect a charge of forty-five.

We all chattered away as this splendid vehicle glided over to Salo. As I suspected, the driver shrugged his shoulders and said, "on the 'ouse.' I didn't argue the point but tucked the twenty-note in his top pocket and shook his hand. We strolled over to the entrance of Fabrizio's, where we were welcomed by Andreas and a very flamboyant gentleman who looked somewhat familiar. It was when Giovanni greeted him, I realised that we had been well 'trumped'! Fabrizio and Giovanni had to be brothers! Andreas roared with laughter and Giovanni looked incredibly pleased with himself. "Andreas has tutored me in the correct and colloquial English. Allow me to introduce you to

Fabrizio, he my kid-brother!" The brothers roared with laughter. "You have no idea, I very pleased when you told me Fabrizio was booked."

"Andreas, where's your mother? I hope she is joining us." Muriel was looking about for the third scheduled guest to attend.

"Oh, don't worry, she's being shown the kitchens as she has one of her nephews working there." Andreas assured us that she was delighted to be meeting all of us and seeing the famous book that she has heard so much about. She must have sensed she was being talked about because she appeared at that very moment. Andreas performed the honours, introduced his mother, Eileen, and she smiled all round, shook a few of the offered hands. I was introduced as the discoverer of the famous book.

"It's a pleasure to meet you Monty. Needless-to-say, I have heard so much about this book and I'm looking forward to seeing it."

We allowed ourselves to be shown to the table and Fabrizio told us that two of his staff would pour aperitifs. Of course, we could choose something different. Just to be a touch different, I suspect, Daniel asked for a beer. The 'girls' along with Eileen, now sitting next to Giovanni, opted for bubbles and the rest of us allowed the waiters to make the selection on our behalf, or perhaps it was Giovanni who made the decision – he and his brother were beginning to act like identical twins. With the arrangement that I had made with Fabrizio, none of us knew what Italian culinary delights were going to be served. As I was just pondering that thought, I caught sight of two trolleys being wheeled to our table. I saw it first, taking centre spot on the top of one of the trolleys was a whole Gorgonzola cheese, so the question of my first course was answered, and other choices paled into insignificance: a spoonful or two of this magnificent cheese, some olives, slices of cucumber and a few cherry tomatoes together with a little bread and this would transport me to food heaven Before I had done no more than gently sniff my cheese, a glass of red wine was placed beside it. Glancing up I saw Fabrizio smile, so I lifted my glass in toasting gesture.

I could see that the evening would stretch ahead to be remembered as an Italian culinary delight of which one's taste buds would be able to recall for years. From time to time I looked to see what my fellow guests were eating, and it was then I realized just how many different dishes Fabrizio and his chefs had prepared. Like me, Giovanni looked to be in food heaven and Muriel sounded ecstatic with every mouthful. Daniel and Mavis, as can be the way with romantic couples, were offering each other different tastings, allowing them to sample twice as much as anyone else; was I jealous?

Giovanni leaned towards me. "Monty, you understand why I was so full of smiles when I realised where we were going?"

"Indeed, I do, 'upstaged' is the expression. By the way, did you know the minibus driver?"

"Sorry, didn't I say? One of many cousins is Alberto. Now, Monty, have you chosen what next you eat. Have lighter aubergine dish." He spoke rapidly in Italian to one of the staff and the only word I managed to catch was, 'Parmigiana'.

"Is vegetarian dish, classic, give room for something more." He and Fabrizio exchanged a few rapid sentences.

Looking at me, Fabrizio translated. "I tell my brother, he is not at his hotel now, it is for me and my staff to make the recommendations."

I didn't think Giovanni was much abashed. Andreas looked up and smiled in my direction. Whatever the brothers may argue about wouldn't alter the fact that Fabrizio's Aubergine Parmigiana was delicious, and as Giovanni said, very light, not too filling. Not remotely like a large portion of a very heavy lasagne and, sad to say, I've had plenty of those (not here in Gardone, I hasten to add). As I put down my cutlery, I found the 'kid brother' at my elbow.

"Do you like fish, Monty?"

"I certainly do, are you about to recommend something in that line Fabrizio?"

"I think you have room for a very small portion of our own Shrimp Fettuccini."

He did no more than raise an eyebrow in the direction of one of his very excellent waiters and this small delight was placed before me while another member of staff was pouring a glass of white wine. I could get used to this incredible level of service. A mouthful of a very attractive dryish white wine was followed by my first forkful of Fabrizio's recommendation: sheer bliss: a light creamy consistency with the fettuccini cooked to perfection and with the shrimps just hot enough but not in any way hard as they so often are. What all the other flavours were, I wouldn't know, but the total effect was sublime. Delicious or not, my stomach was beginning to call for a rest; I followed its wise hint.

I continued to sip the wine and took the opportunity to look round at my friends and found them all very engrossed in the food and drink, talking quietly in pairs generally. Andreas and Ken were chatting away, but I couldn't really hear. Muriel and Eileen were talking nineteen to the dozen, and I could hear place names being mentioned so wondered if they were going down memory lane in the UK. They too seemed to have paused in their eating. No need to mention the lovebirds. Giovanni called over to me. "Monty, you haven't finished, have you? I must recommend something." He caught Fabrizio's eye and said no more.

Fabrizio came over to complete the conversation. "Now, Monty, I must ask you to try just three or four of our house speciality, Polpette mixte. You call them meatballs. Ours are made with four different ground meats, breadcrumbs from our own homemade breads and a large range of Italian seasoning and herbs and a sauce from olive oil and local tomatoes. With it we will serve some fresh asparagus. Lorenzo will pour you a glass of a rich red wine.

"I don't know where I shall put it all, but it sounds quite stunning." I was beginning to run out of superlatives. While I was speaking, I noticed Giovanni nodding what was obviously his approval. He spoke to one of the staff quietly and shortly he received the same dish and red wine. He obviously rates his brother highly; he was now smiling his pleasure at his brother's order. They got on so well, really, quite charming. I was at dangerous risk of overloading my digestive system but the Polpette dish was perfection as was the wine. I hadn't seen any of the bottle labels so whatever I drank was likely to remain a mystery. I determined to take my time with this dish and make it my last, especially as I knew there would be a glorious finale with the sweet trolley and someone, I can't remember who now, had mentioned the ice-cream for which Fabrizio was famous. Another glance round the table and I noticed that I was not alone in easing up on the speed of consumption, even Andreas, and he was several decades younger than the rest of us.

In what appeared to be a general pause amongst us all, Giovanni produced that famous book and for the benefit of Eileen and Fabrizio mainly, I gave a summary of its discovery. I also mentioned my having a facsimile of the dustjacket and how the auction house had chanced upon another copy of the first edition, one which might be considered to be in a hopeless condition but because of their interest and that of their book restorer would be looking quite reasonable for me to collect on returning to London; there it would join my facsimile dustjacket in matrimony, if not exactly holy. Giovanni took the opportunity of congratulating me on my talk to his friends the night before, the English study group. In his own unique English, he described a couple of my anecdotes where I sent books all round the world but to the wrong person; needless-to-say, he made these lapses sound unbelievably disastrous.

Soon after, I noticed a couple of trolleys being wheeled in, not too heavily laden, I was pleased to note, so perhaps Fabrizio had begun to notice that his guests were getting beyond what a relative of mine once described as an 'elegant sufficiency'. He mentioned the house ice-cream, I noticed a Tiramisu and a dish of wonderful looking meringues. There also looked to have been plenty of chocolate used in the preparation of some of the sweets. I could place a bet on Muriel choosing Tiramisu; I wasn't wrong. I fancied what was translated as lemon syllabub. More substantial looking was an Italian Summer Pudding. There was a chocolate trifle, a couple of plates of individual chocolate sized cakes. There were many others and as with previous courses we were all spoilt for choice. However, bearing in mind my resolution of a few minutes earlier I opted for the limoncello syllabub and a little later I tried some Fabrizio's vanilla and strawberry ice-creams. Given how Mavis and Muriel were smiling at each other I presumed the Tiramisu met with total approval. I was happy to sip coffee while other squeezed down more puddings than was perhaps wise.

I don't when it arrived, but I noticed a small glass of limoncello had arrived next to my coffee. It was while I was enjoying this unexpected arrival that I began to wonder how the final bill was going to calculated. I could see embarrassment and stubbornness surrounding the issue. Whatever happened, I had to make sure that the staff were not neglected because at least a dozen or so had helped at our table and that was not forgetting the other parties of people about the restaurant. In the event it was Fabrizio who solved the whole situation, explaining quietly to me that he would calculate the bill and email it through to hotel in the morning. That certainly suited me and hopefully would remove any awkwardness. I asked him to accept a couple of hundred Eros for his staff and he seemed quite happy with the gift. I was pleasantly relieved to note that Giovanni didn't intervene in this arrangement, but presumably he knew his brother's plan. Time was getting on and soon Giovanni dropped a hint that his cousin would be arriving soon. It was Mavis who stood first, clapped her hands and indicated that she needed to speak.

"Giovanni, this was our night in which we wished to show our very great appreciation for all that you done for our 'holiday' – I think that is still the right word – even if you have been out manoeuvring us since the moment we first arrived, and you'll probably still be doing that as we leave. Anyway, just come over here so I can give you a kiss." Everybody laughed but Giovanni didn't have to be told twice although Mavis seemed to get hold of him rather than the other way. As they smiled on parting, there was

Muriel to add another kiss. We cheered and applauded. There followed much handshaking, hugging, embracing, and kissing as many of the staff seemed suddenly to fancy our lady guests! This great 'love in' only stopped when Giovanni's cousin gave some loud hoots from outside. I imagined that Fabrizio's other customers were relieved to see us depart. As we were boarding our very deluxe taxi, Ken took me aside to tell me that he would see Alberto right when we got back to the hotel, and for once I was pleased to leave the matter to someone else.

43. FAREWELLS & DEPARTURES

The following morning, I popped down to the reception desk and quickly settled the bill which Fabrizio had sent over. It certainly didn't seem enough, but I was not going to start a battle and handed over my credit card. The rest of the group had all given me contributions which I would bank when back in Peterborough and all would balance out quite nicely. While I was completing this transaction a member of reception staff arrived and gave some car keys to a colleague asking her to give them Andreas and his mother. I think she saw me looking surprised and knew that I had been of the party at Fabrizio's the previous night. "You have seen an example of our manager's kindness. He sent me over to Salo in a taxi this morning so that I could drive their car back." I smiled approval, thinking yet again how amazing was one, Giovanni.

A while later, our group met for breakfast for the last time, as Mavis and Daniel were off to Venice that afternoon. They were staying there for a couple of days, then flying to Paris. After that I wasn't sure of their plans. I mentioned to Andreas and his mother that I knew their car had been brought over. Eileen seemed surprised but Andreas explained how Giovanni asked for his keys so he could arrange it. Ken and the 'girls' arrived roughly at the same time. Eileen got up and gave him a hug and a kiss, by way of a thank you for some perfume. Andreas waved and pointed out the fountain pen now in his pocket. I imagined one would be going in the direction of Giovanni before the rest of us left. It was a lovely gesture.

Breakfast followed the same pattern as a couple of days back. Two waiters wheeled laden trolleys over with everything that one could possibly want to eat, and shortly after Giovanni joined us. It was as he sat down, a surprising thought crossed my mind, that nobody the previous night had mentioned the terrible events which had occurred as the firework display ended. In fact, we had hardly given it any thought. Was it because it was an event that had had the potential to have been absolutely horrific or was it because we knew the true facts had been hidden from public view and to which we were giving tacit approval? I even wondered if Andreas and his mother had heard about it, quite possibly not.

Giovanni leant my way. "What is keeping you so quiet, Monty, thoughts of going home?"

"No, not at all, something quite different. I hardly like to mention it, but I have just realised that nobody said anything last night about the tragedy at the firework display."

"Very strange, and I can offer no explanation."

And that was the sum total of our conversation on the matter.

"Have you seen this? A gift from Ken." Giovanni held a beautiful looking fountain pen for me to inspect. "Just the thing to have on the desk in my study."

"I don't know a great deal about Ken, but he is most certainly a kind, thoughtful and resolute individual."

We said no more and continued breakfast. Soon after we were saying goodbye to Andreas and his mother. They had been charming company and I was pleased that they had been able to join us for the dinner. I find farewells can be awkward events and theirs had been very speedy. I was pleased that Mavis and Daniel's, just before lunch, was also quite swift, controlled by the taxi and Alberto I supposed. Handshakes, kisses and promises about meeting soon and they were gone. I went upstairs to my room then as the previous night's indulgences were catching up and I needed to sleep for a while. Later I would sort luggage and get packed. Our departure was scheduled for exceedingly early the following morning, so I had opted out of any dinner that evening, and the rest of the day passed midst quiet contemplation and dreamy sleep.

Accounts settled, luggage assembled and 5.00am found Ken, Muriel, and me ready to join Alberto (what a surprise) for our drive to Verona. Giovanni, as genial as ever, was there to wave us off and we were away. I knew no more until Muriel gave me a nudge and I found we had stopped, and Alberto was already unloading the luggage. Not surprisingly, Ken was settling the bill. I slept on the plane coming and I did the same going home. I had already decided to keep to the booked taxi and travel straight on to Peterborough; Ken and Muriel were met by Tony for their journey to Leopold Mansions. Friendly but speedy farewells completed, and we all departed at the same time. I was able to send a quick message to Trumpingtons, apologising for not calling and asking if they would be kind and post the restored 'Hound' together with the account. Some pleasant dozing and my journey to Peterborough seemed to pass quite swiftly. It was only when I was finally home, did I reflect on how so much had happened in the previous nine months and that it had all started when I rummaged in a box of dusty old gardening books.

POSTSCRIPTS

Visiting the new Mr & Mrs Daniel Harrison in their London accommodation and not long after we had all returned from Gardone, I found myself alone for a while, having got up early and gone in search of coffee. I was hoping not to disturb anyone else; in this matter, at least I was successful. The search for coffee took longer than one might have expected but success comes to those who persevere. Sitting in their most comfortable lounge I found myself studying a recent photograph, taken from outside the west entrance to St Petrie's Chapel, also the entrance to Fr Blakeston's house but in combination made a very attractive backdrop for this group photograph. There was a Guard of Honour of six uniformed Police Officers with batons raised to form an archway, not quite gleaming swords but effective none-the-less. Nearest the camera were two rather young-looking officers, perhaps 'illegally' uniformed, namely, Sanjay and his friend, Kieran. Their batons were inconveniently lower than those behind them, so Mavis and Daniel were having to duck and squeeze together to get through, obviously the intended purpose. Behind these two young men were Junaid Anwar and his brother, Kabir, equally illegal in his uniform. At the front, well to the left and right were Fr Blakeston and the Dean looking quite resplendent in their ornate copes. It all made for a very symmetrical and memorable photograph. I looked across to a small table and found another photograph, same cast but different staging: the police formed a 'V' shape leading to the door of the Deanery with Lucinda in the welcoming role standing together with Muriel at the open doorway, Daniel and Mavis just entering the 'V' with the cope-wearing clerics following them.

Two splendid photographs, mementoes of a great autumn-tide wedding. I had eaten three times at the Deanery, a funeral wake, an evening dinner and a wedding breakfast, this last provided at Daniel insistence and expense, by staff from the Cathedral teashop, thus allowing Lucinda to be hostess at her leisure. Not in either of these photographs, but it was nice to remember that Husani, Noura's youngest brother had been at the wedding. On the wall of the lounge Mavis had hung a recent picture, a pastel sketch of Daniel, sitting drinking coffee in St Mark's Square. It was a very sensitive sketch, catching Daniel in a quiet and reflective pose.

Glancing at the two photographs again reminded me of another recent one which I had at my house, standing alongside a 1st edition copy of 'The Hound of the Baskervilles' and in its dustjacket. In my photo, Kabir Anwar and his university friend, Stephen, were standing together, with Stephen's mother to the centre and just behind them, his father next to Kabir, and standing beside Stephen was Junaid. The photograph celebrated the two undergraduates winning the shared prize of one thousand pounds, reward for a piece of computer programming which reorganised very successfully a local industry's manufacturing sequencing processes.

Thinking of this photograph took me to a conversation between Jon Mostang and Sanjay Bhatt which took place at the wedding reception. Jon told had me of it later, he had been talking to Sanjay about his mother tongue and was pleased to find it very good and including some understanding of regional dialects; nor was there any trace of his accent having been anglicized, or he was able to revert to a more 'pure' sound.. He was also very impressed with his level of 'school' French, particularly his use of some quite advanced grammatical structures. He told me, that with Sanjay's agreement, he had visited his school and met his French teacher to organise some additional tuition. He was also getting him started on Latin. He also told me that he still maintained close contact with his old college, so I pondered the possibility of another photograph, well in the future, but showing a young man in academic dress, hood with scarlet trim. Of Sanjay's friend, Kieran, I had at present no clear vision, but I had every confidence for his future too.

THE END

Printed in Great Britain
by Amazon